The Only-Good HEART

Beth Goobie

Toronto

Pedlar Press

ACKNOWLEDGEMENTS:

Earlier versions of the following stories have previously been published. "Somewhere Apart" appeared in *Raw Fiction*. "Nowhere Gone" appeared as "The Feeling" in *Whetstone*. "The Only-Good Heart" appeared in *sub-TERRAIN*. "Nothing But The Hurt" appeared in *Fireweed*. "The Lives In The Cross" appeared in *Survivorship*.

The author gratefully acknowledges a generous writing grant from The Alberta Foundation for the Arts. Thanks also to Peter Gabriel for permission to incorporate sections of "Mercy Street" into *The Spin of Spirits*. Finally, a thanks in every colour to Beth Follett for her careful, enabling editing.

CANADIAN CATALOGUING IN PUBLICATION DATA

Goobie, Beth, 1959-
The only-good heart
ISBN 0-9681884-1-9
I. Title

PS8563.O8326054 1998   C813'.54   C98-930217-2
PR9199.3.G66054 1998

First Edition

PRINTED IN TORONTO

DESIGNED IN TORONTO by Julie Gibb & Christian Morrison of GreenStreet Design

COVER PHOTOGRAPHS by April Hickox of Toronto

for the ones I keep somewhere apart

contents

The Only-Good Heart

The three of us on the bridge over the Elora Gorge, middle of a summer night.
It's stretching out before us—the universe, dark sky and dark earth,
immense, silent, so still you wonder where the breeze comes from, who's
breathing. It's such a gentle thing, the wind sometimes, the way it slips over
your face, your neck and arms, the way you want to be loved. It can bring
you back to yourself, let you be in your skin for a while, drifting between
your own molecules. The way the dark sky drifts, far away, between the stars.
Lennie on one side, Juss on the other. We've been together so long, the three of
us, we fit into each other any which way meaning comes together. Right
now it's this—my arms hooked around the rise and fall of their breathing,
our eyes wide and unblinking, fixed on that black stretch of sky and gorge,
falling up and falling down before us, our feet walking the thin line
stretched between.
Skin feels like this most of the time, a thin line stretched between two ways of
falling—darkness in or out. I know Lennie and Juss live that thin line, I've
held both of them as they've come screaming out of dreams. They've done
the same for me, done it for years, still doing it now we're in grade twelve
and they're the high school super jocks, their bodies thick with the bone
and muscle that drive them down the football field and basketball court,
while mine loses, inch by inch, body fat, body tissue, bodyground fading so
I can float, vague concept of girl between them, lightweight as any kiss of
wind.
Lennie slips his cigarette between my lips and I drag on it like it's the air in his
lungs filling mine. His eyes are on my face, watching every flicker, every
curve, it's a road map to where he's going and he's lost, he's so lost. On the
other side, Juss is quiet, studying the stars, looking for something easy to
dream about.

We've just come from somewhere, it could be anywhere from what we remember of it. It's like a mirror we've been looking into, then turned from, wiping away what happened. Every moment is like that, every moment is there as long as we stare straight into it, getting the colours, the shapes, smells, sounds, the touch of that very exact moment. Imprinting it. Then we move on. Or the moment itself moves on, leaving us grabbing at what was, what has become the vague blurred *nothing-in-motion* we are.

It's like this: Lennie rules the basketball court, knows the moving, the writhing down the gym, ball in his hands, bodies all around him reaching to drag him down as he rises for the hoop, rises in a way nothing no one nowhere can keep down, he's riding air on the force of his own gut smashing that ball *indownthrough*, the net still swishing as he lands, already pivoting to catch the slightest coming at him that might be in motion. He remembers which games they win where, but details escape him. Yesterday, last night, this morning, is always foggy, scraps of it coming up clear—the way the back yard looked out his window when he got up. Or half a sentence his dad stabbed at him over jam and toast: *fucking loser,* replayed the rest of the day, multiplied and coming at him like the entire fucking opposing team and he's got the ball in his hands, it's all he's got, that one moment of ball in his hands, and they're out to take it from him. Lennie plays all of life like that, his heart between his hands, everyone out to tear it away and he's got to get a slam-dunk on it, slam it bruised and bleeding onto the court floor before someone else does. So he's always moving, small fidgets all over him, looking for what's gonna get him, take it from him again.

Juss, on the other hand, he's a very still place, like a corner quiet's settled. When his mouth is on yours, it's all midnight and teal, he touches you like the beginning of a world that's gonna take a millennium to happen and he's gonna be there for all of it. I don't know how he's kept so much heart from what he's been through, all I know is his heart is part of him, like an arm or a leg, flesh and blood, and when he's on the football or rugger field, he isn't carrying it under his arm, using it to score, his heart is beauty inside him, sending hope out and calling it back, keeping all the cycles going the way they're supposed to. Which makes him less of a star athlete than Lennie. Juss stays closer to the ground and knows more of what happens there. Juss talks less but he means it more and he takes hurt up front, right on the skin.

Whereas Lennie and I, we're inclined to duck it, pretend it never happened— shit, fear, pain, all that stuff. Which is why we both need Juss, crawl into his arms and suckle on him while he rocks and soothes us, humming nothing. Which is all there's ever been to say.

I'm thinking about how much isn't worth saying, staring down at that river going on too dark to see but you can hear it running through. And I'm thinking, That's like Juss, constant, always running on through. Then my body catches me off guard like it does sometimes, getting me thinking about something or just staring, not thinking at all. Next thing I know, my arms and legs will start moving, real quick, heading out onto a busy street straight in front of a truck, anything big coming fast. This time my arms work first, sliding off the guys' shoulders, reaching for the rail, my feet digging into the chain link fence, all my muscles, heart included, knitting together for that one wild swing arcing down. But Juss and Lennie are on to me, and their arms hook in tight around my stomach. The three of us lock into panic-quick breathing.

"Get her off the bridge," Lennie says.

I know they won't take their bodies off me until they've got me in the car, driving on to someplace else, but still I'm pushing against their jock arms and chests, wishing myself into wind. I'll just blow up and over, *away.* . .

What we've come from is some job or other, private mansion-type party where we've been sent to work the dance floor, the punch bowl, to strip and take positions upon demand. When we're lucky, the party-goers want to see the three of us work each other but mostly they want in on the action, in on ass and cunt and oral, dicking it at girl and the jock boy who thinks he's got somewhere to go in life. Teach him he doesn't—he'll end up the same place the dick in him has. If he's lucky. Follows all the rules.

Later, called into the upstairs bedrooms for longer sessions with patrons who'll pay more, the guy running the party keeps tabs because he's got to pay a percentage on every cum we give out. Pay it back to the guys who run us, our clan, family, folk, kith, our *Kin.*

But Lennie, Juss and me, we don't want to think about that now. Now is free time. So we turn from whatever tonight was in the mirror and it's *gone gone gone,* like the last breath we let out. It'll be coming back, but this is our pact, unspoken as it is—we pull each other back from the edge when we see the other wobbling, leaning too far over. A borderline patrol we keep up, constant, prowling each other's minds.

Other than that, we just don't think about it.

I'm not crying, just shaking, whimpering strange sounds that come out of me
sometimes when I get tired, too tired, and no one will let me sleep. Just then
that river looked like sleep, sleep so deep you could go down and die in it.

"We'll take her driving," Lennie says, opening the door to the back seat, my
favourite place in Lennie's old green car. Juss and I get in. Right away, Juss
has his arms around me and I sink into his voice and hands like a stone into
that river. Juss going on around me—that's how I'd choose to live or die.

Up front, Lennie pushes PLAY and "One Of These Nights" comes on. He turns
it up, driving the country lanes with the heel of one hand, watching the
moon skim the aching trees while he unscrews the bottle of rye trapped
between his knees.

"Keep it down," he says. "I gotta listen to you."

We don't listen to him. Lennie's always complaining about having to drive, but
I can't think about that with Juss slipping into me, bringing everything he
is into me, the way he says he loves me and we're gonna get married and
the Kin's not gonna stop us. Sometimes I even believe him, for one pastel
moment. You want to give yourself that kind of happiness here and there,
even if you have to take it back again, and he's talking like that now, moving everywhere into me. I let Juss in easy, it's always been that way. Every
molecule has a door or window and when Juss touches me, the curtains slide
open, the doors swing wide and he's there, a hundred thousand, rocking
gentle and deep across me. I close my eyes and he lights up for me, every
one of the hundred thousand of him across that great dark.

"Juss, it's happening. The stars are coming down," I say. "The stars are coming
down into my skin and they're shining. They're shining."

Heat, our hair going damp. I taste sweat on his mouth, lick his upper lip.
Lennie's got one back door tied open, a rope running from the back handle
to the front so we can lie spread against each other, the night air rushing in,
the earth flowing by underneath. Juss always moves slow in me, the longest
cock I've seen, and every time, the words run out of me as I try to tell him
what he's doing for me. He links his hands through mine, raises them above

my head and says, "Shh, don't work me. Slow down." My cunt stops doing what it's been trained to do and just lets love touch, lick and stroke it. Then sound comes out of me like the sun rising and it's gotta touch every little leaf, every blade of grass.

"Dori, you're like fucking a goddam opera," Lennie says from the front seat.

Juss laughs, I can feel it ripple his stomach, but I know he's not laughing at me and I'm laughing too, happy. Because that's what we're made of, that moaning rocking fucking dick-in-cunt motion built the minutes, the hours of every day. Our bones and muscles grew into this rhythm. The Kin sold us before we could walk—*baby toys*. So now it's the way the earth moves under our feet, every step we take. The sun fucks us, the moon fucks us, the wind and the trees, chemistry and the *Eagles*, 1+1 and Jesus Christ, everything has always been about fucking, sex waiting behind every moment, ready to unravel the pretty picture of *This Is My Happy Normal Life*.

The Kin picks up every loose end they can get at and weaves the picture of you they want. You come out looking ugly, so ugly, all cunt spread wide, ready to take anything any size for the camera. The same for Lennie and Juss— they've been made to fuck anything with a hole in it, live or dead, the camera taking everything they've got right up close. But somewhere, the three of us began to pick up those loose ends ourselves, weave them through that fucking motion when it was us together, weave a couple of my loose ends here to a couple of Lennie's there and a few more of Juss's worked in like breath, working in more and more over the years until we'd woven ourselves together, flesh and dreams, and what we got out of it was love. I looked in their eyes and saw love, they said my name and I heard love, they touched my tit, arm, my fucking locker, textbooks, the same floor across a classroom, and I felt love coming to me, weaving itself through every fear-tight muscle. And that's how I learned what it was—*love*. Lennie and Juss taught it to me out of what they knew, which was the way their skin and bones hurt, the way they ached for something different. And I gave it back to them.

So when Lennie parks on the side of the road, strips and crawls back to tip the half-empty bottle of rye into our mouths, it's the three of us touching, just touching. No words, no ugliness, just letting touch do it for us, the way it starts on your skin and moves in, quiet as twilight slipping down between every tree, every night leaf, up through the ground beneath your feet.

When there's three of us, we share it, so Juss lies on his back and I lie on him,
 on my back too, head dropped over his shoulder, and Lennie slides into me,
 not going as deep but farther back. The Kin pairs kids off, trains them as a
 duo and calls them "others." Lennie is my other, we've been together since
 we could walk. There are pictures the Kin took of us going that far back,
 teaching us to be one. And *one* was what we became, Lennie and I. The Kin
 beat us together, put us in with the dogs, hooked us up to the shock machine
 and after, dropped us on a bed and left us alone. Then we'd crawl into the
 other's whimpering, crawl in and put our arms around it, touch, moan, rock
 and cry, his sobbing or my sobbing, it was all the same sobbing, no skin
 between. And when that was past, there was a way to draw closer. The Kin
 had taught us the wild wet wonder of it. The truth of that pleasure was this:
 when Lennie was in me at the age of four or eight, twelve or fifteen, we were
 together, putting pain and loneliness behind us. Pain and loneliness became
 another moment that belonged somewhere else, to someone else, part of
 another life. Over the years, Lennie and I drew into each other so much we
 lost the skins between us. Together we are raw aching flesh, always fucking,
 his blood bleeding into mine.

The way the Kin knew we would.

They drove us together then tore us apart, ripping us into little pieces. I know
 this from scraps that come and go in my head. Like this one: I'm around four
 years old, waking up in a four-poster bed. Lennie's lying on the floor in front
 of a fire that plays half-dark half-light in the grate. He's moaning and I can
 see bruises on him like thunderclouds, so I climb down off the bed. When
 I do, the walls and floor start swinging circles around me, I'm down crawling on hands and knees. Now I know I was drugged, but in that room, dragging through to Lennie's lonely baby sounds, I just try to get myself
 through pendulum swings of *fire floor bed* to that small heart beating weak
 and weaker. Almost going out. Then I touch it and I know I can keep it
 going. I slide my arm under Lennie's thin chest, the other around his back,
 and I rock him rock me, my voice whimpering, weaving in and out of his.

"Lennie, Lennie, it's okay Lennie. It'll be all right."

Finally, he opens his eyes so I can see he's there in his face again, and we kiss
 each other soft as mothers, nuzzling the whimpers away. We don't know
 where we've come from, how we got to where we are at that moment; all we

know is we're together, there's a fire and a bed. So since Lennie can't move yet, I hook my arms around his chest and drag him, fighting the circles in my head and gut. I get him leaned over the bed on his stomach, then I lift and shove his leg and bum until he's all up there, up on the warm soft bed.

We've both wet ourselves. The quilt's damp and we smell like piss but we're used to it, almost every time I sleep or cum I'm pissing so I hold Lennie close as I can and still keep him breathing, pat his loose blonde curls and I tell him a story about happiness.

"Up on a mountain, there's a little tiny village. And in this little tiny village live people with only-good hearts. Only-good hearts that are very big. And in one house lives a good lady with blonde blonde hair. When a little boy or girl comes down the street all lost and crying, she picks them up and takes them inside.

"Inside is a nice big table with soft chairs and a blue table-cloth. The nice lady, she gives you a big cup of hot chocolate with lots of little coloured marshmallows in it. There are so *manymanymany*, you can hardly see over your cup. And if you want more, you can have it."

"I want more," whispers Lennie.

"Then you can have it, little boy. Because I'm the good lady with blonde blonde hair. I always have a pot of hot chocolate on my stove and you can always have some. I need a good little boy like you to be my son. I'll be your mommy and give you hot chocolate whenever you want it. With lots of marshmallows. And you can always have more."

Lennie and I lie quiet for a bit, floating in pictures of the nice lady and hot chocolate; we're tired but warm, safe skin next to safe skin, firelight lipping dark, our aches and pains still there but floating a little way off, just beyond my story.

"I'll be your mommy, Lennie," I say. "And you be my daddy."

"Okay," Lennie whispers.

Then the door to the room comes sudden out of the wall, jumping out of my skin, and they're there, the Kin, coming into the room in their white robes, dead bones dangling from chains around their necks and waists. And there's one dressed as a skeleton, white bones in his arms and across the place his face should be. We're just little, Lennie and I, easy to fool and the Kin are always scaring us, our lives stretched screaming thin and long.

"Where is the dead child?" the dead one hisses, his bone hands reaching for us on the bed. Lennie and I, vivid with fear, are locked into each other like parts of a machine.

The rest of the Kin stand by the fire, staring down at the place where Lennie had been lying, hissing, "Dead, dead, dead."

Everything starts closing down inside like a hundred turtles going into their shells. Heart in a shell, stomach in a shell, each finger and toe in a different shell. Each bit moves away from the others, holding itself apart from the rest so that all the fear isn't together at once.

I close my eyes and see the little village with the gingerbread houses. The smell of hot chocolate drifts out of every window, everything is good and right, I know everything will work out fine if we all believe in only-good hearts. Then I feel my brown hair turn blonde and go up in a bun. I'm the blonde blonde lady with an only-good heart. I open my eyes again and I look at the white robes.

"Lennie's alive," I say. "He's not dead."

I feel Lennie shove his face into my neck like he wants to go inside me and never come out.

"There is a dead child," the dead one hisses, floating toward us, the white robes chanting and moaning, shaking their chains and the metal balls that let out a dizzy sweet smoke. Things swing in and out of my head. Lennie's wailing again, I'm hanging onto him, trying to be only-good. I so want to be only-good. Just let me be heart.

"One of you is the dead child." The skeleton man leans over us, big as a little kid's eyes can make him. "Which one is dead?"

Lennie pushes at me, screaming, "Pick her, pick her, pick her." Then he's just screaming, mouth stretched wide, head gone back, spinning off where there's no coming near him. And I'm lost, I just got pushed out into nowhere, an only-dark place, the white robes whispering, "Dead, dead, dead."

Then a voice speaks clear and clean in my head. No one can hear it but me. "My little one, you are very dear," it says. "You have an only-good heart."

The good and right feeling brushes by me, flows up and out of my mouth.

"Take me," it tells the Kin.

Then it's hazy again, the way most things live in my head, but there's another scrap: I'm lying on an altar and the skeleton man is holding a bloody chunk over me. He tells me they cut out my heart. There's blood on my chest so I believe him, I believe my heart's gone, I can't be good anymore, I can't be the blonde blonde lady, I can't be Lennie's mommy. No more love slipping from my fingers and running into Lennie like all the stars wishing together into one forever sky. No heart, no stars. Only dark.

I try never to let those scraps come back up; they take away the only-good, burst out of me like a door coming out of a wall, the Kin floating in behind. But those scraps, they're *me*, I feel them in me solid and bloody as organs I'm trying to cut out. And the more of myself I lose, the more I hang onto what I have. So when I've got Lennie close like now, and it's free time, Juss carrying us like Mother Earth underneath, I hold Lennie the way the sky holds the moon. I feel him move into me scared like he's gonna lose what he wants just because he wants it and I hold him soft. Everywhere we touch—tongues, necks, nipples, cock and cunt—everywhere I try to be soft fingertips, brushing and brushing, telling him this touch loves him and is never going away. The fear that juggles Lennie's cells slows down, his skin settles into itself so it can feel more than terror, it can feel me. And then the years of us come together and our skins fade away completely and all the love and comfort we ever gave each other is here again, reaching out.

And touching. *Touching.* Baby cries. When Lennie gives out his raw baby cries, I know he's let me sift in deep, I'm touching the baby face he doesn't let anyone else near, he's giving me his greatest need. I let my cunt go still and I turn myself into one big tit so wherever he starts sucking—my neck, mouth, shoulder—he's getting that only-good milk.

It makes me cry tonight, hearing Lennie like this. I can feel Juss's face beside mine, warm wet with tears too, he'd do anything to hold Lennie's babies like I do. Hold them until they get enough and sink into soft baby sleep. Juss and I lie there crying while Lennie moans and whimpers. Then he puts his babies away and kisses me as if I've got need and he's the one holding it.

"Juss, you drive," Lennie says. "I'm gonna fuck Dori on the roof." He's pulling out of me and I'm laughing at the craziness of how his mind goes. Juss wraps his arms around me, protesting.

"Just drive slow," Lennie tells him, already on the trunk. "Maybe give 'er a bit after a while." He gives me a hand up, the trunk giving under our weight so I think we're going in with his spare tire and jack. But then I'm lying on the roof, Lennie settling into me, starting to move like there's been no interruption, hasn't been for the past fifteen years.

Juss stands there arguing with the night but we aren't exactly in mode for a lecture, so he gives up and gets in the car.

"There's bourbon in the cunt." Lennie means the glove compartment. It's Juss's consolation prize because Lennie knows what it's like to have to drive. Somewhere, it could be anywhere, I hear a motor start up, I think of it as Lennie's cock getting into high gear, it sure feels like it. And then I look up past Lennie's mouth and eyes and hair and see the stars. Really dropping down through the dark, onto me, onto Lennie, onto Juss drinking bourbon and finding the way for us through the immense dark night.

"Lennie, you're givin' it to me." I'm crying because I know how he listens in the front seat, listens to every breath I take. Tonight, while he was driving, he tried to figure out how he could give me the stars. Every constellation out of every night he's lived. And now he is.

After a bit, Juss and Lennie switch places, Lennie drinking a little more, picking up night speed. The stars still come down, two glowing at the tip of Juss's cock and tongue. When we're quiet again, Juss lying on me, resting, Lennie gets out of the front seat and stands back a little, cigarette slouching from his mouth. He looks at Juss and Juss looks at him and I wonder if it's gonna happen, it hasn't in too long a while. It gets quiet, just the breeze blowing in from somewhere past Mars.

"Let Dori drive," Lennie says.

Juss is real still a moment, looking at Lennie. "You wanna?"

"Yeah," Lennie says. "I wanna."

Now they've settled it, I can throw a panic. "Lennie, I ain't got my license. I can't drive a lawn mower. All I can do is catch the bus. I don't even sit *near* the driver."

"Just don't go over twenty," Lennie says. He's already half on the roof and

I know I've got to get off or something will give. So I climb down and slam the door to let them know how many stars got caught inside, swirling in my blood.

"How do I get this thing going?" I yell.

"It's on," Lennie says.

"I know that!"

"Put your foot on the brake."

"Which one's that?"

"The one to the left. Got it?"

"Yeah."

"Now slide into first gear. It's straight up."

"Okay."

"Take your foot off and let 'er roll."

I do and we're moving, sliding on into the dark. Lennie's got the *Eagles* on low, half the bottle of bourbon left. Once I stop wobbling side to side and stick somewhere around the middle of the road, I pick up the bourbon and take a couple swallows, just to straighten things out. After all, I still got stars whirling in my head. And with those two up there, taking down their skins and sliding deeper and deeper into each other's dark, it's up to me to pilot through this night. It's free time now. We've got several galaxies left to go.

Child of Doors

The room is cold, angry with light. I lie on my back, too small to shift over a shoulder onto my stomach. In the folds of the blanket beneath me, a flannel darkness, but I can't move toward it. Somewhere in this giant space of unending light, a loud grinding noise repeats itself. I've been here cold, pissing, shitting and lying in it, an infant's forever; time is the pulse of gears grinding, fine vivid tentacles vibrate through me. What I know is the shriek of ears, the wail of a mouth, the ache of shut-tight eyes, the skin between my legs a membrane cold-burning and alone.

And I know wanting. *Wanting, wanting.* I overflow my skin with sobs, wails I send out in search of mother hands, mother voice. Rooted in heart and the tips of nerves, a tiny longing energy floats around me. Against this, the huge grinding noise cuts deeper. The Body opens into a raw red wound.

The *longing* released. Vague baby shape, transparent as a wish, the *longing* hovers a moment over the three-day-old infant's Body spread naked and wailing, then drifts around the room. *Wishing mother hands, wishing mother voice.* The open doorway, too far for The Body's eyes to bring into focus, comes close-up into the *longing*'s gaze. This is the first door: escape from grinding sound, burning skin, the overwhelming light. Through the doorway into a hallway, immediately shadowed, the horror of sound and light placed further back. Lost, the *longing* drifts in the upper hallway where every other door is closed, then floats down the long stairwell of the old house to the first floor. There are different sounds at the end of this hall and the *longing* travels through another open doorway into a large white kitchen.

Here a woman stands at a stove cooking soup. She listens to tendrils of sound coming from a small radio; these tendrils are gentle as fingertips that come and go, soft-moving. Sometimes a man's voice speaks smooth as water, then more of the sweet wisping sound. Something about the woman, the way she stands, tells the *longing* that she also listens for sounds beyond this room. Several times she leaves off cutting things into the bubbling soup to listen at the hall entrance for the upstairs grind of gears in the blinding light, the infant Body's thin cry. In the kitchen, the infant *longing* can't cry out but it can be near the woman; it can't touch her but it can watch. Hovering just under the high-up ceiling, the *longing* watches and waits.

Until the woman turns off the soup and quickly climbs the stairs toward the noise and the white glare, goes into the room where The Body lies, hoarse now with a wail that is only a bubble in the throat. The *longing* follows, hovering in the doorway. The woman crosses to the tape recorder by the window and pushes a button. The grind of gears stops, leaving a solid block of silence broken by tendrils from the downstairs radio and the infant Body's whimper.

"There there now," says the woman. She turns off the brilliant glare and the room becomes a shadowy green, its light filtered through the maple at the window. A hum begins in her throat. "Twinkle tiny star up far," she sings. "Come and go and there you are."

Up near the ceiling, the *longing* continues to watch as the woman cleans off the stretched-open place between the infant's legs, washes and dries it. Watches as the woman takes a smooth jelly from a jar and begins to rub slow circles onto the soreness. *Slow, slow* as she continues to hum. Up by the ceiling, the *longing* watches the infant Body send all its feeling into the skin between its legs as the finger draws its circles, *slow, slow.* The only touch, the only gentle sound all day, The Body soaks up what it can get, its whimpers fade into the skin of its throat, quiet. Then a single cry as The Body shudders, shudders again. The *longing* stays up by the ceiling and watches until the woman puts on a diaper and wraps the infant Body in a blanket. She opens her blouse and slides a nipple into the tiny mouth.

Now the *longing* sees what it wants, slips slowly back into The Body, clean and close to its warm large-breasted mother, the nipple wet and milky in its mouth. Rocked back and forth, sucking and sucking, eyes large on the breast and the mother's slow singing mouth, The Body and *longing* come together again. As the *longing* slides in through The Body's inner shadows, it brings with it a first memory of doors, sees an open doorway in the infant heart, and slips in there.

I suck against flesh, am rocked by arms of flesh, listen to the lilting voice of flesh above me *hum sing cool green shadows of this loving place.*

Watching over the woman's shoulder, I'm carried through a life of doorways. Each door means a change in light and dark, hot and cold, the voice of the woman or man, how I'll be touched. Even their voices are doors that open and close moments. Sometimes I'm laid on a back yard blanket, I kick my feet in soft-knit booties up through the sun. The man's voice floats warm, he lies by me and holds out a finger I grab and pull. "Twinkle tiny star up far, come and go and there you are," he sings. Happy shrieks burst out of me; his chuckle opens a door to further happiness.

Sometimes I'm laid on a table. Nearby, the man's voice curls tight and thin. The woman takes away my clothes and different doors come open, they fall open the way my legs fall apart, the man leans over and around me, no voice, just the heavy grind of air in his throat. As something softhard rubs between my legs, the man makes an edgy whine. The rubbing goes on and on, pushes harder. Sounds grind out of my mouth. I want to go through doorways to some other place, soft as a blanket, where someone sings above milky flesh. I'm looking, looking for a door, the door in this room is too far away and The Body must be carried to it.

"Not yet, Larry, she's too young," says the voice of the flesh, arms and breasts that *feedrocksing* me.

The softheavy rubbing moves up my chest and face. I don't want chest and face. There's a door, there has to be a door. Then I see a door far down a dark hallway, vague and shadowy as a dream. I've never seen this door before, or this hallway. As I lift up with the *longing*, The Body is left behind, down and under the man. I float along this new dark hall to the new door, it opens as I come to it and lets me in. Into another place, another room, where a different woman waits for me. She looks the same as the one who carries me about, singing, feeding, undressing me for the man, but this woman lives only in a room of green whispering light, there's never any grinding noise here, only a milky breast and "Twinkle Tiny Star Up Far." She's my *mother.*

This room and this woman are mine, they come from me. The door to them is rooted in The Body like a nerve, somewhere near my left shoulder, deep in, a place the man hasn't touched. The room leaves The Body the way a wish does, hovering just beyond The Body's reach. But I've found the door to my *mother*, and I can carry myself through it. I travel to my *mother* whenever I want or need.

When I can roll and sit propped, I learn new sounds and feelings. There's the birth of fire, the way it begins with a scratch, a pretty orange wave that dances like happy shrieks. Then the air turns into *everywhere fire*, the man holding the flame close and hard-burning, pushing in where there's no hole.

I learn the way needles grow out of hands and air, they go into me anywhere, not just the already holes. Sometimes the woman and man sing the song while they push the needles in. The song grows as long as the hurt.

Twinkle tiny star up far,
Come and go and there you are
When it hurts you go away
When it's nice stay there to play
Twinkle tiny star up far,
Come and go and there you are.

The woman sings it soft, the man sings it hard. Quickly I learn the meaning of the song's sound—needles or fire. The song itself means *find the longing, find the door.*

The woman often picks me up and walks to the bedroom doorway where I feel the *longing* start to shift as if about to float out and down the hall. "Door," the woman says to me. She walks in and out, in and out, so the ceiling and walls blur and she repeats, singsong, "Door, door, door."

She smiles at me like the woman who resembles her in the cool green shadows room, my *mother*, and she says, "Dora. Your name is Dora."

I learn to lean the *longing* into my shoulders, pull up off the heavy anchor of my bum and crawl in and out of doorways myself. I crawl back and forth, back and forth, from the dark hall to the white kitchen space, and happy shrieks burst out of me. If I don't like something, I look for an open door. Then I start crawling.

I've learned *open* and I've learned *close*. I've found more doors inside The Body that open onto other places of soft colours and sounds. Some of the colours move and sing like people, like the *longing* of people, like my *mother*. I close my eyes and find the inside door I want, then go to the place where the *longing* is the colour I need.

The man and the woman own all doors outside The Body. Often they talk to me about *open* and *close*. They make the sounds big in their mouths, stretch their lips wide and repeat the sounds while I watch. It makes me sleepy, the way I used to feel when the woman carried me back and forth through doorways saying, Door, and making the *ceilingswallsfloors* run together like window rain. Soon I feel sleepy whenever I hear the sounds *open* or *close*, my eyes get *widestaring* and my inside doors, *my doors*, do whatever they're told.

The man touches my hole. "Open this door." It opens. "This is my door, little girl," he tells me. "My door." He holds up a small thin object. "This is a key. It makes a door come open. I own the key to your door. Now I'm going to come in. Into a big room just for me."

One night, I wake to see a small fire kept on a candle on the dresser leaping fearful in the dark. Then its light jumps onto a knife in the man's hand. When the woman uses that knife in the kitchen, things get smaller and smaller. I start looking for doors.

"Be quiet, Dora," says the man. "Be quiet or I'll give you a spanking."

The woman and man are robed in black. Inside, my doors are opening, *everywhere opening*. I want only one door, the one that will take me away, so many doors swinging *crazy open* make me dizzy. As the man opens my clothes, the fire jumps scared in his eyes and along the knife. Other robed people come in carrying candles; their faces go *peekaboo* in the dark.

"Sa cri fice," says the man.

Behind the robed people, on the other side of the room, a new door appears. There's never been a door beside my dresser before, but now I see a new door begin to open very slowly, a door deeper than any I've ever seen. This one doesn't start in The Body. It sits in a thick darkness at the end of a very long hall and it pulls at me, lifts me up out of The Body and lands me on the floor between the people's feet. They don't see me, they're looking at The Body I left behind in my crib. I'm crawling fast, so fast, I don't know how I can crawl so fast, somehow I have to keep away from the man's knife. I crawl through the people to the other side of the room, then down this new hall. Fast, faster. I lift and crawl through air.

Back around The Body I left behind, the people chant, "Sa cri fice."

The knife enters The Body burning hard as fire. Even out of The Body, I can feel it. As the knife goes in, I see the new door in the new hall open wide. I think I'm about to crawl into a new place with new colours and sounds, a place with more of the *longing people*, but this time everything in that place comes through the door to me. Through this door pours every colour I've seen behind all my inside doors—all the colours of *longing* rush together toward me.

The Body is losing blood quickly through a stomach wound. Even though I'm out of The Body, my stomach also bleeds from a knife gash. I lie down in the hall and watch the colours of the *longing people* flow toward me. For a moment, they surround and hold me, then flow into me through my stomach wound—first the black, then the white, then the many colours. Once the *longing people* are in, this wound closes and disappears.

I lie alone in the new hall and wonder what's happening to The Body. As I begin to crawl back to it, the black *longing* oozes out of me. He's the largest of the *longing people*, and he's like the man with the softhard between his legs except he's not-man. He picks me up and we float down the new hall into the room where The Body lies in the crib, covered with blood, the robed people standing around it. Suddenly the black *longing* blows fast and hard. The bedroom door slams, blowing out the candles. The people scream and push.

In the darkness, the black *longing* carries me to The Body and lays me back into it. The Body is different now, very cold and no *thumpthump thumpthump* travelling through it, no *whoosh whoosh* coming through the nose. The stomach feels cut and wet like the dinner the woman makes. The black *longing* places his hand on The Body's stomach. The wet shrinks back inside and The Body's wound closes. He puts his hand on The Body's chest and the *thumpthump* starts. He breathes into the nose and the *whoosh* comes back.

"Dora," he says to me, "you will be the place wherein heaven meets earth meets hell. You will be dearly loved. Beloved."

When the black *longing* slides into me again, he slides in through my hole. Slides in like quiet dark going to sleep; I don't have to stretch the hole big, there's no pain or fear. I see the new door from the new hall has come into me, placed itself inside The Body, between my legs. It has become my door and there's no key.

I open my eyes. A man looks at me and screams. The people whisper and point, push at each other, trying to get out of the room. They close the door and I'm alone.

Inside, the *longing people* drift their colours through my arms, legs and stomach. They feel like happiness, I float with the *longing* into sleep.

The *longing people* open and close my inside doors, come and go from the other places. Sometimes they float free of The Body into the air, swirl their colours, light and dark, about the room. The man and woman watch them, talking to each other in sharp whispers. They call the *longing people* "spirits." I let this word hover on my tongue. It drifts the way the *longing people* do, so I give them this sound too. *Spirits.*

Each spirit is a different colour. Each colour has its own sound. The dark spirits have deeper voices, the light ones sing with higher notes. Spirits of the same colour speak in the same pitch. I lie in my crib watching the spirits play, and I talk to each one in the sound of its own colour. The spirits circle the air above me, round and round, as I talk to them like the green and yellow light at my afternoon window, with the lilt of a tiny wind.

The light spirits spin clockwise. The dark spirits turn counter-clockwise, the same direction as the circles the woman and man draw between my legs with the jelly. The largest blackest spirit stays closest to me. He has told me his name: Behemoth. Often he lifts me out of my crib and holds me, gazing down at me like my *mother*. Sometimes he lies in the middle of the air with me on his chest and floats in circles that go slow as sleeping. Then it's as if I'm in the middle of awake-dreams, breathing colours and images that swirl around me. I can hear voices, laughter, screams; smell perfumes, smoke and burning. I drift through the stories the spirits show me, follow them with feelings in The Body until the spirits let the stories fade away. Then I lie on Behemoth's chest and tell him *my* stories. Say his name to keep him close. This becomes the sound of happiness.

There are other spirits that come and go, but not through my doors inside The Body. They come from other places, doors I haven't seen, doors that are not inside me. Some of them stay low to the floor and hiss in corners, twisting as if made of fire. I stand holding my crib bars and talk to them in the green-yellow sounds, sometimes a soft blue. Then they go quiet and suck their thumbs. Some nights, the spirits that come from the unknown doors lift me up and take me in their spins, showing me more awake-dreams. The man and woman watch from the doorway, whispering, but when these spirits are in the room, they don't come in. Sometimes when the woman is alone, we giggle back and forth but if any spirits are out, she never enters the room.

Black, red and white-robed people come more frequently. The man gives demonstrations.

"Hold out your finger." The man takes out a knife.

I know I must be quiet. The cut is a thin pain widening to bright blood. I want to suck it better.

"Open the red door," says the man. "Fix it."

My inside doors are many colours. Each spirit comes through a door of its own colour. The man only knows about one red door, I find this one and open it. The red she-spirit floats through the door and down an inside hall to my finger. As she hovers inside the cut, it heals and disappears. The red spirit retreats inside her red door and closes it.

"That's incredible," say the watching people.

More and more frequently, the man brings people to watch the spirits work.

"Fix it," he says.

Different spirits regenerate different areas of The Body. Yellow and white spirits heal wounds in my face, green and blue spirits heal cuts to my abdomen. Dark purple and brown regenerate my feet. Behemoth heals my hole.

The man tries to call the spirits to do his will. He cuts high in my chest and says, "Now I want the dark blue spirit to come up to this wound." Or he tries to instigate a battle. "I want the light spirits to open their doors. Come out and line up in a row. Now I want the dark spirits to open their doors. Come out and attack the light spirits. Banish them from this body."

The spirits don't listen to him until the night the man brings in the Dark Master. By this point I can run up and down halls, in and out of doors. I can go any-where very fast, and I talk very big so my sound fills up rooms. I remember words and the feelings they cause, I remember the man's words, *Dark Master*. When the unfamiliar man enters the room, I know by the feeling that it's him.

I'm standing in my crib watching the spirits play. I clap my hands at their spins, so they've circled my arms and legs, hips and head, and I'm centred by their spinning. Happy shrieks burst out of me.

The Dark Master walks in alone and watches me.

"Hi mister," I say.

The spirits continue spinning as he walks to the centre of the room and raises his arms. At this gesture, the spirits' movement slows. The Dark Master begins to turn on his bare feet, faster until he's one dark spin. He lifts from the floor and all the dark spirits in the room swoop to join with his spin. Other dark spirits come through the window and zoom into the spin. The dark middle of the room swells, spreads further out.

As it spreads, the darkness deepens as if reaching further into itself through a door in the air to something else. Even though the spin hasn't yet reached me, a place breaks open inside, a huge cut that bleeds its own darkness into the rest of me. Everywhere inside, darkness spreads like the Dark Master's spin. It isn't the blackness of Behemoth. This blackness twists and hisses. A dark sound cries from my mouth.

The light spirits drift, lost in the room's corners. At my cry they come together in a circle outside the black spin. Slowly they begin a wider clockwise spin of light around the dark spin. As they do, they call other spirits of light in through the window—pale pink and blue, yellow, green, blue-white—all of these join in the spin of light around the spin of dark. The air is heavy with the feeling of pushing against something too great. I press against my crib bars and when I whine the spin of light speeds up.

For a long while the two circles of spirits run against each other at equal speeds. Then they shift together and touch, darkness and light mixing at the edges, and from this touching rises such a song of *longing*, of wanting to come together, to find what's needed for happiness. Further and further the spins move in through each other until they merge completely. They lift from the Dark Master and move through the air to come down around me, then sink in through my skin. As they spin through each other inside me, the inner black cut heals and disappears.

Slowly the spirits separate into their own colours. My spirits begin to drift into my doors. The rest float out the window in swoops and spins. I wave *byebye*, then look at the Dark Master who stands in the middle of the room.

Since Behemoth came, I can see everything in the dark. Now in this dark room, I see the Dark Master so clearly I can see *into* him. As he stares at me, I look through and into him, into his dark halls and doors. I look everywhere, into every room, behind every door, and I see nothing but angry dark—dark spirits everywhere, hissing and screaming, sitting heavy in their hurt. I wonder where all the colours went and why there's no happy dark. I feel the dark in him reach toward me, angry throbbing hands that want to pull me out of all my spirits into his dark and scared-bad places.

But my spirits flow out of The Body, hover around me so I glow yellow, green, red, black with Behemoth, together and balanced. For that moment, the Dark Master's angry spirit hands cannot penetrate my spirits, so he turns with a hiss and leaves the room. The orange-brown spirits lay me down, making mother hands, brushing them over my face and hair until I go to sleep.

Doors onto the dark, The Body full of them, hallways of doors running endless tunnels through heart, arms and legs, gut. I build more and more of the deep dark doors and they take me farther and farther away. Some open onto stars and planets, some onto places of energy that move like colour breathing. I find a place of black nothingness inside Behemoth. When he spins, I go into his centre and *become* nothing, I lie mid-air and there's no breath, no heartbeat, no light. The tiredness fades, the sad-crying in my stomach, the heavy fear in my mouth disappears into Behemoth. When I return from him, I leave it all behind. The Body feels bigger, thicker, as if all my fingers, toes, eyes—everything is renewed and belongs to me again.

Usually The Body feels like a sad curtain, torn and floating. Other girls and boys have come to live in The Body, coming and going when the man or woman call them. We have to share The Body and I'm supposed to wait behind an inside door with my name on it. When it's my turn to surface, The Body often feels like someone else's—a hand will move differently, not know how to hold a spoon. Or the voice will be squeaky when I don't talk squeaky. Or it won't think right, the body won't remember *my* name or *my* teddy bear or *my* favourite dress.

"Don't be so stupid!" I slap the face. Then The Body remembers me.

I want the other children to disappear. Toys and colouring and church and company for dinner happen to them, not me. I want to colour with their crayons in their books. At night I sneak out of sleeping, and colour on the walls. When the other children are punished, I retreat inside Behemoth.

I know the other children can't dream-awake with the spirits. They can't fly with Behemoth to the stars. So perhaps I pity them. All they know is their one door. They don't see anyone else inside so they don't realize there are other children in The Body. When they colour, they colour loneliness in all its shapes and shades. Sometimes they draw spirits and they don't know what they've drawn.

The man has appointed me *Doorkeeper*. It is now my job to make and keep all doors. I keep track of everyone inside. When the man needs a new child, he calls me up into The Body. He inserts a needle into the skin and instructs me to make a new door. The Body must obey without crying or twisting its face so I send the needle pain in behind the door where a girl named Klarrenord lives. The man has decreed that it is Klarrenord's job to feel needle pain, but she must cry alone behind her door without knowing what's happening. All alone so no one can hear her and be bothered by her wailing. Then The Body can perform the required task without complaining.

"Doorkeeper, make a new door," the man orders. He inserts a needle high in The Body's leg. I direct the pain to Klarrenord, then go inside, down the long hallway that leads to that leg. There are five other doors nearby. I wave my hands counter-clockwise around the needle tip, round and round. The man requires a dark door here.

"Doorkeeper, make a new door," the man chants.

The new door appears, dark as the man's eyes. I surface into The Body and look out the face.

"Doorkeeper, did you make a new door?" the man asks.

"Yes."

"Yes, what?"

"Yes, lord and master."

"Obey," he says to me.

"Obey." He requires these words. I prefer *doll* and *ice cream* and *piggyback* but they belong to the other children.

"Submit."

"Submit." *Yucky words.*

"I own you."

"You own me." *Yucky yucky stupid.*

"There will be a new girl who lives behind this door. Her name will be Sepperintowski. Sepperintowski will do everything I tell her. Sepperintowski will like especially to cut with knives. Sepperintowski will like to cut anything I tell her to cut. If I tell Sepperintowski to cut a puppy, she will cut a puppy. If I tell Sepperintowski to cut a man, Sepperintowski will cut a man. If I tell Sepperintowski to cut herself, Sepperintowski will cut herself. But when Sepperintowski cuts herself, Sepperintowski will not feel it. Someone else inside will feel it and that someone will be Klarrenord. Klarrenord is already there and Klarrenord feels pain for other children. Is Klarrenord listening?"

"Yes." Klarrenord is behind her door but her voice comes out The Body's mouth.

"Klarrenord will feel the pain when Sepperintowski cuts herself. Sepperintowski will only come out when I call. She will never come out on her own. NEVER. Or Sepperintowski and Klarrenord and the Doorkeeper will die. Sepperintowski will come out when I speak her name or when I touch The Body like this."

The man taps seven times on the knee of the leg with the needle in it. Then he draws a counter-clockwise circle around the kneecap.

"I am calling Sepperintowski," he says.

I find my door and retreat deep into Behemoth, into the nothing-dark. Just before I close the door, I see Sepperintowski float up the hall to the main door that will allow her to surface into The Body. Her face twists thin, her eyes burn a bright yellow. Quickly I close my door and sink into the nothing-dark to sleep.

The man requires more and more regeneration. Sometimes he cuts off my fingers, sometimes he operates on The Body and removes organs, then commands regeneration. The spirits reclaim The Body parts, float them back into place and set up an intense glow until the tissues fuse and mend. Sepperintowski learns to cut and operate on The Body. When she commands regeneration, the spirits obey her. This becomes the pattern of being alive: cut apart, heal together, cut apart, heal together. Everything breaks down into smaller and smaller pieces, but I'm still able to call them all in, know their names, keep track of them.

Until the man begins to call the hurting spirits, the ones that carry pain and suffering as their only message to this world. Dividing the dark and light and colours with so much fear, there is less and less coming together, less knowing, less *longing*.

I'm lying in the middle of night. Huge and complete, the moon lacks nothing. Behemoth and the other spirits float in the room, larger tonight like the moon. Outside the window hovers an unfamiliar spirit, black and full of knives. I watch Behemoth talk to it, discovering what will be required.

The man comes into the room holding a lit candle and a curved knife. He glares at my spirits, hissing a small sound. When he turns toward me, every door closes, I can't leave The Body.

"You're going to give me something now," the man says. "If I get it real good, you'll get a candy."

As he takes off my clothes I wonder, *Chocolate or caramel or peppermints?* "Chocolate?"

"Shut up." The man raises the knife, turns to the window and summons the unfamiliar spirit. Quickly it floats in through the window and hangs above me. It's a man spirit. Air twists as if it hurts while it's in him, as if in a scream.

The man leans in on me and says, "You are my slave. The Power will come into you and you will give it to me."

He makes several cuts on the sides of my hole. I try to send the crying to Klarrenord but it catches in my mouth. "The blood is calling you," the man says and the spirit comes into me, as if all the cuts are doors, straight into the hurt. Screams swell in my mouth.

Now the man comes in too. The spirit moves like knives cutting and the man is another huge knife and I'm going to come all apart for dinner. Behemoth hovers, a black cloud over us wanting to intercede, but the man has invited the spirit in.

Then I feel the new black spirit move out of my cuts into the man. More and more of the spirit leaves me until it has fully seeped into the man. When the man pulls out, his eyes gleam red. He blows out the candle and his eyes continue to burn.

"I'm going to rule the world with you, little bitch," he says. "You'll give me The Power."

He starts to spin black circles, then lifts and flies out the window. I've never seen him fly before, it must be through the black spirit's power.

Behemoth comes down around me. The red spirit flows to my hole. Together they heal the wounds, but there's a scared hurt that won't go away, even when the light blue spirit curls in around and cradles me.

I keep remembering there was no door that allowed me to flee. The man trapped me in The Body and kept me there. I'll have to find more secret doors.

More and more doors in The Body, but not doors that I've found. The man discovers them through needles and fire, the screams in my mouth. He no longer needs me to build these doors into The Body, perhaps The Body has learned to obey without the Doorkeeper. The man inserts a needle and commands a door of white light to begin. The door shapes itself out of fear and pain, then a spirit of hissing white comes through it and rises from The Body to speak with the man.

I close my own door quietly. I don't want to see any more. I crawl into Behemoth and disappear.

The woman tells the other children about *school coming soon*, teaches them numbers and letters as preparation. I'm not supposed to come out of my door during the lessons, so I make an inner window and watch. I learn addition, subtraction and reading, learn it more quickly than the other children, even though they're up front. I decide they're somewhat stupid. When they see a meeting place they think it's a cross, and they think six is just any other number.

One afternoon, as I practice the new numbers in the back yard, I discover the reason so many bad things are done in sixes. I count the main doors through which the spirits enter and leave The Body. When I place my arms out and my feet together, spirits can enter all six doors at once: blue-white spirits descend into my head, black spirits rise into my feet, colour spirits enter the four ways into my heart, front and back, left and right. That's how the spirits come and go when there are no needles or fire. You're a meeting place for all of them at once, balanced, strong. You *know* things, the way they are.

That afternoon as I discover the meaning of sixes, I stand thinking in a meeting place. It's sunny so nobody can see the spirits come and go, but the woman glances out the kitchen window and she notices my position. There's a yelp. "DORA!" The back door slams and footsteps run toward the back yard. I know it's about to get bad so I retreat behind my door and slam it. Then I peek out my window.

As I go inside, a dumb girl surfaces. She doesn't know anything about sixes. The woman grabs The Body's arm and shakes it, then drags the dumb girl crying into the house and hits her bum six times with the wooden spoon. That night the man lights candles and calls Sepperintowski. Sepperintowski doesn't know anything about the good spirits and the good six doors. The man gives Sepperintowski a knife and makes her kill six puppies. He tells her the number six is always bad and black and it means she has to kill. Then he takes her hands and spins her six times counter-clockwise. Through the dizzy learning, Sepperintowski connects counter-clockwise to killing and the dark, not Behemoth and the night and the huge everything-heart that holds the planets and stars and *all all all the things that happen, all of it together.*

The man and woman continue teaching the dumb children about crosses. They teach that a man named Jesus died on a white cross so humans could have eternal life. The dumb children believe them. There are constant lessons about crosses killing people.

"No!" I yell through my window. "Not a cross. A meeting place. A MEETING PLACE!"

But they don't hear me.

At night the man and woman take Sepperintowski to a different church where a black-robed congregation holds candles and chants. A black cross sits upside-down at the front. Everyone chants, "Sacrifice. Sacrifice to the Dark Power." Often Sepperintowski is given the knife to perform a sacrifice.

One night there's a woman tied down on the altar. The congregation performs the whirling devil dance, spinning counter-clockwise, *round round round.* I want to stop the lies, I want to show Sepperintowski something different. I shove up until I surface into The Body and stretch out my arms. I place my feet together and make a meeting place in my heart. I call all the spirits, all the pretty blue-white and yellow ones, all the dark tree greens and apple reds, the garden dirt browns that smell like the sun. I call the darkest black from the quiet places where it's stronger than anything. I call Behemoth who's my everything-heart.

When they come through the night into that church, the spirits are streams of light and dark flying toward the six points of my meeting place, flowing into the six good doors. I feel strong, so strong, strong enough to open any door, strong enough to call anything or any place to me.

The congregation stops whirling. They back into the corners of the church, try to run out. I stand in that meeting place, lit up and full of the dark at the same time, and I tell the people over and over, "Not a cross, a meeting place. A MEETING PLACE."

One little boy walks over to me and touches my shining face. "Can I do that?" he asks.

"Yes," I tell him.

He's only three and wobbles trying to find his balance, but the spirits come into his meeting place in all their colours. His face is full of happiness, everything come together.

We walk to the altar where the woman is tied down. I touch the ropes and the spirits release the bonds.

"Where do you want to go, lady?" I ask.

She looks at me, crying. "Home," she says.

I touch over her heart. I see a place, a red brick house somewhere far away, and I know they stole her and brought her here where no one would know her.

"You'll be all right," I tell her.

I ask the little boy to help. He stands on the woman's left side and touches above her heart. He places his feet together and sticks his other arm straight out. I stand on the other side of the altar. I have to stretch to reach the boy's hand on the woman's heart. Then I stick out my other hand and place my feet together. Both six points, a together-meeting place.

"Can you see her house?" I ask the boy.

"Yeth," he lisps.

He *knows* what to do. We close our eyes and we *wish*. We wish for a happy family in that red brick house and we send the *longing* into that woman's *mother* heart. I feel the spirits rush into her with all my happiness.

"Oh my god," the woman whispers.

Then she's gone. The spirits carry her alive body away to that red brick faraway house.

The little boy and I hold hands. The spirits are leaving and the congregation closes in, but I feel right and good. I know what's *real real* behind everything that's wrong. I know this is happiness, that it's truly mine.

There's the swish of robes coming close. It's so dark, I can hardly see the little boy's face. He squeezes my hand.

"I like you," he says.

Nowhere Gone

I am playing. It is with the plastic farm animals and the tin barn. I am playing that the piggy died and we are having a sad church time. But then I hear Daddy's feet coming on the stairs. I don't want Daddy coming on the stairs. Because that means the playing is over. Now the door knob is turning so I go away. I just go away like when you breathe in air. You feel it come in and then it's gone. I go in with the air and then I'm gone.

Eyes stretched wide as sky. Chest all squished and can't breathe. Mouth coming apart like door coming out of wall. Hole gets bigger and in the middle stands Daddy. My eyes play tricks like when you stare at light and everything goes opposite. So now he's all dark, all the light dark and the dark light. My chest all squished and can't breathe.

Pumping feeling between my legs. *Boom boom boom.* Daddy makes that come. *Can't move look at him tell me what to do so I can do it and no yelling.*

But he doesn't tell me, *Get undressed and on the bed.* He says, "Get up and come downstairs we're going out." He goes away. That's better because sometimes I can't stand up when he's there. My legs get too afraid and I can't walk.

I hang onto the railing and go downstairs. The ceilings in our house are faraway up. Sometime when I get big I'm gonna reach up and touch them. I hang onto the railing and look at the faraway ceiling while I go downstairs. In the kitchen, Mommy has my coat. She tells me Daddy's waiting in the car. I go out the back door and get in the front seat.

My Daddy always scares me. He makes my mouth go away. He makes my tit nipples burn like fire and between my legs it's like water running and lots of times I pee. Just when he walks in the room, I pee. I sit in the car seat and I squish my legs together and try to not move. Because now the air's gone all hard and if I move, it'll crack and break all around me. Then he'll be mad for sure.

He puts on the radio and the windshield wipers and I watch them go back and forth. Sometimes the same as the music, then not, then the same again. It wipes everything out of my head and I just stare and then I'm nowhere gone.

Dashboard. Wipers. Rain. Fuzzy feeling in my ears and then everything clear. Daddy's music on the radio, lady singing high up, lot of violins rubbing like tree leaves.

"I'm taking you to see a nice man." Daddy's hands are monster big on the steering wheel. I think sometimes I'm stuck to his hands. He moves them and I move too, even when I'm across the room from him.

"I'm taking you to his house and he'll play some games with you. You know the games I taught you. You play those games the way he wants and I don't want to hear about any complaining out of you."

"No, Daddy."

"What'd you say? Speak up."

"No, Daddy."

"No Daddy what?"

"I'll be a good girl."

He drives like he's mad at me—real quiet, but the quiet roars off him like crazy invisible dogs ready to jump.

"When you get to the house, you put on the clothes in that bag there."

There's a grocery bag on the car floor. I leave it where it is. If I look too soon, I'll get the weird feeling. Like everything inside is melting, things going too fast, running together, I'm drowning. Drowning in sounds coming up my throat. Scared sounds. I won't look until I have to.

We drive to where the rich houses are, up a back alley and a driveway with three cars. Big cars. I never been here before. Daddy makes me carry the bag. When he knocks on the back door, a lady dressed like the movies lets us in. Black dress and white apron and cap. She's got black skin.

This lady takes me to a bathroom lots bigger than ours and tells me to get changed. I try to find a place where no mirrors can get me. I don't like mirrors to get me because I can't go nowhere else—everything's grabbed tight in the seeing-you place. Especially with no clothes on. So I look hard for a corner where no mirror's watching and squish in between the toilet and the wall. I have to bend over the toilet because of the toilet paper holder but I close the lid first. Even though it smells like flowers in there.

I take off all my clothes. My underwear smells dirty, like I wore it too long. I shove it deep into my red pants. I put my socks in the pant legs. They're all brown on the bottom part. Then I pull off my top quick and reach for the bag. I keep my chin stuck out far so I can't see the rest of me, no clothes on like that. Never want to be with no clothes on like that.

If I see part of myself that's supposed to have clothes on but doesn't, I get scared. There's stuff living in those parts that will jump out at me. It's like those parts will just burst open and horrible things will come out. That's what lives inside those parts, so I don't want to see them. I stick my chin way out and only look down when my hand goes into the bag to pull out the new clothes. Feel the clothes, soft and smooth, sliding in my hand.

Feel me in my head, soft and smooth, sliding away. *Away.*

Don't want to wear soft smooth clothes. Bad clothes. Bad clothes for a bad girl. I'm not a bad girl. I'm good. Good. Please let me be good.

I come up like a tongue ready to lick. A cat looking for badness. I'm the badness and I like it. I always want to laugh when the others are crying. When someone's hurting, I just got to smile. Cuz I'm the badness and that's what badness does.

I get unstuck from behind the toilet and go look in the mirrors. Big ones that let you see your bum and tits from behind and in front at the same time. The bruises are there, places where the badness is showing, and I can tell I still got no tits yet. I keep waiting, but they don't show up. Mommy says maybe in six years. I go get the bag, pull out the red and black doll clothes and put them on. Then the garter. I forgot it once and the man told Daddy so now I never forget the garter.

The lady comes back and she helps me with the make-up. I like the sparkly stuff around my eyes with my lips all shiny. The lady even curls my hair but she won't put the red stuff on my fingernails when I ask. I watch her put the lipstick away in a velvet purple bag and she catches me looking.

"What's your name, honey?" she asks me.

"Marilyn Monroe." I'm lying but Daddy told me to say that and anyway, I like
lying. See what you can make people think.

"You know what you're doing, honey?" the lady asks.

I know what she's thinking. She's feeling sorry for me and wanting me to be
like the others. The goodies who always cry. I never cry. I'm the *badness*.
I get the evil eyes out and look at her with them.

"I'm here for the birthday boy," I say. I stick my lip out a little.

Her eyes get big and she looks away. "Yes honey, you are," she says. "How old
are you? Six?"

"Old enough to know what's in a pair of pants."

Now her face starts falling in. Like there's nothing there holding it up. I smile
cuz that's what I want.

"Want me to kiss your ass?" I ask. Just to make sure she doesn't get those sorry
eyes again. Her face goes back to normal and her eyes get real cold.

"You must be the devil's child," she says.

I smile again.

"C'mon, let's go," she says in her order-around voice.

I follow her out the door, wiggling my bum while I walk. Getting it working.
They always want the bum to wiggle. Like it's dancing. Or like it's trying to
get away. It's hard to know which way a guy wants it before I see him. I look
at his eyes and then I know. But right now I don't know so I practice both
wiggle ways going down the hall.

The sorry eyes—you gotta get rid of them fast. I let one lady go sorry on me
once and one of the others came out and pushed me back in. The other one
crawled up onto this lady's lap and hung on bawling her eyes out. I couldn't
get out again and the man waiting for me got real mad. So no more sorry
eyes. Not with all the bawlers I got hanging around inside just waiting to
get out.

We go down a big hall with nice carpet and up a wide staircase. There are little
holes in the wall with statues of just heads, and pictures of trees and the
countryside. The lady takes me to the upstairs hall where there are more
pictures and lots of doors. In one door, I see a little girl's bed with pink frills
and lots of toys on it. I want to go sleep in that bed.

The lady stops and knocks on a door. "Your guest is here, sir," she says.

"Send her in," says the man.

The lady looks at me one last time. I think her face is gonna start falling in again so I stick out my tongue. Then I wiggle my bum like I'm dancing. She clicks her tongue and opens the door. Then she walks away real fast.

I watch her go down the hall a minute. I can tell she's a real nice lady. The bawlers in me, they want to run after her. I turn fast and walk in the room, wiggling my bum like I'm supposed to.

The man's sitting on the edge of the bed. He's wearing a housecoat with his legs apart but I can't see his thing yet. He's sort of old and fat and he's got a cigar. He looks at me like he's figuring out what he wants.

"Close the door, little girl," he says.

I close the door and turn around again. He's still figuring things out. I turn around a couple of times, wiggling my bum like my Daddy showed me. That's so he can see the merchandise better. Daddy says that helps make up their minds.

The man gets up. He goes over to a record player and puts on a record. It's old music, with a lady singing but not like Daddy's music. This music feels like it's got soft hands and they're on you, heading for the bad places. I stick my tits out and pretend I'm six years older.

"You dance for me, little girl," the man says.

I dance like Daddy taught me with his metronome counting so I got it right. I lift my arms and wiggle and count. I close my eyes and listen for the badness in the music. I got to find all the badness and let it come in to help me. Cuz I'm starting to feel like a bawler and I can't be a bawler, I got to be bad. I keep my eyes closed real tight and listen hard for the badness and just wiggle and wiggle into the badness. It's there between the notes, the badness. Wiggle, wiggle, one two three, until I hear a spot big enough for me to wiggle into and then I'm only badness and the body's gone far away.

She's bad but I'm the fucker. She wiggles around and then I take it. I come out into the eyes and look at the asshole. Housecoat open now. Prick big like his cigar. He lies down on the bed.

"Come here, little girl," he says.

First I take off the doll clothes. Then I climb up on the bed and lie down beside him. Pretend everything's all right with me. This is how I pretend. When I was little, I saw a chain saw on a tree stump. It cut real good and I thought it could do what I wanted. So I made up another chain saw inside me and now I get it going, cutting everything inside apart like that tree stump. When he tells me to put my hand on his prick, I cut that hand off so it's on his prick doing what he wants but it's not my hand cuz I can't feel it, cut off like that. When he tells me to suck him, I cut my head into two pieces and I go into the top part. While my mouth sucks, I stay in my eyes where nothing happens. When he starts poking me, everywhere he pokes me, I just cut that off. Soon I'm like a piece of meat for supper, all cut up into chunks that stick together but they're still apart from each other. So they're all bloody but nothing goes from one piece to the other. He can do anything he wants to me and I'll find a piece somewhere to go and be gone from it. And I just wait in that piece and I watch what he does to the other pieces but I don't feel it. Because the feeling is in another piece, and it's not me.

I figured this out. It's the feeling they want. The feeling in me. Any feeling they can get. So they can take that feeling and hurt it bad. I learned. I learned how to take the feeling and put it away in deep, way far away from them and way far away from me. So I don't feel no more. The feeling's gone so deep inside, I can't get to it. Even when I want to because I don't know where it's gone. Maybe there's a bit of it in each piece I cut off. That's good, I guess. Now I can smile while he pokes me. I smile and I say things my Daddy told me to say.

"You've got such a big one, mister. Do you do this to your little girl, mister? I like you, mister. Can you put it in me again, please?"

Sometimes, even though I don't feel it, I can see the feeling when he's pushing extra hard. Then I see all the chunks I cut off inside. In each one there's a face. Just for a second. A different face in each chunk.

They're all bawling. Except for one. She's looking at the rest and she's laughing.

And then there's my face on top of all the other faces. My face hanging onto that lipstick and sparkly eye stuff. Until he's done. I shine and smile. And when he goes away, I do too.

The Lives in the Cross

We're building an acrostic. The Kin says it's because I'm in grade one so I'm old enough. They say I learned my Up and Down and Front and Back and Left and Right really good so I can do more. Sometimes after, They give me a sucker. Sometimes not.

When I was very little, we started the cross. I didn't know Left or Right yet, so they'd say, "Side, side," and wave on one side of me or the other. Then I'd know where. They did the same things to me then as They do now. They would make it hurt very bad, like fire but there was no fire. They called it electricity or The Zap for short. It felt like small lightning. They would put round things on me called discs, with wires off them that ran to a machine. Then it would start to hurt. The electricity would come and hurt bad. They'd yell things at me, bad things. And a devil would come in, all red or black, or a bad angel all in white, and hiss at me and I'd get so scared, I'd want to go anywhere away.

I thought The Kin was just trying to help me understand how to get things right. I thought when everything went according to The Plan, God stayed happy. Then there was no need for anyone to get punished. They were teaching me about the Cross and the Way and the Truth, and They said I was learning it good. So I was glad about that. But it still hurt and I got scared. I wondered when I would learn it all enough so the electricity would stop and go away.

Then I learned about The Lie.

This was when I was around five. Soon after I figured out The Lie, I finished the cross. I thought maybe then I would be done with the electricity. But They told me I was old enough to make an acrostic, so I knew I would have to work longer.

Sometimes I think my heart is too little to carry such a big cross. Plus an acrostic. Because I'm only Dorell, not a Jesus person. But I don't think I can tell the Kin that. So I just keep going on.

The cross is a funny world. It's made up of levels, levels of trying to get away. It wasn't there in the beginning but They helped me make it. I can remember some of it very good. Other stuff is more blurry. There are six ways to go out of the body and into the cross: Up, Down, Left, Right, Back and Front. Each one of the six ways is full of different places. The Kin calls them "levels." If you go out of the body to the Right, there are different levels there, one after the other. Each level is different from the one before it and each level gets further away from the body and the electricity. But you have to remember how many levels you travelled or you could get lost. And you have to do everything They say.

Unless you learn about The Lie. That's what I did. Then everything changed.

Daddy brings me to the doctor's office. Or Mommy. Way back, they would carry me because I couldn't walk yet. Or I'd walk too slow. In the waiting room, we sit and wait. If it's Mommy, she reads me a book. If it's Daddy, he reads a book and I sit quiet so I don't get hit.

When the nurse says so, Daddy or Mommy carry me down a hall into the Operating Room. It looks just like any other doctor's room but it has a special name. The name makes me scared. Whenever they say "Operating Room," they say it angry as if they're telling me to keep it secret or bad things will happen. Everything that happens in the Operating Room is very very secret, only for the Chosen Few to know about. That's why it has a special name.

Daddy and Mommy go away and leave me in the Operating Room. I don't want them to go away, but I suck in my mouth. That's so I won't say nothing about it. Because I did once and then I got hit.

The nurse gives me two pills. They make me feel sleepy. Then she takes off my clothes and puts me on a table. She puts the straps on me so I can't move. She turns on the light above my face. It's very big and bright. She goes out.

When she comes back, the doctor is with her. He's a baby doctor. All the Mommies and Daddies like him. I see how they smile at him in church and when we go downtown. So I smile at him too.

The doctor never smiles at me here. He does in church but not in the Operating Room. He pushes over the machine and puts the glue on me and then the cold round discs with the wires running off. So now I know the electricity will come.

Next he tells me a story. It's a story about where we're going to go. The story tells me what it will be like there.

"Up Up Up is a land of angels," he says. "It's a land where everything is white and clean. The angels are friendly and they sing happy songs. They play harps and sit on clouds. There are many white crosses there. When you go to Up Up Up, you'll be happy. There will be no devils and there will be no dark."

For a moment I'm happy. Because last time I came to the Operating Room, the doctor read me a story about Down Down Down. It was very dark and in a grave under the floor. When I went out of the body and travelled to Down Down Down, there were dead people there and I got put in a coffin. I got very scared. So today I'm happy to go to Up Up Up. I never been there before.

"Can you see Up Up Up, Dorell?" the doctor asks me.

I nod my head. I can't really, but if I tell the truth I know I'll get hit. And if I squint hard, maybe I can see some angels. Happy with harps.

"Up Up Up," says the doctor. "Say it. Up Up Up."

"Upupup," I say quick and loud.

"That's a good girl. Up Up Up."

He turns on the electricity and I scream. I can't help it, it hurts so bad, and I know it's going to get worse. Then the door to the Operating Room bursts open and a devil comes in. A devil all dressed in black with horns on his head. The nurse screams, waving her hands.

"Gotcha," the devil yells at me. "Gotcha, Dorell. Gotcha."

I'm jerking from the electricity so I can't watch the devil jump all around me with his pitchfork. The doctor keeps saying, "Up Up Up."

Up Up Up. Gotcha. Yellow orange fire. Up Up Up. Black devil gotcha. Red yellow fire. Up Up Up. Yellow white fire. Gotcha. Up Up Up. Up Up Up. Up Up Up.

Up. It starts to happen. As if I'm a white sheet pinned to a clothesline and the clothes pins come loose and a wind picks the sheet up slow, lifting me higher and higher, away from where I'm tied down, away from the electricity.

Now it doesn't hurt no more. It's easy, I lift into Up where I been lots of times. Up is still in the same room, just under the ceiling. I stay in Up a minute and look around even though I'm not supposed to.

There's a lot going on in Up. The nurse is up here too, and the doctor. And the devil, but he's a lot different in Up. Here he's like the doctor and nurse—a person, not a devil. They all float up by the ceiling and look down at the bodies doing stuff in the room. They just watch.

There's a couple of other me's up here. They look just like the body, little girl persons, but if a real person put her finger in them, it would go right through. In Up, no one is hard like a body. In Up, you mostly just think and watch what is happening below. The Kin call the place where the body lives Real.

Up here, I don't have to feel like the body. I like that about Up. Except it can get boring in Up. Because you never feel happy or good, even when the body reads a bedtime story. You just watch.

So I wave at the other me's in Up and they watch me go past, on into Up Up. But before I go into Up Up, I have to go through the first Changing Place. This is the ceiling. The Changing is funny weird but you get used to it. It happens everywhere between levels, even in Side Side, but each Changing Place is different. When you go out of the body into Up or Down or any-where, you turn into tiny waves. Everything you are is moving in little waves. Tiny ripples. If you go up, the waves go faster. If you go down, they go slower. When you go into Front or Back or the Sides, the waves change colours but you don't always know how fast or slow they'll go.

I done this lots of times. I know the waves will get faster at this Changing Place but not a lot faster. The ceiling has a light in it so I use it for the Changing Place because the light waves go quickest and I'll get there faster. I move into the light waves and keep going up. The waves are a yellow white, then it starts to get blue like it's supposed to, and then I'm through the first Changing Place and in Up Up.

In Up Up, it's all blue. Up Up is the sky and it loves me here. Everywhere is pretty blue with no bad thinking. No one here has bad thinking and everyone is blue like the sky. There are lots of other people in Up Up, blue and floating around. All thinking good thoughts. I think this is what peace means in church. Peace is all-blue.

There are so many all-blue people in Up Up, I think that's what the sky is made of. People thinking good thoughts. I have lots of me's up here. Maybe even a hundred. Sometimes when I'm in the body reading a bedtime story, I start to feel all-blue and full of peace. I know one of the me's in Up Up is listening to the story too and she likes it.

I want to stay in Up Up because it's nice here but I keep going because the doctor told me to. And because the body is still screaming. I'm glad I can't feel it. I can see the body in a small circle way down below me, screaming and screaming. But none of the other me's in Up Up can see the body. They get to keep the peace they've got.

Up Up Up. I never been there before. Coming to the top of Up Up, I wonder what it will be like. The doctor said full of nice angels with harps. And white crosses.

I see the Changing Place between Up Up and Up Up Up in front of me. Sort of invisible but sort of there. It looks like a brick wall but see-through. When I go through it the Changing will happen again. I know going to Up Up Up, the waves will go even faster. The electricity is so full of fast waves, it's *fastfastfastfast* like a million waves all in one. I'm scared maybe Up Up Up will be like the electricity. But the doctor said it will be nice, so I go on.

The first part of this Changing Place is blue, like Up Up. It gets to be a softer and softer blue until it's almost white. I can feel the waves in me moving faster. Then I see the white really-fast waves ahead of me. I turn into them and I'm moving up very fast, like a zoom.

I'm through the Changing Place and in Up Up Up. Right away I see them. Angels, all over the place. With their harps, singing. Some of them talking and having tea in little china cups. Close by there's a big white gate with a white cross on each side. It's hard to see shapes with all this white but when I stare I can. I walk to the gate and there's a big angel with a book. I think this must be the Angel Gabriel and the Book of Judgement.

But no, it's the doctor in a white dress and wings. And he still has his glasses and bald head. So I know the nurse is probably somewhere in Up Up Up too. And Mommy and Daddy and everyone else I know, all going in white fast waves. I found them everywhere else I went in the cross, so far. All the levels.

"What is your name?" the doctor angel asks me. He doesn't look too happy. He's frowning. A white frown.

"Dorell," I tell him in a white voice. High up and talking fast and pretty.

"What is your birth name?" His voice is high quick too. Not as pretty as mine though.

I can think so quick here. "Dorene Grace Hall."

He flips some pages. A lot of pages, more than the phone book. Finally he stops and reads.

"Dorene Grace Hall," he says. "I see you have been forgiven and washed clean by the blood of the lamb. Do you understand that you have died and gone to Heaven?"

I get mixed up. No one ever said I had to *stay* in a level before. The doctor sent me to levels but he always called me back. I think this time he's saying I got to stay.

"I don't know," I say.

"Look down," the doctor angel tells me. "Look down to Real."

There's a small dark circle in Heaven's floor. When I look down through it, I can see the Operating Room. The electricity is off and the body is lying still and quiet.

"The body is dead," says the angel doctor. "But no matter, you have been forgiven and granted permission to enter the gates of Heaven. Dorene Grace Hall, you may enter."

So I go in. I don't know what else to do. I don't know how to go back down to Real and if the body is dead I don't want to get stuck in it. Then it will go into a grave in Down Down Down, where I got sent to last time.

I walk around Heaven for a long time. It's all right. There's no bad stuff and everyone flies around and has tea. They sing a lot of the "Hallelujah Chorus" that Daddy plays at Christmas time in Real. And there's no electricity. Just a lot of white tea and Bible stories. It's sort of like always Sunday—white churches and white preachers preaching white sermons. There are white crosses all over the place.

Everywhere I go, I can see the small dark circle in Heaven's floor with the body in it down below. I don't think I'm supposed to, so I don't tell anyone. Because this is how I know the angel doctor lied to me. I can see the body isn't dead, it never went really dead. It was just asleep for a while. Tired of the electricity, I think. And I think the doctor angel knew that because he's a doctor. A little after he told me the body was dead, I looked into the dark circle in Heaven's floor. I saw the body open its eyes and get up. I could tell another me had the body. I could tell she had a headache and her eyes were all red from the pills but she was alive and still in Real. Then she got a sucker and she went home.

So I know They lied to me here in Up Up Up. In *Heaven*. That's not the way it's supposed to be in Heaven. So now I'm suspicious. I'm suspicious about the doctor angel and all the other angels and the quick white waves that make me feel clean and happy. Because A Lie got told here and that makes the white a dirty-white. Some of this white is bad.

I turn into a spy. A Heaven spy. Looking around and trying to figure it out. I walk all around Heaven, looking and looking for how The Lie got here. I find so many angels, all quick white waves. I find some other angel me's. They look happy and drink a lot of tea. They read their Bibles and sit quiet. I don't tell them about The Lie because I can tell they like their white place. It's their peace.

Then I think about going more up. Further up into Up Up Up to see what's at the top. Maybe I can find God and ask Him. So instead of flying back and forth, I make my wings fly up.

Most of the other angels don't ever look up or down. They just stay around each other. Even the other me's. I fly up a long time, through more white. White sky, white clouds. White night, white day. No sun or moon or stars, just white sky. Higher up, I see some other angels. They fly up and down like messengers. Like kids at school carrying notes to the office. These angels look very busy and they don't pay attention to me.

I don't see God anywhere. Not anywhere in Heaven. I think I would know God if I saw Him—I seen enough pictures. But I don't see anyone that looks like God.

Finally I get to the top of Up Up Up. I see the next Changing Place between Up Up Up and Up Up Up Up. It's a wall of huge white fire. I wonder how to do this. Then, way far over, I see an angel come through the wall of fire and go down. The angel doesn't look burnt, not a bit. So I know this

Changing Place isn't a real fire. If I'm careful I won't get burnt. It looks like my waves will have to go fast though. Very very fast.

I think I can do it, but I'm worried that I don't have permission. I'm supposed to stay dead and saved in Up Up Up. But I'm so suspicious, I think I'll go into Up Up Up Up and see if God can tell me about The Lie I found in Heaven.

I fly quick into the wall of fire. The Changing happens fast here. Quick fast hot. And then only *screaming white never going to stop* fire. Not fire. *Electricity.*

Up Up Up Up is a level of electricity. All electricity. It never stops, it never starts. You're just there in the middle of it all the time. I know right off that this is God. Up Up Up Up *is* God. This is how God is, white punishment. Heaven is white peace, God is white punishment. Now I know this, I don't need to ask God any questions. I see that every time the body gets the electricity in the Operating Room, God comes into the body and kills it. God takes the soul He killed and sends it to live somewhere outside Real, somewhere in the levels in the cross. Then the body is reborn with someone new in it. Like a John the Baptist baptism of fire.

In Up Up Up Up, I know all this right away. Everything is so quick here, I learn it all at once. And I know I'm not going to stay here, I'm not going to be part of the electric fire God. I make all my waves go fast down through the Changing Place of fire. I keep going until I'm through and down into Heaven. Now everything seems slow here and not so white. Less white than a screaming God.

Now I know I can go to different levels on my own. I don't have to stay here either. So I zoom down past the angels, past the angel doctor at the gate. I don't say a word, not even Hi. I just make my waves ripple into the Changing Wall until they slow to the blue sky colour. Does it ever feel slow here now. So full of peace.

But I don't want to stay here either. And I know I don't have to. So I float down to the ceiling. My waves go even slower and when I come through the ceiling Changing Place, I'm not in the Operating Room. I'm in my own bedroom. This happens because the body is in my bedroom now. I float and watch.

There are a lot of me's in this room. The ceiling is full of them. All the me's outside the body float and watch. Some are in the ceiling light. Some are in the dresser lamp. Others hide in the dark places. Under the bed, in the dresser drawers. In the closet and behind the door. Even in pockets and shadows and cracks in the floor. Some are in the mirror. Lots of me's go into the pictures the body draws and sticks on the wall. Or stories the body writes, books the body reads. Everywhere, another little bit going away. To save itself apart. So the Kin can't get at it.

Now the body is reading itself another bedtime story. It's a book about rabbits. Rabbits helping each other to be happy. Pictures with lots of colours. These colours have slower waves than Heaven with its lie-white and God with His hurting-white. I think I want to go into the picture colour green for a while until the body goes to sleep. Because right now another me is reading the rabbit story. She doesn't know about me and she'll get dizzy and afraid if I push her away. So I wait.

I go into a rabbit's green jacket. Green is my favourite colour. The waves go soft as a breeze in the trees. When I hear the body breathing slow as sleep, I slip into it.

It's nice to feel the sheets all warm. My skin heavy around me. My heart is thick and wet and such a slow *pump pump pumping*. Everything feels thick and wet and slow like a tongue. I like this and I like sleeping. Sleeping is one of my favourite things.

I'm very afraid during the next trip to the Operating Room. This is because I know the doctor angel saw me go back down. And Daddy takes me back the next day, so I know it's because of my spying around and finding God.

They put the straps on me and then the discs and I start to cry. I think they're going to send me into God and Up Up Up Up but they don't. The doctor says I can't leave. When he says that, all the me's in Up and Down and Front and Back and both Sides, they all crowd in close so I can't get out. I have to stay in the body and take the electricity the whole time.

God comes into the body. The white screaming electric God. God hurts way more in the body than in Up Up Up Up. The hurting lasts a long time. It makes me poop and pee and my eyes see blurry. My ears are loud bells. When it all stops, I'm too tired to cry.

"You do what you are commanded," the doctor tells me. "Submit. Obey. I own you."

I want to say yes but I can't move my mouth. The doctor and nurse stand there a long time and all they say is "Submit. Obey. I own you," until there's nothing else in my head. When I get my mouth working, I say it back.

The doctor tells me I'm getting a new sign. A sign is a picture. Every me has a sign. Before this, my sign was a girl walking, like on a crosswalk sign. Because that's what I did—I walked between levels that were close in.

My new sign is a bird. It's a weird bird. It's all drawn in waves, and all the colours are there. I look at it and I get the feeling that the Changing is about to happen.

"This will be a sign unto you," the doctor says. "This will be your new sign. It means you have a new job. You will be a Traveller now. You will travel the far-out levels. The only time you will be in the body is when I call you back. Do you understand?"

I start to cry. I don't want to go back up to God. Or down to the grave. The nurse slaps my face. I keep crying. She slaps it again. I suck in my mouth and stop.

"When I call you back to the body, you will tell me what you found."

I get surprised here. I thought the doctor knew everything out there.

"You will tell me everything you find," he says again.

"Yes," I say, thinking.

"Submit," he says.

"Submit," I say. I'm still thinking.

"Obey," he says.

"Obey," I say. Thinking as fast as God.

"I own you," he says.

"You own me," I say. I think maybe when the doctor calls me back into the body, maybe there will be a way to look around real quick in the head and find the bedtime stories the body read while I was out and gone. All the stories I'll have to miss while I'm out travelling. I love the bedtime stories. Maybe I'll figure out a way. I hope.

"I'm going to send you to Up Up Up Up Up," says the doctor. "That's the night sky. There are a lot of stars and planets up there. I'll leave you there for a long time. When I call you back, you'll feel this."

He holds a small machine over my heart. It sends a new kind of wave in, bright and strong. It goes straight and then it quick jerks to one side. Like a heart gasp. When he does this, I see a new colour I've never seen before. The colour is making a sound. The doctor keeps sending the new wave into my heart until I learn this colour and sound, the way it hurts me. Whenever I feel it, I know I'm supposed to come back to the body because it's calling me in.

This time the doctor doesn't read me a story about Up Up Up Up Up. All my thinking tells me the doctor doesn't know about Up Up Up Up Up. He's never been there. I think maybe he's never been to God either. But then I think he has. Because he's mean like the God waves. White-hurting mean.

The electricity starts and I shoot out. This time I travel quick through each Changing Place. I fly quick as I can through God, though all of God takes longer to get through than Heaven. To get through God takes a very long time. Then there's a new Changing Place. It's like a million faraway stars, all pretty colours mixed together.

I go through this Changing Place and come out into black. The waves are going faster than God to keep me so far out but the waves aren't scary like God. Everywhere I turn and look, there are things. Pieces of rock. Floating colours. Stars—one is pretty close. They're bigger here.

This is better than God. I start off looking around. I look a long time. And when the doctor calls me back, I tell him some things. If he hurts me, I tell him more. But I know something now. He can send me Up or Down or all around but he can't go where I can go. He can't go past God or Satan and I've been past both. I wonder if maybe everyone in the Kin is like the doctor—stuck between God and Satan.

When the doctor starts to build the acrostic with me, I know I can tell him anything I want and he has to believe me. Because I find new levels he can't go to. I find levels he's never even heard about. Sometimes he doesn't believe what I tell him. Because he knows about The Lie. He's been to Heaven.

I been there too.

Brother on the Bridge

For God so loved the world, He sent His only begotten son.

Sometimes, walking home from the Christian school on Lewis Street, the sky
falls soft, a pastel pink-blue colour that falls into Cartright River, into sidewalk cracks too, and the hole in my running shoe. And I'm so happy, I feel
the love of Jesus everywhere, like the world's made up of His dying tears,
drops of water running together into one swirling happiness. And I feel like
I'm everything too, like my skin is happiness that doesn't have to stay in one
place and I can go out of my skin into the black trees, the way they hurt
happy against a sunset. Like when it's March and there's no leaves yet, and
everything is waiting for the resurrection.

If God didn't love Jesus, He wouldn't have sent Him to die.

The Orford Road hill is so steep. It comes down at you like God's forgiveness
when you're climbing it. When I turn and look back at my brother, I feel the
sky push heavy on the small of my back. My birthday is coming soon and
I'll be eleven. This morning while I was hiding extra brown sugar under my
Shredded Wheat, before I poured on the milk, Mom said, "Now you're
almost grown-up, you'll be given more responsibilities."

My brother Ian will be eight this summer. It's still cold out, but Mom already
gave him his spring haircut. His red curls are almost gone. He looks thinner.
His arms and legs look longer. I love my little brother like God loves Jesus.

"Hurry up!" I yell.

Ian's banging his orange lunch pail against his legs every step like it's on purpose, and he's going to break his thermos. He does that and Daddy will drag
him into the pantry for the wooden spoon and I won't be able to eat because
Ian never cries if he can help it but he groans, especially when he gets
punched, and his groans get into my mashed potatoes so they're lumpy in
my throat going down and I want to throw up. Every day I want to save my

little brother from getting hit but I don't know how. He doesn't listen to me, it's like he *wants* to get hit sometimes. When I tell him how to smarten up, he looks at me and laughs. Like a hyena.

God loved Jesus so He sent Him to die.

I have lots of Bible verses memorized. They use up a whole bunch of my head. I like to say them out into the air, into the trees and ground while I walk. Then I can put them there inside what's going to be leaves and flowers, and I can touch the world like God did. Sort of create it all over again, and make sure the Word stays put. When I feel extra close to God, I can see Jesus dying on hydro poles or nailed up on the RCMP station door.

Just last week I saw Him dying on the RCMP door, His blood shedding for all the criminals who kill people and get traffic tickets. I'll never get a traffic ticket. I'll drive carefully so I never hit a baby. My kindergarten teacher hit a boy in my class and he died. They said it wasn't her fault, he ran in front of her car, but she had a nervous breakdown. I bet you she never drove her car again either. I bet there was a lot of blood. I bet that kid thought he was Jesus, just before he died. I bet God let him pick someone, just anyone he loved, like his Mom or his little brother, just before he died so he could save that person from eternal damnation.

Ian catches up and stomps by, just like I haven't been waiting for him very patiently. My back hurts from standing on that Orford hill, just like someone mean is trying to shove and push me all the way back down again. To where the RCMP station is, at the very bottom.

Suddenly Ian ducks down and pokes his hand under a lilac hedge. He pulls out a dirty Coke bottle and holds it up and laughs. Like a hyena. I start to run at him.

"You got to share!"

He backs away. "No way. *You* never do."

"Yes I do." His hair is too short to grab, so I take his shoulders and shake him. "You give it to me."

"You're a fatty."

I can't hold onto everything, my lunch pail and books and Ian, so I stop shaking him. We stand there panting and staring at the sidewalk. I forgot all about the street while I was shaking him—the cars going by, the houses, the traffic light switching red, green, yellow at the corner. A little bird starts

singing nearby and the song gets into my ear. Something nice and pretty. It
makes the air go deep into my chest, like the smell of a flower. You can't see
it, but when a flower smell is there, it takes up all of you.

"You gonna buy some candy?" I ask Ian. You can buy bags of broken candy for
two cents or an empty pop bottle at a store up the street.

"I dunno." Still staring at the sidewalk, he shrugs. Then he holds the bottle out.
"Here, you can have it."

"Don't you want it?"

"It's too dirty. They won't take it at the store anyway."

There's a puddle on the sidewalk from last night's rain. I take the bottle and
swish it in the water, then I give it back to Ian. Just before he takes it, the
sunset touches the glass so it glows. Right there between our hands, and
we're both touching it. I look at Ian and he smiles, real happiness, which he
hardly ever has.

"C'mon," I say. "Maybe we'll find another one."

He runs ahead. "I'll look. You can have that one."

That makes me feel like he loves me so much, I feel all spread out against the
purple-pink sunset like a black tree and I think, *If only God would let me die
and save my little brother from all his pain and suffering, I'd do it, I'd do it right
now.* Just like Billy Graham always tells us on TV. Sacrifice *everything* for
Jesus.

I run after Ian, careful not to let my thermos bang. Once, the hinges on mine
broke and the thermos fell out and I was so worried, I sat at the supper table
crying and crying, I couldn't stop, it was like everything was melting and
running out my eyes. But Daddy just looked at me and said it was an acci-
dent and he didn't spank me and I felt so much like I had real happiness
then, I cried even harder. I was seven, like my brother is now.

When I catch up to him, Ian's crouched down on the sidewalk. He's set his
lunch pail and books on the edge of the curb and they're almost falling into
the street. I just shake my head and move them onto the sidewalk. A Jesus
hanging on a Yield sign at the corner lifts his head and nods at me. Then He
drops it and goes on dying, bleeding soft purple-orange-pink across the sky.
Jesus' love is just *everywhere* if you know how to look for it. I pat Ian on his
short red curls.

"Don't," he says.

"What're you doing?"

"Found some gum."

It's Black Cat and it's fresh. I can tell because it's stretching easy when Ian pulls at it and he has to work it off the cement. Someone stepped on it. Black Cat is the best kind of gum because it never loses its taste no matter how many people chew it before you. I think I'll grab it away from him, then I look at the Yield sign and see the blood dripping from Jesus' hands and feet and the big sword hole in his side. So I don't. I let Ian pop it in his mouth and chew away.

"Did you check it for stones?" I ask.

"Yeah. Not stupid." Ian picks up his lunch pail and books.

"You want me to carry your books?" It's just his spelling notebook and some math sheets. They're working on subtraction.

"Okay."

Ian marches ahead of me like a soldier, swinging his lunch pail wide, so I can tell his heart feels big and proud. He stomps right through puddles like they're not there, getting his runners wet. "Hey Dorene," he yells. "You think they'll have pink peppermints?"

That's one of the kinds of broken-up candy they sell in the two-cent bags. "I dunno."

"If they do, I'll let you have them."

I know he hates pink peppermints, so I don't say thanks. Sometimes I think my little brother wouldn't make a very good missionary. That's what I'm going to be when I grow up, a missionary to deepest darkest Africa. When the natives cut me up and boil me in a pot, I'll be just like Jesus and when they eat me, it'll be like a Lord's Supper. I wonder for a bit if they sell two-cent bags of broken-up missionaries at African jungle corner stores, and it makes me giggle. I tell Ian and he laughs like it's the biggest joke.

But Jesus on the Yield sign doesn't think it's a good one, so I stop laughing. Ian giggles all the way down the block. I don't think my little brother sees very many dying Jesuses along the street. At least, he doesn't act like it.

Once he told me he thought *Jesus* was stupid. He was hanging by his hands onto the up-and-down rails of the bridge over Cartright River. On the *outside*, his little feet dangling. This was when he was six. I was standing on the bridge, screaming at him to watch out. "You're gonna drown and die!"

I screamed. "You want to drown and die?"

Ian was criss-crossing his hands, going rail to rail. That was how he got across the whole entire bridge. And the whole time, he laughed at me. Like a hyena.

Cars just kept driving by. No one stopped. I think he got scared half-way across. I saw it when he looked down at the dark rushing water. Then he looked back up at me and laughed.

"Jesus is stupid, Dorene," he yelled.

I almost took my foot and jammed it on his fingers, I got so mad. No more feeling sorry—he deserved to drop into the river for that. But I didn't, I just turned and walked away.

You don't say those kinds of things about Jesus. You just don't.

For God so loved Dorene, He sent His only begotten son.

Ian got all the way across by himself. I guess it wasn't really a surprise none of the car drivers noticed his little fingers around the bottom of the bridge rails. Just his lunch pail sitting on the sidewalk. And the RCMP were probably busy catching murderers. So if he'd dropped into Cartright River, it would've been all my fault. Some days I feel so guilty about that, I can hardly walk across the bridge. I see Jesus hanging off each rail and dripping tons of blood into the river until it's almost pure red.

Suffer the children to come unto me.

I keep getting a dream about the bridge. It makes me wake up with the blankets twisted through my legs and arms and I'm sweaty. In the dream Ian is hanging over the bridge, only it's me holding onto him and I see my fingernails are digging blood out of his hands. And this time we're both screaming and I don't know how long I can hold on. *I don't know how long I can hold on.* I think maybe this dream is Jesus punishing me for walking away on Ian that real time.

In another dream I get, Ian is lying on a cross. I'm kneeling over him, nailing his hands to the bars and I'm yelling, "I love you." I have to yell loud because he's screaming and not listening to me, and he has to hear God's will.

Suffer the children, suffer the children, amazing grace to come unto me.

At the Christian school, we sing hymns every morning and pray. The school is at the end of a street full of lilac bushes and in May lots of the houses hide behind their walls of purple flowers. Next to the school is an old house no one's lived in for a hundred years. It's like an old person dying in front of you, or like a moaning ghost. Sometimes I sit in my desk and I can't stop looking at it. I feel like it's trying to tell me something. Something about dying. Like it's slow and sagging and it goes on forever. Those old rusty nails keeping that house together are pulling the rotting boards apart, tiny bits at a time. When it's raining hard, the sky gets so dark I can hardly see the house through the trees. Then it looks like it's sunk into the ground. A grave opened up and said, *Come unto me now, come unto sleep.*

One day Ian and some other boys went over there and looked around. I can't believe they did that. I'm not sure Jesus even likes me thinking about that house. He spends a lot of time hanging on His cross right over the front door, dripping bright red on the porch and windows and everywhere, saving that old house from its dirt and sin so when it does die and go to Heaven, it'll be fixed up and painted white and feel real happiness. When I see Jesus dying all over that house, I know I don't have to worry about its pain and sorrow, and I can concentrate on my times tables again.

It takes us a whole hour to walk home from the Christian school. The kids on our street think it's stupid that we go to a weird school when there's one for everyone right around the corner but Mom and Daddy want us to be with Christians all the time. The girl down the street, her dad's a minister, and she goes to the public school but they're Anglicans. I guess some people are more Christian than others. I'm lucky God sent me to live in a very Christian family.

For God so loved the world, He sent Dorene to live with her father and mother and her little brother Ian.

Sometimes I rewrite the Bible and put myself in it. The Queen Dorene version.

I look at Jesus dying on a shed door and He nods again. I smile at Him and pretend I've got blood leaking out from a crown of thorns and nails in my hands. People in robes cry and wail all around me.

Father forgive them, they didn't love Dorene enough.

Now the sun is almost down. Blackness is coming up from the earth like a painting going on around us. Someone invisible is painting a wet dark up from the ground, first into tree trunks and branches, then bushes and houses. Up from the basements. Windows are turning on, soft and pretty. This is my favourite time of the day, in between things, when the light gets turned down and everything is a soft dark that's easier to look at. Easier to walk through,

friendlier. Darkness makes edges softer so that when you get close to something, you don't feel like you'll get cut. I skip to catch up to Ian. He's waiting
outside the store that sells the two-cent bags of candy.

"You can pick the bag but I get to pick who eats what," he says, mad-like.

I let the dark go into my mouth and make my words soft. "All right."

Ian stomps up the store steps and pushes open the door with its Canada Dry
sign. The bells on the string jingle and the man at the cash register looks up.
Ian stomps up to the counter and holds the Coke bottle high in the air. He
glares at the man like the man's going to say, "Now get out of my store you
little rat."

The man never says things like that. He even takes dirty bottles from Ian. I've
seen him say no to bigger boys who bring in gucky bottles but he's always
got this little smile on his face when Ian stomps into his store.

Ian stands there a bit, holding the bottle high in the air and glaring at the man.
Then he says, "My sister cleaned it in a puddle."

"Did she now?" The man nods at me and then he looks back at Ian. All of a
sudden I think, *He likes Ian, maybe he should take Ian home to be his own son.*
And my heart hurts all over because I know it, he'd love him and not hit him,
not *ever ever.*

"She did it for me." It surprises me that Ian says that. "So you would take it."

"Well, let me see it then." The man takes the bottle and looks at it all over, really
slow. Ian is hardly breathing, his eyes all squinty and his shoulders hunched
way up.

"Hmm," says the man. "This looks like an extra fine bottle to me. And you say
your sister cleaned it in a puddle for you?"

"Uh huh." Ian's shoulders are coming down a little.

"Well. . ." The man strokes his chin. He's got the little smile. "I think this is a
two bag two-cent bottle today, young man. One for you and one for your sister."

Ian's eyes practically shoot out of his head and his mouth gets huge. It looks
little when he's got it shut but my brother really has a really big mouth. He
twists half around and stares at me. Then this smile shoots out of me and
this smile shoots out of Ian, and they bump into each other in the air.

You can almost see it, those smiles bumping into each other, just like when the
sun touched that pop bottle we were both holding.

"Hey Dorene, you get a bag too!" Ian says.

The man has this big grin on, like he's having the time of his life. He probably
has his own kids and doesn't want any more. I move over fast to get a bag
before he changes his mind. Ian has his face all screwed up, staring at the
plastic bucket that has the two-cent bags of candy.

"Help yourself," says the man.

Suffer the children to come unto me.

Candy's not a lot like suffering. I just take one off the top but Ian keeps
staring, his eyes all squinty again.

"Can't make up your mind?" the man asks.

Ian tears his eyes from the candy bags and looks up at him. "Do you know
which one don't got those pink peppermints?" he asks.

I hold my breath. He's going to get hit now for sure. But I got a bag, so we can
share it. I'll take the peppermints.

Suffer.

"You don't like pink peppermints?" The man doesn't look mad.

"No. They're stupid."

The man's smiling again. "Don't like them much myself. What do you like, sir?"

Sir?! Ian swells up big and tall at that.

"Caramels. Tootsie Rolls. Black Cat gum. Like this." Ian opens his big mouth
and shows the man his gum off the street. I nearly die.

"Well," says the man, "I think we can manage that. For *this* extra special cleaned
pop bottle, that is."

He takes out a small brown bag and opens up the containers of Caramels and
Tootsie Rolls—the *not broken* ones. He fills up the bag extra full and adds a
couple of Black Cat gums. Then he twists the top and hands it to Ian who
takes it with both hands like it's a precious prize.

"Thanks," he whispers.

I want to ask this man to adopt my brother. *Please, Mr. Nice Man, he needs a
father like you to be nice to him.*

The man looks at me. "And today, I'll fill up your bag with something extra too.
What would you like?"

I come close to the shelves that hold all the different kinds of small candy.
I know what I want, but I look at them all for a bit. All those kinds. "Jelly
beans," I sigh.

He takes out the small metal shovel and shovels in jelly beans until there's no room for any more. Then he hands the bag to me. I have to take it with both hands so it won't spill onto the floor. Right away, I put it in my coat pocket. I have big coat pockets.

"Thanks!" I say.

"Don't spoil your suppers," says the man. He gives us a small wave as we pick up our lunch pails and books. Going out the door, Ian stops and looks back at him. Just stands there for a moment, gone all still, and looks at the man behind the counter. The man looks back. His face is full of soft darkness. The store lights are on, but not too bright. It's very quiet. No one else is there. I wonder what Ian's thinking, his head to one side, looking at the man like that.

"You take care of yourself, sonny," the man tells him.

Ian's face moves a little, just like water—his eyebrows and his mouth. He stands a little longer and then he says, "Yeah." We go out.

We cross Orford Road and turn down Mabel Street. Up and down the street now, it's two colours. As if someone took a grey pencil and drew over everything except the windows which are squares of yellow-orange light. Some places you can hear music, it's like the house walls turn into voices singing or a symphony. Two more blocks to home.

Ian's chomping all his Tootsie Rolls first. I knew he'd do that because that's what he always eats first, even at Hallowe'en. I'm trying to suck each jelly bean slowly, and I'm watching the darkness, the way it takes away all the differences. Now my face looks like anything else—a bush or a tree, a fire hydrant or the faraway sky and I can make my eyes two stars. I feel like I belong with everything else, just walking with my little brother between the yellow windows.

I don't see any more Jesuses dying along the street. Maybe They're taking a break from all that blood.

Ian's really quiet beside me. All I hear is him chomping on those Tootsie Rolls. He's a disgusting eater but he likes it a lot. I think maybe he's thinking about the store man and peace and love like I am but then I hear him gurgle as he swallows a big chunk. The bag crinkles when he pokes in it for another Tootsie Roll.

"Dorene?"

"Yeah?"

"You think if we looked hard in the train yard we could find more bottles and wait until it rains and we can wash them real clean and say you washed them all in a little puddle for me and then you think he'd give us extra candy again?"

His voice goes piping high and quick all the way through and then there's the sound of the Tootsie Roll wrapper and a big suck as it goes in his mouth. I think about the man's face in the store in the softest shadows and that small smile there for us both. This big breath comes into me and makes a clean space full of real happiness.

"Like as if he really likes us?" I say back.

Ian takes a big breath too. "Yeah."

"We can try," I tell him.

"Tomorrow?"

"Yeah, tomorrow."

That night I have a different bridge dream. Ian's hanging off the outside by his hands and I'm screaming, "You're gonna drown and die!" Everywhere, Jesuses are dying and Ian looks scared. His hands are crossed over each other and somehow they got stuck like that, and where they touch they're bleeding, just tons of blood pouring out. Then from under the bridge, out of the black running water rises the man from the store. He's huge. When he's standing, his head is higher than the top of the bridge. He's dripping all over the place, seaweed and fish in his hair, and he takes both his number two fingers and puts them under Ian's little underarms. Then he slowly lifts my brother up over the rail and sets him on the sidewalk.

Cars just keep driving by.

The man stands there with his giant face looking at us and we look back at him. Ian's head is on one side like it was in the store just before we went out. His hands stop bleeding. It's quiet.

Then the man says, "You take care of yourself, sonny."

Ian looks at him a long time, like he's figuring out what that means. "Yeah," he says.

The man disappears back down into the river. We look through the rails at the water awhile, watching it go away. Ian picks up his lunch pail.

"C'mon Dorene." He takes my hand.

We go on.

Somewhere Apart

They kept Billy Wheeler in an old farmhouse, deep in the countryside. It felt deep in the middle of far away, the house closed in by large heavy trees, the bedroom where he was chained to a metal-frame bed ending a long-shadowed hall, echoes coming off the bare walls and hardwood floors. I always came to this house feeling lost, as if while driving to it the rest of the world and time fell away into a blur. I could remember nothing behind me; ahead only him.

I was twelve. I would climb out of the family car into an Ontario heat wave that rippled into my chest. From the side of the house came the rattle of the black dog's chain, a creeping growl. The first porch step felt as if it would give under my foot, like flesh, another heartbeat there and gone. Inside, the house was milky cool, rooms stretching out high and dark, another hall running to the kitchen at the back. Nothing was furnished, the place had the feeling of an empty heart, wisps of old curtains at windows. The couple who kept Billy were always there. They were in their mid-50s, stocky, with a European accent. They would nod to my father, he nodded to me, I climbed the stairwell to the second floor. The creaking old wood splintered the silence ahead, as below the adults began to discuss weather, farming, the encroachment of government bureaucracy into the affairs of private life.

The banister was cracked, rough against my palm. Old wallpaper ran by my fingertips. At the end of the hall, the door to Billy's room. There was always a ruffle of wind from the open window at the end of the hall. I would stop there for a moment, not sure why I stood, head bowed, listening; no angel ever spoke to me, touched my forehead with gentleness or wisdom from beyond. I always looked once out the window, watched the maple leaves coil in the heat, their motion like *something* that slid invisible in my throat.

I worked it down, way back down. Then I placed my hand on the door knob and opened.

He was also twelve, blonde-brown hair, an accent from the deep South. He would be sitting on the far edge of the bed, face turned over his shoulder toward the door, dressed in the cotton pyjama bottoms they allowed him, one ankle shackled to the foot of the bed. Or lying on his back. Always, when he saw me, the fear blew out of his face and a smile came, passed from him to me. That is how I remember him most clearly, his face changing from fear to happiness. For me.

One afternoon, the European couple released him for an hour and we wandered to a nearby river. Sometimes they allowed this, having shown us first the dog trained to track and kill. We removed our clothes and, giggling, slid into the water and then into each other, sunlight running over the small dark waves, through our slow-moving bodies. Then we sat close to the shore. I straddled his lap and we were kissing, touching light, following patterns in each other's fingertips. Taking away what was coming to him.

He gave me a phone number and asked me to call for help, made me repeat the number over and over, the digits drifting from our mouths like the leaves already turning here and there on the uneasy trees. That sequence of numbers mixed with the sweet sensation of his stomach against mine, his hard cock between us, the water warm on the river's surface, cooler further down, going by, going by.

"Tell my mother," he said. "Or my sister. Her name's Rosie. My sister's name's Rosie."

Sometimes he hardly seemed able to remember, though he'd only been here a few months. It was as if he peered back through years when he talked of them, his face twisting into a soft confusion, shaking away a dizziness. I asked him once how he had gotten here and he looked at me with such sadness shifting his gaze. Then fear.

"I don't know," he whispered.

It was night in his room, we were wrapped together in the one dirty bedsheet, the room lit to a fierce black and white by an almost full moon. His mouth on mine so the words and their fear took up space in mine.

"I've just always been here," he said.

Knowing what that meant, that there was no coming and going between time, what is and what was, what you were and what you are. Somewhere out there, Billy Wheeler felt he had once had a family, a sister named Rosie. He could remember a house, blurry as a dream; he said he floated through it like a ghost, unable to touch anything. He would hear voices in another room and come round a doorway, his mouth opening. He told me his mouth was always open, ready to call out at the first sight of them. Though they blurred into walls and furniture, hazy in a hazy light, they were still human—mother, father, sister—something that moved in flesh, blood, bone, body heat like his. But whenever he saw them, they were always leaving through a window, another door. Never looking back.

Whispering the numbers again, I traced his mouth, open in that helpless cry never released, even in dreams. It was wet with tears, they collected along his upper lip, a warm quivering ridge, splashed over into his mouth, into mine.

"I'll call," I promised from the bottom of summer in that riverbed, and kissed his throat. Again, he made me repeat the number, it came off my tongue fluid as hope, a whip-poor-will's song.

I first saw him at the meetings, a pale shivering form pushed out of the dark into the circle around the fire. We were all in white robes, standing hand in hand in our family groups, oldest to youngest after the father, so I was between my mother and brother. I could see my friend Lennie and his family nearby. We were swaying a little, dizzy from the drink of Jesus' blood, my mother with her head back, her voice floating pure in her throat, singing "Precious Redeemer" with the rest of us.

They pushed the strange boy into the light, his naked skin flickering like fire. Arms wrapped around his chest, eyes darting. Bruises and whip marks on his skin.

"A boy with no family," the priest intoned. "This boy is outside the circle. He lives outside the power and forgiveness of our Lord Jesus Christ. He has been sent to us to decide his fate. The company of Brothers must decide his fate."

I knew then he would die, knew it as the drugged dizzy swaying in my throat took away singing, took away all words. Death shivered in that thin boy body, death in someone we could set apart and watch, learn the way death stalked, circled in.

It was a slow approach. The first few meetings, I watched the boy from a distance. He was always naked; I could see rope marks around his throat and wrists, skin lifting a little from whippings on his back. He was never still; eyes, arms, feet moving restlessly, shadows twisted across his face. At every meeting he was pulled forward, hands chained, and forced to kneel as the priest intoned, "This boy is without a family. He is outside the circle."

"He is outside the circle," we replied, the wind leaning down through the trees, heavy upon us.

"He must die," the priest chanted.

Then someone chosen would step forward, moving safe inside the rustle of a white robe, and place the mark of death on the boy's throat, the black X. Maybe they saw how I watched him, his body shifting in and out of the dark like a whisper of human light, how as soon as I arrived I was looking to where they kept him chained to a nearby tree until it was time to bring him into the circle for the ceremony of the shunning, the heaping of shame. Setting the one apart, preparation for sacrifice.

I was chosen to present the mark of death at the boy's fourth gathering of the Kin. My face and finger blackened in ash, I was pushed into the center of the circle where he waited on his knees. My every breath a rubbed-raw terror. Every sacrifice took place in the center of the circle—every death, every punishment, all pain. As I stumbled on the edge of my robe, the chant of the Kin began. "He must die, he is without a family."

The boy lifted his face as I approached. He knew the ritual. He would be tied to a cross which would then be placed upright at the edge of the clearing. Here he would hang while we went on with the meeting. Finally, he would be untied and led off into the dawn. Fading into the other parts of a fade-in-fade-out life, like all of us.

He waited, his chin up. I could see his mouth open and trembling, his eyes staring fixedly away; panting, rapid and shallow.

He must die. He is without——

My brain shifted suddenly, a maple in a huge wind blowing through and gone. And then someone pure and new stepped into me; she glowed a translucent blue-white, clearer than the fire, and to me she said, *Forgiven, he shall live.* She took my black finger into my mouth and sucked it clean. Then she knelt my body down in front of Billy Wheeler and touched his wavering lips.

Silence. Only the fire crackling, the circle stunned, wind warning the trees. The boy's eyes came from far away, from set apart, back to the circle, to me. We saw each other and we knew. He would die and I would live. It was the way the heart beat, the way the wind moved in the trees, the way darkness grew between things. But he was no longer set apart. I had joined him.

I began to live Billy Wheeler. That night and every meeting until his death, I was made to kneel naked and chained beside him, though no black X was placed upon my throat. I was taken with him outside the circle and tied to a second cross at the edge of the trees, too far to speak to him, close enough to see his face turn toward me. Staring. Both of us staring. Eyes watching the other as pain and fatigue worked into shoulder and elbow joints, extending into burning claws. Seeing the light dance across the other's sagging head, the shudders that came and went in the bent shape. But not alone. I walked toward his death with my arms held as wide as that cross. I longed for it, wanted to take it from him into me, a quick breath, a last heartbeat, the falling dark and then gone, leaving him to step alive into the white shifting circle, take my place as the living-on child of the family, the everlasting Kin.

Late spring and summer, the Kin met several nights a week on farms or in provincial parks. I had hung without speaking opposite the strange boy perhaps ten times when, just past Canada Day, my father drove me through a maze of country roads, late morning and Vaughan Williams pouring from the car radio, to the farmhouse where the boy waited in the upper room. I did not know why we had driven down the long rutted driveway between trees bent into their whispering; I was never told where we were going, or why. It was always a matter of sacrifice, some payment due. All children born to the Kin pay for their sins with their flesh, legs spread wide while a Brother pushes deep into them, hissing about sin and evil and what the devil makes men do. So I thought, as we walked into the shadow of the front porch, that I had been brought here to receive a Brother's sins, carry his stain in my flesh. When I was told to go upstairs into the room at the end of the hall, I expected to find a white dress to put on, to lie down on an altar, a cross or a bed, and wait.

When I opened the door, the boy was poised frenzied on the edge of the bed, body turned toward me, leg pulling the ankle shackle tight. When I saw him, shock rammed into my chest like crossbars, across, down. The room tilted twice, swung around. Images of fire, white robes in a circle, boy on a cross. Eyelids heavy, I was swimming in darkness so huge there was no edge to it. Breath gone deep. I held onto the door knob, pushed up, pushed back up toward this bedroom, the one window, its faint light. When I opened my eyes clear again, I brought the images with me; I knew who he was, this boy set apart. The boy meant for sacrifice.

I watched his mouth close, his arms lose tension, come back to hover near his body. All across the room his heartbeat, *thudthudthud,* the walls sweating.

"Is. . .is anyone else coming?" His voice was low, cracked.

"I don't know." My own slid from me like a hot July wind, ruffling my lips, my tongue, into many leaves. I turned to look back but there was nothing except the hall, its empty doorways. This room with the thin shaking boy chained to an old bed. *Condemned.* I stepped in and closed the door. "Who are you?" I asked.

"Billy Wheeler," he said.

Walking across the room to that bed, I became someone else. By the time I reached him, I was someone I dream about, someone who exists in a pastel blur, glowing with gentleness and extreme love. I sat by him, touched his face as he began to cry. *Began to die.* The last of his life, his cheek warm in my hand.

"I don't know why I'm here," I said.

Reaching again to touch his face. Bruise on his forehead, his eyes puffy, sleepless. Touching and touching and touching, fear along his cheekbone, the wail kept in his lower lip, the curled-in terror in his throat. Sharp swallows under my thumb locking part way down. All this he carried for me and I wanted to take it back.

Slowly the shape of his face changed, the cheeks not so sucked-in, the forehead letting go of its tightness so the skin floated a little under my fingers. His eyes lost a little of their squint. Our breathing now parallel, in rhythm.

When he touched my face, I thought my cheek would shred in gory strips, the skin sizzle and shrivel black. *Death hand.* His fingers traced my mouth, my eyelids. I felt myself lose the demon in him or the demon in me, whatever it was that hissed evil and sudden doom. Our faces and bodies curved together and we rocked slowly, not speaking. Not wanting words, one mouth touched its half-sob to the mouth watched all night long on the opposite cross, brushing away its loneliness, its unutterable fatigue. I unbuttoned my shirt, he placed a hand around my breast, movements that took care of themselves like breath in the lungs, as simple, as necessary. Then the pure one in me, the one glowing blue-white, spoke to me again. *Forgiven,* she said. *And love shall be.*

The Kin did not interrupt any of my moments with Billy Wheeler, moments of his life or his death. For the Brothers were giving him to me, it was obvious they intended him as a lesson concerning the way of things, the purpose for which all things were created. None of this was discussed with me; they allowed it to sink unexplained into the pores of my flesh. I climbed those old stairs, a tunnel of soft blurred light glowing in the middle of such darkness, my joy running ahead of me down the long hall, flinging open the door to see his happiness, happiness that meant me.

Each time I touched first the wounds I found on him, the bruises, the nicks where pieces of skin had been gouged out, the scrapes. For weeks, a scab ran along the whole left side of his chest, festering from an untreated burn, fluid running freely from the cracked surface. He lay there sobbing, sucking in the hot air so desperately; I heard it vibrate down his throat, the infection fingering its way past his flesh to his will, his will to live, to live past this, to live past what he could see and feel, to live for what was beyond. To live free.

They let me treat that burn, let me feed him pills to kill the pain, smooth on the salve, lay hands on him that pulled the infection out of his flesh as if it was death itself I called out of him, summoning it to myself. Begging it into my own skin. *Leave him be, leave him be, let it be me.* With each visit he became more and more childlike. I would find him sitting cross-legged on the bed staring at me as if his whole life walked into the room with me. Settled in my arms, he curved into my chest. Once or twice, he called me *Mama.*

"I'm not your Mama."

He did not answer.

I wanted a knife so large it would cut the throats of all the Brothers in one slice. As we hung from our crosses Billy and I locked eyes, locked breathing, locked the pain and fatigue growing in our stretched joints, dividing ourselves further from the rest of the congregation as it swayed in its white robes, singing "Precious Redeemer," "The Old Rugged Cross."

Over the summer he seemed to settle into the infinity of it—the wind in the trees, the air in his lungs—everything came and went beyond his reach, his choosing. He talked less and less and stared for long periods out the window. One afternoon we sat in the river and I held him against my chest. So quiet, nothing but the endless breathing, the scab peeling, time leaving him.

"I think the trees are real pretty, don't you, Doris?" he murmured. "They look like they're always sleeping."

Dreams of somewhere soft, the ripple of an endless peace. I could feel Billy Wheeler's dreams shift in his skin, dreams of a small boy being rocked. The day after he gave me his phone number, I waited until my house was empty, my parents out grocery shopping, my brother throwing a frisbee with friends at a nearby park. Then I dialed.

"Hello?" a woman asked.

"Hello? I know Billy Wheeler?" My voice floated up, smoke from the fire in my throat. At the other end of the phone, a long silence. "He needs your help," I said. "Please."

Then I was sobbing. Violent with release, the tears burst out of every pore in my face, throat, all across my arms and chest. "Please, please, are you his mother? Come and help him."

She waited, somewhere in Louisiana, for my sobbing to subside. When I was quiet enough to hear, the woman spoke to me, she spoke so clearly.

"We don't have a son named Billy Wheeler anymore," she said. "You tell him to be a good boy and do what he's told."

Then a click and a dial tone as Louisiana cut off. The phone slipped from my hands, ceiling, walls, everything sliding out of place, plummeting down, down. When I next saw him, I sat by him on that bed, wove my arms around his neck, our bodies now strands in a braid, wound together.

"I called your mother," I whispered. "She said she loved you. You are her morning star. She wants to help you but she can't. She thinks about you every day. She said she cries."

For one moment he believed me, the pain of this loss complete in his face. Then he let it pass by him, something too enormous to contain in the stretched membranes that kept him together; it became something that had to do with someone else, another time, another place, something that was never intended to mean him at all.

Only once did he refer to it. Late evening, the harvest moon close to rounding itself, low in the moan of trees. We were sitting in the darkening room, side by side on the bed's edge, having moved into and through each other with all the gentleness we could give. Billy's ankle still shackled, the chain ran over my foot to where it locked around the end of the bed frame. The tense wires criss-crossing our brains had relaxed, we floated with the soft wishing of the curtain at the open window. My hand in his. Breathing.

He turned to me then, the light so dim I could barely see his mouth move. His shoulders suddenly rigid, chin jutted out. My hand in a tight grip as his voice spoke, coming from somewhere deep, looming huge in his flesh.

"I will take over the world," this voice in him said. "I will kill every last person in it, including you. And I will start with my mother."

Then Billy's shoulders slumped, his hand once more limp in mine.

"Billy?" I whispered.

"Mama?" he asked.

Finally, the meeting under the harvest moon. When I saw the black dog chained to a nearby tree, I knew blood would be given. When they pulled me from the cross and shackled me onto the altar built from field rocks, I knew the dog was there for my blood, the devil's jaws ready to tear me open and claim my sin. Terror took the trees, the white robes, the fire, danced them together until nothing stayed in place. Everything was owned by fear. Wordless, I was screaming, Let me live, let it be him, let it be Billy Wheeler, not me.

As if I had been heard, they took him from the first cross, shackled his ankle to a long chain and made him kneel before the fire. My mother stepped forward, finger blackened in ash, and drew the black X on his throat. She sang "Precious Redeemer." The notes settled into me, small odd gifts of peace, for I knew myself redeemed, welcomed back into the family.

As Billy Wheeler was made to stand and approach me, he was sobbing, his thin body shaking off sparks, his hands flexed rigid at his sides. Reaching but nothing to reach for, not even me. Behind him, the white robes chanted, "For we have sinned and he must die."

They made us come together one last time. Shackled down on that altar, there was only one way to get away from what I had wished upon Billy Wheeler now almost dead upon me. I moved into sex pleasure, found every aching throb, pushed mindless into it; I let his small hard cock take my body out of sin, out of terror, out of flesh to somewhere else, a place we had created for the two of us alone. His tears fell on my face as he sent me there, leaving him behind this last time.

The Brothers watched us carefully, listened for the way my cries caught in my throat. As I peaked, seeking the expanding edge of deepest pleasure, they pulled the chain around Billy Wheeler's foot. He held onto me, fingernails digging into my shoulders, his face hooked into my neck. Through the orgasm beginning to blow wide in me, I heard him cry out. His screams cut off pleasure, I came back to his body sliding from mine, his nails dragging down my breasts, stomach, legs. A slight thump as he hit the ground, was held flat on his back, a small red X cut over the black one on his throat. The dog released toward the scent of blood.

I could not pull my eyes from Billy Wheeler, his life or his death. I saw the dog leap, saw the jaws descend onto the thin lines of blood. Saw Billy's rigid legs and arms slump as his voice passed into mine, screaming, until a hand pressed over my mouth, the side of my head hit hard, the night blacked out. When I surfaced into lopsided vision, a dark throb in my head, I was covered in blood. Still shackled to the altar, I knew it must be his, there was no way to get it off me, I would carry this stain all my life.

Unless I saved myself from it, the fate of memory, of knowing. I folded up that summer, the deep green, heat-stroked time of it, the old creak of the staircase, echoes running down that empty hall toward the one window of light, the closed door with my love beyond it. He sat waiting for me, I so wanted to save him, his heart shackled to that metal bed frame, I wanted to take him somewhere away. Every touch, whisper, every minute of joy my fingers touched in him, the way we came together, welcoming. I folded it up, tight as a thin line somewhere inside me, somewhere apart.

And as the Brothers intended, never after that summer did I search as deep for pleasure. Pleasure always reaches for that deepest place; in me that became the place Billy Wheeler lived and died. Still, moments escape that thin line, rise in pastel bubbles to the surface and I remember: I am twelve and I am sitting in the warm shallow water of a riverbed holding a tow-headed boy. He says his name is Billy Wheeler, I tell him I don't know why I am there. Then his voice, clear and soft, says, "I think the trees are real pretty, don't you? They look like they're always sleeping."

There is no scab on his chest, no bruise on his face, no blood that can be seen, only the dream of a smile on his childlike face. I have taken these wounds away, I have that power now. In memory I keep Billy Wheeler safe in my head and heart, safe from pain, terror, safe from family and Kin, safe somewhere apart. There was a large red-brown maple outside the window of the bedroom in which he was kept; he would stare at it for hours, let the leaves drift like fingers on his face, his skin. When I think of Billy Wheeler, I see him sitting on that bed watching that tree, mother love, in the Ontario heat. I think of him wide-eyed, always sleeping.

Then the blue-white voice speaks to me, pure, in deepest tenderness. *Forgiven,* she says. *And all shall live.*

Wanting to Know

The beat of the drum is a slow black throb that comes from every direction, rises from the earth floor, oozes in through walls. In this place the beat of the drum is always, it has been forever, the beat of all drums the beat of this drum. When it is heartbeat, then I am come into the texture of the body: I am the beat of blood in the mouth, the beat of air in the lungs, the beat of cum in the cunt according to the beat of the Dark, its slowed time, the ripple of Under Time brought into the sacred now.

We the congregation walk the long water system aqueduct beneath the night city and its sleepers, the myriad of low-glow streetlights above us like a brain at slow ebb. We the congregation walk the aqueduct to the beat of the drum, through the downward drifting dreams of those who sleep above. For long pulled moments we step into their dreams, their heartbeats slow to the pulse of the drum that walks our feet, they dream images of black robed figures slow-shuffling, low-chanting. Then we are gone, passed further along the tunnel into another sleeper's dream.

Each time, we enter the Underground by a different gate, follow the system of tunnels to the round door under the cathedral. A door with six locks; we stand back as the high priest performs the secret ritual of opening in counter-clockwise order. Next, the slow pace through the maze under the church. Here the walls close in, the way doubles back, twists and turns on itself, every path but one a dead end. From behind comes the death click of the circle door. Ahead the high priest leads, followed by six drummers and the deep blood beat of their hands.

To enter the Inner Sanctum is to enter Satan's soul. Here pulse slows to what is almost-not. You stretch between heartbeats, to lift an arm or a foot is a gesture of great significance. Years between breaths. Between each mouth of air, the sink into the open grave, the cold raw-cut earth. With the next beat of the drum comes the pull upward into blood, bone, moment in heart and lung, the look out the eye. Darkness, circle of robed figures around a fire—even its twisted light leaps in slowed time. Six drummers, their backs to the wall. An altar, before it one robed figure, the hood thrown back. A girl of thirteen, her eyes wide, staring, pupils deep purple. She wears braces, the only clue to another world, zone, forelife. In her hand, the curved Slayer knife.

Seeing this is one long suspended moment, one stretched beat of the drum. Then there is another sinking fall into the open grave where you lie suspended, wait the upward pull of the next drumbeat into body, the look out into this room where you see the Slayer, the rise of her slow arm, the groan of firelight along the knife blade.

You are the congregation. I am the Slayer.

I am made of old fire and the Dark. I come into this body the way a dream comes to flesh, slippery, slow-floating. I touch but cannot be touched. The body can die but I cannot. Slayer, I am part human, I am all Death, know the preparations, the drugs, the ceremonies. I have studied every nerve end the body carries, every organ, every filament of brain. I know the many ways life leaves the body, how to pull its energy out as scream or silence. Every kill dedicated to the Dark Lord passes through me, I am made up of their passing. Each death that passes leaves part of its energy with me so that I have become the pulse and shift of a great dying moan.

At my beginning the body was four, I came out of its sixth death. They killed and rebirthed the body five times before my coming. Once by earth, once by fire, once by water, once by air. Once by shock, the last by word. After five deaths, the child born to Satan's Kin must learn to die by word. This is the sixth way to the regions of the Dark Power and those who do not find it die in the flesh and do not return.

I found the power deep in the Dark below the nether regions of earth. Deep in the zone below what is solid, below the region of shadow, earth and grave. Deep into what is only-Dark, pulse and throb. Where what *is* exists beyond death, beyond the touch of flesh, beyond fear. When I came into this child's flesh I brought with me the pulse of that place, its knowing, which is this: death itself is nothing to fear. It is gift, gate to eternal truth and what lies beyond the shallow time and knowing of what man fears and calls *life*. My entry into this flesh was the final death and rebirth. No more needed to be done, all had been accomplished. The Slayer had birthed into the child and death had conquered the body of life. She named Dorene Grace Hall became child of the Dark, daughter of Satan, able to travel by thought and word to deeper zones and worship in *being* there.

In the deeper places there is no distinction between self and not-self, it is all Dark and throb, vision of The Seeing Eye. Here in this region of Upper Dark under the cathedral, I have been called by the drum into a limited place, limited by breath and heartbeat, but I flow beyond this girl flesh, I exude to all corners of this room, I throb from the drum that called me. This girl body is not enough to contain me though she is a beginning, a beginning deeper than most humans can bear. I am the Dark, I am what they call Death, this congregation turns slow counter-clockwise circles, suspended in the energy I bring with me from the Down Side because the body of this girl is Door, Gateway beyond the Kin's minions to the power and throb of the Dark Lord, Satan Himself.

Coming here, this girl was not yet open to me. She received the drug of preparation to slow her pulse, bring her to an entry frequency point. To almost non-life but not quite. Part human, I can bear a heartbeat that carries the length of six slow counts between each beat. No quicker. Even that sometimes is too much and I must retreat. I am the Slayer, I am the Dark; I will not tolerate much of colour, the quick of sound, any taste but that of drug, blood and the tearing of meat.

The boy child gave its final breath several stabs ago but I continue the working of this kill. With each lift of the arm I pull the energy of the nether regions into this room; it takes a millennium of effort. Then the downward stab carrying the weight of the Dark Lord Himself, His need to feed and be satisfied. Give of flesh under blade. No struggling in this child; he had been given the final drug. Screams are sounds too high-pitched for my frequency, I would sink beyond them out of reach, far from this place of human being.

I cannot describe the power, the energy that comes off a young kill. One human child carries enough to feed the Dark Lord for minutes or a congregation for several months. The rich and famous pay for kills that grant them extra afterlives. I the Slayer, I am the Gateway that takes the kill energy to the dimension to which it is ordained. This child of two had much to offer as sacrifice; his dying went through me as the changing of winds, a great passing by.

What I seek now are the most tender places. A corpse contains yet further energy that can be caught after a kill. It must be hunted down and directed, for if it is not pulled into the Gateway, the energy escapes and continues as an energy form called into a region *against* the Dark. For there are other forces, the frequencies of Colour, the frequencies of White. Each of these energies struggles for power, the power of energy which is matter, the power of energy which is non-matter. If I do not gather the complete energy of this death it could move into a region of Colour, be it blue or green. Perhaps yellow; I felt in his drugged pulse a predominance of the quick. The blade continues its mission to sever what made this boy's life connect, what caused these nerve ends to feel. I meld with the blade, harden and thrust. Slice into what is soft, razor it, taste the shot blood in my mouth.

Always I seek the blood of the heart early on. The heart must be cut off from its pulse at the beginning for there is a calling out, a call that goes on beyond the voice in the throat, a call for the continuance of life, a pulse which I am not. The pulse of life refuses to let me be, does not let me feed, would starve me out. Strong as I am, the girl Dorene Grace Hall is stronger. Always the battle between us, even as I rule the body. For when I come into the body, she is sent out to an upper zone to dream of girlish things—horned unicorns, flying, singing. But she refuses to partake of all that is offered there. While she hovers in those regions of pastel light, she listens, listens for any cry toward life, even from this boy child chosen to become sacrifice. Dorene Grace Hall would struggle toward the slightest sound of his plea. And if she pushed back into the body I would be pushed out, returned to the regions from whence I came. To the Dark Lord's vengeance.

So the preparation must be sound. The Slayer goes deepest into the Dark, beyond the reach of the high priest. The Slayer's body must be taken earliest into advance rites. For the body alive does not understand Death and its requirements, does not comprehend the need for Slayer. The body of Dorene Grace Hall fights my coming; every time she struggles against the Kin, knows not what approaches or how, simply that there is something in their intent she would deny.

The preparation for Dorene Grace Hall is longer than most. Several days, the Kin keeps her deep in a drug, chained to a bed in a room lit by rushlight and candle. Processions come and go, the ceremonies of the True Lie and the Living Death are chanted, repeated slower each time. Every stretched syllable takes her deeper into the Dark, further slowing her pulse and breath; the room's rushlight sinks with her, a dying ebb. Dorene Grace Hall never goes easily into death and when she reaches it, it is only with the surrender of greatest intensity: her frequency matches that of the Dark Lord Himself. Other humans allow small echoes of the Lord through them into the kill rituals. Dorene Grace Hall *becomes* the Gateway to His voice and motion on earth. A premonition of His second coming. Perhaps His true first.

Sometimes this girl dreams me. In her forelife, when she lies sleeping in her bed or sits at a school desk slipped into the low ebb termed daydreaming, I feel her frequency drift toward that which calls me up and into flesh. These are odd moments, for when I the Slayer am not in the body performing the ritual kill, I sink deep into the Down Side, into the regions of the Dark. But it is as if, at these moments, the brain of Dorene Grace Hall, in dream or daydream, goes on a quest, as if unknowing she seeks me, the Slayer, out. Then the black that surrounds me, its slow pulse, changes. Another frequency fingers the atmosphere of my Dark, the faintest ripple touches here, there. If it is allowed to continue, places in the Dark begin to fade. I can see out, I can see the faintest colour lighting her face, the face of Dorene Grace Hall in sleep or thought.

Sometimes she weeps as she lies asleep. Sometimes, as she sits in a school desk, eyes wide and staring at a vague sky, I see she has slowed to a state of shock. Her lips move faintly, she has my name on them. Soundless, but there in her mouth, she has its shape, taste. *Slayer.*

Then I cannot take my gaze from hers. My eyes held by her purpling gaze, she stares into their night side. Holds me, fierce. *Owns me.* Until the power of the Dark can pull me off. Or until her body gives out on her and she slides into a faint on the school floor and I am rescued, let loose from her flesh, her knowing. Freed into the deep slow pulse of the Under Earth.

Here existence slows to the state of no connection, so far from the reference point of event that history never was, matters not. There are plans of great significance afoot and this girl body holds a central position in the Kin's activity. Details of human life are allowed to occur to Dorene Grace Hall; she attends her life of family, religion, school and peer interaction. It is of no relevance to the greater course of events. True history exists only with my entry into her flesh, when her time life is sent upward and hangs suspended above the body. Then I enter the flesh of human history and change its pulse, beat its true heart. Redirect its course to the eternal regions, those beyond the restrictions of flesh and time. The minions guard this girl body carefully. For we move toward the Final Purpose, that time when we will conquer all other regions of Colour and White, when all will be reigned by the Dark. Each kill energy I release contributes to this Grand Climax when all will exist in the Dark nether regions of no pain.

I believe this is the reason Dorene Grace Hall seeks me out. She searches for life beyond the pain They hook into her. For pain is a constant attack. She is surrounded by those who are well-trained: parents, peers, doctors. Church and school have been carefully selected. She is not granted much in the frequencies humans call love and acceptance, only small portions at odd intervals. Allowed much of this and she would root her energy too deep in her own flesh. Her energy is a powerful source, well beyond that of any human she knows. And so there is a constant and carefully planned assault on her flesh, designed to force her to flow out of her body, to live around and beyond it in dimensions where she feels herself loved and cherished. By family, by friends. Places of energy but not of flesh. From these loving places, she catches glimpses of other dimensions that she considers to be not real— dimensions in which she is sold as whore for Satan's Service. Dimensions of demon feed. Dimensions of Slayer. *These* are the real places.

It's all in your head, Dorene, she tells herself.

It is. And it is not. What exists in her head are echoes, the reflections of the many lives of Dorene Grace Hall. She has been divided many ways by the Kin. At her conception, the stars, the planets, the worlds of Dark, Light and Colour aligned, came together and touched their meeting place into her. Dorene Grace Hall became a nerve network of all frequencies of Dark, Light and Colours. Most humans contain a basic frequency network. Dorene Grace Hall is a prism that reflects frequencies never before seen: new blues, conceptions of green, imagined yellows. Her every nerve is a gate to another dimension of energy and power. Through her, the Kin has discovered many new frequencies and dimensions. They have carefully tortured and trained each nerve with needles and shock, turning nerves into gates of fear so that the worlds they open onto may be twisted into frequency dimensions that the Kin can manage. Through careful training, each nerve learns to call in whatever frequencies, dimensions and beings the Kin requires. With the body sufficiently prepared and its nerves pressed in a specific sequence, then I, Slayer, am called from my dimension into her flesh to feed the Dark Lord's appetite.

The Kin serves both the Dark Lord and the Lord of Light, feeding them both from the kill energy of ritual sacrifice so that they may fortify their regions of Dark and Light in their war against one another. Though I am of the pulse of the Dark, I understand those who serve the Lord of Light; do we not obey the same laws, albeit in opposing frequencies? However, there are worlds that I sense in Dorene Grace Hall, worlds of Light, Dark and Colour to which she connects that are different, that do not demand death or sacrifice. Their frequencies are incomprehensible. The nerve gates leading to them do not open in response to pain or fear. Who they are, what purpose they serve, is beyond my comprehension.

Just as I cannot fully comprehend her. Dorene Grace Hall. The way she reaches even now into this Dark to touch me. So many times my Dark has faded into the stare of those eyes. Seeking, hunting me down, she wills herself to find the frequency necessary to match mine, meet me at my fullest. *She must not. She must not. She must not.*

She would love me. She would reach her flesh glowing with its nerve ends of *greenblueorangescarlet* toward me, nerve ends with their glimmerlove, glimmerfear, glimmerpain. I exist in No Pain. I struggled so long against the limitations of her flesh to come here. I exist now beyond the demands, the screaming body; I am no longer required to live those dimensions. If she succeeds—if those nerve ends, those Christmas lights of *baby born for sacrifice*, that *life* strung twinkling through her flesh—if that *lie* touches me, all will be lost, the Death Dark I maintain will dissolve. I will die into her and she will die into me. Dorene Grace Hall will be lost, she will trance-walk into a midnight kitchen looking for the butcher knife and slice her own throat with my found expertise. Or she will let her lungs slide deep into the city river. With my knowledge she would succeed. I have gone into each Death Gate. I know how to give and receive of it.

I, the Slayer, am her only salvation. By resting apart from her, a dimension of her life remains carefully guarded from that desire in her to know, to connect. Each thought tentacle, each small pink wish she sends toward me must be severed as I sever all life, slicing it as an artery, a portion of heart. I must keep myself in the Dead Zone, keep her seeking frequency separate as the zone of *life.*

It is not too much to sacrifice for her, this girl body, this Dorene Grace Hall. It is all I can give her—this separate place, this divided heart. I am her peace. I am her guardian. I watch her as a shadow in the Dark, from afar. Always her distant heartbeat calls to me, slowed so that I can hear it from the other shore, six counts between.

I will guard her with every kill I dedicate. From this place. From my frequency against hers.

Blue Moon

The worlds are always close, drifting in and out, their endless labyrinths of doors stretched in all directions. Here in this world of Real, I walk high school corridors dressed in jeans and tee shirt, carry graph paper, duotangs and *Julius Caesar*, caught like everyone else between the clang of locker doors, leaps of laughter, the scent of du Maurier. But I can step out of it, step out without permission, travel the worlds further than my keepers and owners. Get past the guardians of fact, out into the breath of myth and mind. The doors are there for everyone and most kids use the basic ones, slip out of their bodies and push open the closest door. Generally, it's one leading to sex, a quick slide into wet dreams of flesh, or a door back into the morning's parental advice: *You're an idiot. Why can't you get your head on straight? How many times do I have to tell you. . .*

. . .to find the door out, out of the parameters of an adult world where you're forced to sit, pen in hand taking down all their philosophies on quantum nothing, bell curves, another novel with an evil heart beating at the center of its plot. *Step out, child, step out into a life of your own making, a landscape you create out of your own desire, a world where no one but you build the walls, doors, skies you fingerprint into your skin.*

Or so I used to think. Now I realize most of the doors I find have been there long before me, that I'm usually walking onto someone else's turf. Sometimes the maker of a particular world is there to attack or welcome you, sometimes she's off exploring another door. Some doors lead onto collective unconscious landscapes that everyone encounters, worlds that have been around since the first mind and the first door. A cave mouth onto a long tunnel of dark. A pit of fire, or a field of fluffy clouds. Angels, demons, gods. Then there are worlds more complex—some shudder and grind in

Picasso's angles, shivershimmer like Van Gogh, bloom into Georgia O'Keeffe. These days a lot of kids head for doors onto the wild west where they can ride and shoot like *Butch Cassidy and the Sundance Kid*, moan and blur into *Blue Lagoon*. You don't have to see the movie to enter these worlds—the modern collective unconscious—just find the door and someone will be waiting to hand you the gun.

Just as many kids hang around *The Gulag Archipelago* or crawl through *The Crypt*. Depends on how you're feeling on a particular day.

On this particular day I walk into Chem, drop my books on the desk, and make an intelligent perch on the stool. The teacher looks as if she straddles two worlds, anchored in one full of ancient leather bound books of spells, boiling test tubes and vampires waiting for a full moon. My lab partner is heavy into well-organized braids and pleated plaid skirts—sturdy knees and rosy cheeks will march her steadfast and obedient through a life of family values and low-level doors. *Yes dear, yes god, yes oh dark lord, I obey without question.*

I glance over my shoulder. Len and Juss toss me sunlit grins from their desk by the window. The teacher gets going, words flap dark and heavy as drugged bats from her mouth. Street traffic goes by in a trance of wheels and gears. Small panes of glass divide the outside light into squares of shifting green leaves, one tree split into many dreaming places, they *dancefloat* on a wind that whispers of better places, lifts each leaf easy as a wish, as hope.

Airborne, I hover over Len and Juss. My body sits on the other side of the class at its desk, writing down something about CO_2. The guys don't know I'm here yet. Juss records the teacher's instructions with his habitual alacrity. Len's half-hearted about everything but sports: he counts on borrowing Juss's notes and mind. The usual gaps loom on his page. I slip into his ear and whisper, "Len, Len, Lennie, it's Dorell. Step into the fourth royal blue door on the right."

Once you're out-of-body, the labyrinths of doors lose their hazy quality and come clear into focus, each one a different colour. Labyrinths of white light head upward, black labyrinths throb downward. Colours branch out more or less laterally. As I turn left into a blue hallway, my frequency adapts to blue—sturdy, serene. At the fourth door on the right, I turn the knob and enter.

Inside, I wait for the guys. They're right behind me, wearing blue grins. I take their hands.

"C'mon."

"Where are you taking us?" Juss asks.

"I want to go far out."

"How far?" Len's always game but he likes to know direction and time zones.

"I dunno. I feel like blue and I feel like a moon."

"Blue moon," Juss muses. He's into the poetic, anything on the tips of his fingers turns gentle as a song.

"C'mon." This room is full of ways to further dimensions of blue. Holding their hands, I turn us to face a window. The wall is blue, the window frame is blue, so is the sky beyond it. Closing my eyes, I begin to see what I want. I focus, tune my mind and send out the mental image of something I've seen in a dream, something I want to bring close. I move deep into the blue of it, listen until I can hear the voice of blue. Then I let it come singing from my mouth.

The song floats from me like the scent of night flowers. All over I feel myself lip out cool and fragile as petals. Still I send out the song of blue until what I'm seeking approaches. I open my eyes and there it is, coming into focus. A slow-turning royal blue moon.

"You got it, Dorell." Len's fingers squeeze mine. The moon is just beyond the window. I reach out and touch its nebulous boundary, my hand goes through and into it.

"Looks solid," Juss says wryly.

"It'll hold us." I swing onto the windowsill, legs out.

"You sure?" Len reaches for me but I know this place, my feet are already walking that blue. I jump.

"Shit!" Len yells. "Dorell!"

I turn and look at them hanging out the window, their faces a smudge of fear, but I'm fine, faith is keeping me here and everywhere the dream of blue stretches, blue as a baby's deepening eye.

"C'mon!"

They look at each other. Usually the worlds have roads, stairways, something like a path to follow. A sign to indicate *The Way*. Not just a colour, not just the pulse of atmosphere and you. *Everywhere, beginnings.* Juss shrugs, Len shrugs back.

"She's still here," Juss points out.

"It is a lovely shade of blue," Len notes.

They take the leap but can't find their feet, end up floating on their backs as if two giant mothers engulf them in their arms and soft-rock them back and forth. I watch this for a bit, grinning. Len and Juss don't seem to mind, they look as if they've forgotten all about me. Len starts to suck his thumb. There's the sound of a woman humming, the whole moon turns into her human throat. Len and Juss float in an unblinking stare, their eyes deepening to more of this landscape of baby blue.

When I lie down, the moon's surface has the texture of a field of flowers. I hover in its scent and let the guys get their fill; they were never treated to this when they were true infants, they can catch up on a little of it now. And I'm getting some of it too, a different type of breathing. It comes in everywhere I've got skin—the scent, the soft in and out of it, a sweet milky taste in my mouth and that song wishing on as if it'll last forever, no more night and day, no more sleep and awake, just this dream of endless mother blue.

Forever is more quality than quantity. After we've gotten what we need, Len and Juss find their feet and pull me up. It's like walking air but we're air too. We walk and walk this peace, uninterrupted. I'm wondering if we've landed in a dimension of the one baby's brain that's never been wounded, never heard a scold, just the swish of window curtains and a lullaby voice. Then I sense a different pulse approaching on the horizon, figures of white light descend onto the blue surface. Not cherubs. These angels tower huge, fry at a sizzling frequency, their outlines snap and waver. In each hand, the sword of judgement flames electric white.

I know two things when I see this horde of violent light: this moon has never seen angels before, and we brought them here. I know from travelling the worlds that angels are killers and what they hate most is any living human pulse, especially a teenager's. But they'll attack anything they find, and when they finish with us, this blue moon will be laid to waste.

"What're we going to do?" Juss asks.

Len steps in front of me, forgetting, as is his tendency, that I'm the leader in the dimensions. The line of white fire is a horizon drawing steadily closer. The angels rearrange into the fighting formation of a white cross and continue to approach. Where they march, the blue dream chars to smoke, releasing a startled newborn shriek. Louder and louder the wails rise out of the moon's flesh.

I want to come back here. It cannot be wasted.

"Len, get behind me."

When he doesn't, I yank him. My energy changes, I let it take shape: huge reptilian head, dinosaur body, dragon wings the width of this moon. Black and deep as the unforgiven, my mouth roars an opened throat, ember red.

Lifted back and down by the thrust of my wings, I swoop in an arc deep into the moon below the angels, then rise behind them. Beyond the angels, I see Len and Juss facing the tribe of judgement, two guys in jeans and rugby shirts. The baby screams go on and on. My form collapses, I become a pool of darkness, a black hole sinking beneath the angels. Going down, going down deep into the moon. Now the spin—I swing into a counter-clockwise spiral. Not so much fast as deep. Deeper. Vacuum packed.

Their cross wobbles uncertainly across my surface as I begin to pull at the angels' flickering feet, pull at those commandments of fire: *thou shalt not, thou shalt not, thou shalt not. . .*Each angel is sucked down, flames and scalds me before being extinguished. The sword is the last wound and it cuts deep: *sacrifice, submit, obey, sacrifice, submit, obey. . .*Even as a black hole, I bleed red. When the last of the killing light has been put out, I spin a circle of wounds, a rounded groan.

Lose the rage, its power, let it spin itself out. Once again in a girl's shape, I lie splayed on a field of blue. The baby wails subside to whimpers, the woman's hum starts up, vibrations across my back and legs.

When I sit up, I see scars across the landscape, char marks from angels' feet, slashes of fiery swords, the travelling cross. This blue moon will go on, but it'll never be the same. And it's my fault, I put it on the map of the gods. They hadn't sniffed out its innocent frequency before I landed here with the mess of my life, the stench of my foul mouth and bad attitudes, my desire to go looking for what was *in the beginning.* As Juss and Len run toward me, I roll into a ball and cry.

"Dorell."

It's Len, then Juss, kneeling beside me. They push against one other to pull me up and into themselves. Somehow they manage to keep it equal, the three of us mashed together in a rocking grieving hug.

"There's nowhere to go, Len." I can't stop. "I'm looking for it, some place where they can't find us, some place where we can go and be free, but there's never no place, no place anywhere I can find."

"Shh, Dorell," Len whispers. "Shh."

Len touches with his voice, Juss with the lyrics of his fingers. Soon the mother
song lilts through me again, the three of us rock, our eyes fixed in that early
blue stare, all questions about trust. When we're soaked in blue, we stand,
slow-moving, a dense wet sponge of peace. Beneath us, the jagged scars of
judgement cross, criss-cross.

"I'm sorry, baby heart," I whisper.

"It's not your fault." Len's voice is fierce.

A quick memory flames in the dark pit of my gut. *Angels.* "Kill them all," I say.

"Yeah," whispers Juss.

We walk back to the window, listening to the mother's song, the odd baby
gurgle—there's a smile holding the sound now. I jump onto the windowsill,
look back, wonder if the history of the human race ever allowed a blue
moon to last long, even suspended far-off as a faint glowing dream. I've
taken its blue into me now and I swear I'll keep it in my blood, my bones,
the tissue of my brain. I try to hold onto it, keep it conscious, but as we walk
to the door I feel its frequency begin to fade. On the door knob, Len puts
his hand over mine.

"We went somewhere I've never been," he tells me. "I never knew it could be
like this."

"I've dreamed it," Juss says.

That doesn't surprise me. Juss's eyes are the deep down colour of that moon.

"Don't forget," I whisper.

We walk the blue labyrinth to the entry point, kiss quick, then float out into
Chem and the divided world of Real. I come into a body bent over a page
of impossible equations, a Bunsen burner and a test tube full of vile white
guck.

"Man, were you spaced out today," my partner complains, tossing a braid.
"Freaky. You kept getting this weird look in your eyes. They changed colour."

"Huh?" I ask for clarification.

"Your eyes. They changed to blue and you kept staring at nothing. I had to do
the whole experiment by myself."

"Hey—what colour of blue?"

"I dunno. Your eyes are supposed to be green. Don't do that again, or I'll ask to switch partners."

I'm soaked in too much blue residue to argue. I glance over at Len and Juss to check out their return to Real. Juss is a genius at split focus; he's probably recorded every teacher grunt and mumble. As usual, Len will have let most of Real go by.

Catching the weight of my glance, both of them look up. Even from here, I can see the quiet blue of Len's eyes. Some scars, but a moment of peace trusted by his flesh.

Nothing but the Hurt

Walking down the long hall, cold ghosts flicker my cunt, whirl round and round the edge of the hole. Nipples two small skulls. Just cold, everywhere damp; skin's got a November sky falling through it, turning the bones to slush. Especially the knees, and the halfway place in the throat where a swallow locks in. Now the shivering starts and the chemical burns—tears in the eyes.

Everywhere I'm fighting it, fighting what's coming up strong through me. I want to turn and run, run up against the last locked door, smash myself into a million dying stars. I tried it once, a long time before I got tits and a beaver, long time before I knew what they were for. The stars lived. I needed them. For when the dark got darker.

They wear white coats and they call each other *Doctor.*

"Doctor Fleiss, could you pass me that syringe?"

"Doctor Johnson, could you tighten that arm restraint?"

Doctor Bull Shit, could you knock her one good on the side of her head please?

Thank you, Doctor.

My dad opens the door to the lab and we walk into the gag of antiseptic, me on Pinnochio legs, jerking every which way every step. My dad walks through his smile to talk to the white coats setting up by the stretchers. I see Lennie and Juss sitting on blue plastic chairs by the wall, trying to hold in their piss; I go over and sit by them. Lennie's between us, Juss leans forward and lifts an eyebrow at me, trying to grin.

"How're you gonna cum for me today?" he asks.

I touch his mouth. "Any way you want." Then I lean onto Lennie's chest and put my arms around him. "You seen what they're using today?"

"Needles," Juss says back.

Lennie doesn't talk, just sits with his head back, breathing *slow slow slow*. I listen to him almost not breathe until it gets so I want to go into his chest and pull out the next breath myself.

My dad laughs and goes out, saying he'll pick me up in three hours. *Three hours*. Lennie jerks when he hears this. I glance at Juss; he's digging his fingernails into his hand, biting his lip. I know they've got a football game tomorrow. It's a big one. Those needles are gonna tear at what they need to move.

Dr. Fleiss pulls down the screen on the wall, so we know they're almost ready, the projector ready to roll. He turns to us and snaps his fingers. Finger snaps go through like shock; when I hear them my head comes up, ready to move as required. I can't stop it. Automatic function.

"Come come," he says. "Why do you have clothes on? Remove them please."

Finger snap.

Strip.

Without looking at each other, we start to pull off shirts, jeans, underwear. It feels like you're pulling off something that won't come off, it's stuck to you, pleading, another skin you've got to take a knife to. The lab's cold as ever. Lennie huddles, shivering, staring down. I forgot to shave my armpits; I'm gonna stink this place up bad.

Juss has his eyes on the equipment trays. His mom's a doctor so Juss knows his way around this stuff more than we do. He's frowning a few thoughts.

"What?" I whisper.

He shakes his head without looking at me so I know he's still working on it. Lennie's dad is an artist, mine's a cop, so we're not much good second-guessing here. In a couple of years they'll start training us for this stuff, we'll be doing it to the younger kids the way some of the older kids, the *trainees*, do it to us. For now, it's a one-way identity clause: *guinea pig*.

"OK—you girl, you come here," says the eloquent Dr. Fleiss, snapping his fingers.

Twitch across my brain and I'm walking across that damn cold floor.

"Lie down."

There's a white sheet on the stretcher but it's still cold. Dr. Johnson straps me into the usual position—wrists by my head, knees up. He feeds me one capsule with water, checks the clock.

"Ten after two," he mutters.

Two-thirty, I'll be getting dizzy, floating away from what I want. A faraway sort
of feeling tells me I want to hang on, grip tight to what I know: *I'm in the
lab now with my loves Len and Juss and they're gonna hurt us and I'll be so fucking stupid brain-dead, I won't even know how after, won't remember one cum or
scream.*

So I watch as long as I can, watch as they strap Lennie in next to me, his face a
white colour close to dead, I know he's wishing his heart would *stop stop
stop.* Sweat jiggles on his upper lip. Closed eyelids whimper. He told me
sometimes he says the Lord's Prayer forty times before the drug takes him
out of it, and he doesn't even believe in the hereafter. Or the here and now.
His fists are clenched tight, his hands will ache later from gripping nothing.

Juss is still figuring out the equipment tray as he's strapped in. It's his Lord's
Prayer. Put up three tombstones with our names on them, we'd be happy
enough: Here lie Dori, Lennie, Juss, closer in death than life. Fuck you.

They adjust the head rests so we can watch, turn off the lights and run the porn,
heavy duty, no one shy about nothing. No screaming yet; this one's the early
bird. I'm doing the Pavlov dog thing—the movie is the bell, my cunt's slobbering. If I looked over, I'd see Lennie and Juss hard, beginning to leak, but
my head's strapped in. Thirty or forty 3D movies, each in its own reel, are
running side by side just under my skin. Every picture is different but I'm in
all of them, *fuckmoanshifting*; each one works my nerve ends further open,
taking away what I know, what I want, my *name.*

So when the doctor slides in the vibrator, straps on its harness and presses *Go*,
I'm ready for anything, I'd fuck a cock with balls the size of planets. My
eyes still closed, I'm floating in my inner movies, the colours of the drug, the
groans coming off Lennie and Juss. They've got vibrators strapped into their
asses, the drug is sending spider legs through their brains, and what gets me
is I'm watching their bodies turn *Fuck Me* in my head and I want their cocks
in me anywhere even though it's gonna be bad, even though there'll be
bawling, there'll be screams.

"Lennie, love me Lennie, Juss, touch my nipple, lick my neck, I want your lips
on my face Lennie, I dream about your fingers in my skin going right
through Lennie, you got my heart in your hands and you're loving it and it's
beating love for you Jussie, it loves you Jussie Jussie Juss." Pulling names into
this nothing place, small bits of human colour. *Lennie. Juss. You're what*

I know. Don't leave me, don't leave me here all alone.

They start the needles in the tips of fingers and toes; it's easiest there. I'm alone, no one's coming to help me and the dark's set in. Everywhere I'm dark, thin lines of pain coming at me, light from the outer edge; I move away from it into what's better, into the *sweet cum black fire* flicker twisting through me like sound, electric Clapton. I don't want to get burned, I want to *be* the burning, move into *arms, legs, head, black dancer flames.*

They move the needles. Needles in the back of my thigh, the lower curve of my tit. I've got to move further into that *sweet fuck fire*, hunt it down, suck it into me until I'm a livid cum that'll never give itself up. Tits, cunt, ass shifting fire. *Burn*, keep everywhere shifting black heat, the needles moving again and now they've got me, the white coats have me where they want me for the next movie they'll be making, me in the starring role begging for it, *begmoanpleading* for a *fuckfuckfuck, fuck me deeper, fuck me away from this,* as the needles take themselves into my cunt lips, pin them open. Two more slide pure and thin into each nipple, and the last, god, the last shines its scream straight into the base of my clit, the heart of everything true and good.

Where I live. My place of joy, of love for Lennie and Juss. Now the enemy's here, the *painfearhorror.* Another slides into my open ass. I gotta take it straight into the fire, gotta let pain and sweet fuck mix and merge until one's the other, I can't tell them apart, they're the same fucking fire stretched everywhere.

All I feel is *Fuck.* All I want is *Fuck.* All I scream is *Fuck.* I am *Fuck.*

Needles slide out slow, moment of coldwet cotton batting, sting of antiseptic. I'm still glowing embers here and there, the rest of me charred black, numb. Fire roars over the horizon, taking with it everything that happened, the feeling, the knowing. I want the knowing but I'm too tired to run after it; beside me I hear Lennie heavy-breathing, taking himself down, *slow slow slow.* I let him take me with him, let him breathe in and out of me, *slow, slower.* Breathing in *now,* breathing out *then,* longer and slower letting out the *what was,* Juss doing the same on Lennie's other side.

But my dad said it'd be three hours so this isn't all of it, we're gonna have to bring that fire back burning over the same ground. The doctors let us rest a bit. I want something to drink but I know better than to ask for it; you never do this stuff with anything in your gut. You throw it up, you die on the

choke, leaving the doctors with too much to explain, even with reputations
to match their starched white coats.

Doctor Fleiss, could you pass me that explanation, please?

You mean the one in this bottle, Doctor Johnson?

"You all right, Dori?" Juss asks.

"Yeah. You?"

"Yeah. Len?"

Lennie doesn't answer right off. He's still counting out his breathing. The doctors
are taking a coffee break. They've left us alone, still strapped in, of course.

"Yeah," Lennie says finally. "What's next, Doc?"

"I think it's ultrasound," says Juss, low.

"What's that?" I ask.

"My mom used it on me a couple of times." That's all Juss will say, though we're
poking at him with words sharp in us. *Fear.*

"C'mon, don't be a wuss."

"Juss, no secrets."

"Juss, you fucking shit."

"It hurts," is all he'll say, as doctor shoes click down the hall toward us.
The door opens.

"OK Dori, we'll move you to the bed now." Doctor Johnson undoes my straps,
helps me walk because I'm stiff. But on the bed it's the same position, joints
bent back into their neon whine. There are straps here too, but at least the
bed is wider than the stretcher. That means I'll be fucking Lennie or Juss or
both, not just the tease of a drug which is better but it's Juss's voice I'm worried about, the way he won't tell us how this is gonna hurt.

Ultrasound.

I never heard of it.

"What're you gonna do next?" I ask Doctor Johnson as he's tightening my wrist
strap, though I know better. He hits me fast across the top of my head, then
goes over to the counter, unlocks a pill drawer and starts clinking bottles.
Part of my head shoves a black cloud around for a bit, then shrinks it small
so I can see Doctor Fleiss getting Lennie out of his straps.

They hit the side of your head so your hair covers most of the evidence.
Sometimes I get them back by moving my face straight into the hit so some
of the bruise shows up where you can see it. They have to think about how

hard they hit next time. Slows them down a bit—thinking. It's a shock to their systems, having to think about you, even a little. After the dog started slobbering to the bell, did Pavlov think about it?

They tell Lennie to lie on me. He's hard right off and I'm wet, bells for each other. Soft as anything, he touches the back of my neck, his secret way of taking us somewhere else, just for a moment. Strapped down, there's nothing I can do back, blink or twitch a nostril without Doctor Fleiss picking it up. I look into Lennie's eyes, look at their medium blue with darker flecks, pupils like black moons. Stare while the doctors wheel over a machine. Stare and stare at what's home.

A long time ago, Lennie's eyes turned into a place for me. A house full of rooms he lets me come in and move around. There's no empty space in eyes, no air. You've got to be real careful moving around in there—it hardly ever happens that someone will really let you in like this. Once you're in, you've got to be so gentle, slow, because you're moving through an eyeball, real body stuff.

In Lennie's eyes, it's all blue. There are big patches of it, you move from one cell to the next, each its own separate place. Like an onion skin, the membranes transparent, thousands of cells stretching all around you. Endless blue, with darker blue lines running like streamers. Maybe they're veins, maybe nerves. On the tip of each one is a tiny picture. I look around and I can see pictures of all the things Lennie's ever seen because he's kept them in his eyes—memories of his summer house and camping, his sisters, school classes, throwing frisbees, sinking the ball through his driveway hoop. And Juss and me, we're there too. Smiling. At him.

There are bad pictures too. Today will end up somewhere in there and I'll find it later, when he lets me in again and I've forgotten what happened here. And when I find it in his eyes, I'll remember. I'll remember Lennie. I'll remember Juss. And I'll remember *me*.

They tell Lennie to slide into me. All along where I'm touching him, my skin dissolves so it's just sweet breathing, his and mine floating, merged. My voice gives away his name over and over, even though the doctors are listening. "Lennie, Lennie, love me Lennie, love me Lennie, Lennie please."

But no kissing. That's the lab rule, never any kissing though you're crazy for it. I watch Lennie's mouth, a dream moving through me. When he puts his mouth against my neck, I turn my neck into lips touching his and then my real mouth can hardly say his name, just sounds going higher and higher.

The doctors tell Lennie to lift up and fuck me slow. Doctor Fleiss holds a gadget connected by a curvy cord to a machine. He flips a couple of switches, turns a knob and adjusts a small screen. Then he holds the gadget against the right side of my stomach.

At first I think, *This is weird, this is stupid—doesn't he know it doesn't hurt?* There's just a warm throb going into me in waves. Over by the counter, Dr. Johnson turns on a tape recorder. A deep sound pulses from it, a dark red wave of sound that matches the throb coming from the gadget. It reminds me of an electric bass but I don't think about it much with Lennie in me, smile at him to let him know I'm all right.

Is this some kind of joke?

Then I know what Doctor Fleiss wants, the waves start to feel like hot metal, slicing through, scooping out moans. The dark red sound coming from the tape recorder gets louder. *Try not to cry so Len won't worry* but tears blur him out. Not Doctor Fleiss's voice though, telling me what to do. His voice so calm, like everything's okay, everything will be all right if I do what I'm told. *Please Doctor Fleiss, I want to be all right. Tell me what to do.*

"You know Dori, you know what to do. You will go away now. This is too much for you. You will let someone else come. Pain will make this someone else horny. She will like this pain. When she hears this sound and feels this pain, she will feel horny and she will come to fuck. Her name is Jezebella and she comes to fuck. Come to fuck, Jezebella. Come to fuck."

He says it over and over, the words and the deep throbbing sound turning into red waves of water pushing at me, getting bigger and bigger between Lennie and me, Lennie standing on a shore, I'm in the red water, the dark red sound still pushing at me. Now I see the water take shape, the shape of another girl rising, face, arms and long black hair, her eyelids painted a heavy blue, her lips a blood-red and moaning, her cunt going, going like mine never does, harder and faster and deeper, *deeper* than I knew anything could go, *deep* as those pain waves, *deeper* still. I see her for a moment between me and Lennie, all the fierceness of the earth rising through her, ready to fucking tear down the sky.

Then she pushes me away—Lennie, the shore, pain and the dark red throb, everything a speck of horizon shrinking fast, and I'm curling into a small ball, a baby going backward into a foetus sucking its thumb, eyes closed, floating in a place of untroubled blue.

Eyes open. It's bright. Cold. Fluorescent light hums, pulses on everything in this room. White room. *Lab. I'm in the lab.*

I can hear sob-breathing, quick, two sounds of it. I turn my head, see Lennie and Juss slumped naked against the nearby counter, getting over something. My eyes blur but I can see theirs are a smudged red. Something got bad.

The body opens like a gate to take me back. Pain swings wide in my neck, shoulders, elbows, all along my back, hips, knees, ankles. Everywhere. Even my hands and feet throb. Face and mouth stretched. A black hurt comes from places inside. I can see my kidneys, liver, stomach, my bowels all lying close together like they're supposed to. Black shadows grow out of parts of them and I can't say what this feels like, I've never felt it before, there are no marks I can see—no cuts, no bleeding. Nothing but the hurt.

I lie still, try to keep my mouth closed, not give anything off. Tears slide off my nose and mouth. *Don't ever want to move.*

"Open your mouth, Dori." Doctor Johnson feeds me the sweet thick syrup that will put this pain out. I've swallowed it before, I'd take it any time, any how, anywhere. They start to unstrap me, slide my legs flat, but a scream cuts out of me, bloody.

"Boys, you come here," Doctor Fleiss says.

The doctors fade off to the other side of the room and now Lennie and Juss are here, bending over me, their fingers and breath soft as a breeze. *Touch, touch, love me.* Over and over they say my name as if it's something that belongs to them, something in them that's beautiful and true and they're calling it to them, *Dori*, a slow sun coming up out of all that's dark.

Dori, Dori, this is who I am, this is how I'm loved.

Their voices and hands drift like laudanum now, a pastel sunset blurring into, down, through me. I know what's good and what I need; as the drug slips me into sleep, I take Lennie and Juss with me, Lennie's voice, Juss's fingertips, slide them around me like a blanket, a womb, a skin always moving, always love.

This time I sleep with them, not alone.

Sky Camp

The Appalachians rise in the distance, a purple-green Gregorian chant. Sometimes Dad drives me here, sometimes it's a small school bus taking a weekend pack of trainees in one load. Today, kids play poker over the backs of seats, read comics, write Fuck You on dirty windows. The older kids stake out the back, working their way into each other's zippers and breathing. It's been a four hour drive with stops to pick up kids along the way. Now we're almost at spy camp, the bus turns right onto the dirt lane that will take us to the compound set a few miles in from the secondary road. I've been seeking since Ottawa, when I left the back of the bus and found a seat to myself. Wanted to sniff out the atmosphere, find my way into what they've been doing in this area. I know some of the codes I'm not supposed to, and I've found some frequencies they can't track. Yet. They will, they're always watching for this type of activity, but every time they trap me in a particular colour sound, I find another frequency and go seeking again.

I've been working a pale yellow. You'd hardly notice it in the fierce light of the sun, tiny pink flowers in the ditch loud with light. On a day like this, very pale is most efficient. I move into the energy of a thin yellow, adapt to its frequency and slip out of the pores of my face, neck and upper chest with it. Just a thin pale yellow, I slide through the bus window into the air.

It's thick with frequencies of human thought, memory, feelings. And other dimensions—dimensions of energy, some of them human, most of them not. Some are indigenous to the area, contain the local spirit life. Some are military experiments testing out new frequencies, their effects on plant and animal life. They go the distance to discover some of these frequencies—a foot from your face there can be an energy dimension that's been brought in from some far-off galaxy to hang invisible above a farmer's field. Suddenly, corn in the area grows thick and strong, or withers brown. There are inexplicable weather changes. Freak accidents. UFO sightings. Shadows and ghosts.

It all connects. Changes in energy flow and density, changes in dimensions. Dimensions thicken the air, make it throb differently. Getting into another dimension is a matter of finding the correct frequency, adjusting to it and travelling with it out of your body. Human dimensions are easy to enter: people work within a pretty basic pulse and most of the dimensions they carry are the usual ones—fear, shame, sex. Keeping track of human dimensions is habit by now. Meet someone new, scan their frequencies, slip into the dimensions they keep *around* themselves. Find out their past, the memories they've sent outside themselves so they don't have to think about them. Most of the bad memories will be behind them. *Just put it all behind you, dear.* Banished memories start small, but the worst ones grow, pulling more and more energy off your body. You think you've gotten rid of a memory but its frequency keeps invading your brain like a scab you've got to keep picking. Eventually you learn to send the memories so far out, their frequencies don't reach you anymore.

The drawback is once you've sent them out of yourself, you can't defend your memories when someone else picks up on their frequencies. That means someone can slip into one of your memories and do whatever he or she wants. That can cause you a lot of damage. Whether you're in conscious contact with a memory dimension or not, it's still active and it's still you, *the cross you carry.* When someone is attacking you in a memory dimension, you may not be aware of it but you *feel* it—headache, groin ache, mood change. The trade-off is that you can do the same to everyone else. Discover their past, know their weak points, take revenge. Visit their fantasy lives. *Read their minds.*

Spirit dimensions are more complex. Most of them are hostile, looking for *sacrifice*, some way to feed off you, suck your energy dry. But the level beyond this is the real challenge. That's where the rules disappear and the only thing left is your ability to *adapt*, change frequencies, become whatever's out there. If you can tune into this level, you'll find the experimental dimensions set up in your own neighbourhood. Invisible, but altering *your* frequencies. This afternoon, coming through Ottawa, I slid into one that blew my mind. Something new they're doing with hatred, tuning it to a high pitch and weaving it into radio waves. Just let it slide through frequencies of opera or *The Doobie Brothers*, into the receiving flesh of the human mind. This dimension's frequency was close to the yellow I was using so I shifted and slipped in briefly as we drove through it. Huge yellow white throb, energy in the shape of a gigantic transmitter weaving its ugliness into radio frequencies that were broadcasting all over the Ottawa area. Its pitch was too high to be picked up by the human ear but it was still sliding every listener into dimensions of old wounds, not knowing why their moods had suddenly gone bad on them. I pulsed with this frequency as long as I could, learning from the inside out how to defend against it. Then I returned to skin and bones, looking for comfort.

"Dorell." Lennie shoves in beside me, leans past and looks out the window. Grey-white specks of the compound startle and dance through the maples. "Bunk with me?"

I know Lennie's dimensions like my own. Better, probably. "I dunno. I have a date with Major Kalinski."

Major Kalinski is the human version of the midwife toad. Lennie grins and blows a fart on my neck which gives me the giggle-shivers and that's the end of that. We unload in front of the dormitories and Lennie and I find a room with two double beds. Juss shares the other with his training partner, a girl named Gwen. There's not much to unpack since they dress us in Legion uniforms out here, military looking, a light grey. I've got purple stripes on my sleeve, a designated Seeker status. You don't usually get Seeker until you're twenty-one; they tagged me early.

It means I'm cut off from the rest of the group after Introductory Prayers and the Statement of Dedication drills. Usually this goes on after breakfast, but as this is arrival day, we get lunch, then take our positions in the circle around the flagpole. Today it's a white flag, a black triangle pointed down at the center. There are different flags, each one signifies a particular training dimension. I join in on the ceremony but I'm past basic training; the black triangle doesn't refer to my schedule. I feel sorry for the rest of them. They'll descend into some of the dark and heavy dimensions throbbing in the compound's underground. They're ugly and the pulse is long and slow, extended so every second feels like forever. Tonight I'll be holding Lennie and he'll be shaking.

"My country means nothing," we chant. "I have no country. I have no citizenship outside the Legion. I have no family. The Legion is my family. The Legion is everywhere. The Legion is everything. The Legion is my Lord, my God, my Way, my Path, my Truth, my Shining Star."

We do marching drills, practice the patterns of the pentagram in the circle, the six-pointed star, the triangles, the Cross and The Seeing Eye. Finally, Lennie and the rest of the group head off to the pressure chambers for black triangle training. I follow Major Kalinski past the front office, through door after door of security codes, deep into the compound where specialty training takes place. They keep a lot of dimensions in here. Mostly Gateway dimensions—thresholds onto other universes. Major Kalinski and other military brass can get into the Gateways and the found dimensions, but they're limited Seekers. That's why they have the job of training. Trainers are educated bullies. Seekers are educated victims.

Innocence is merely restricted access to information. Paranoia means *you know*.

In the security area, the air pulses and throbs. Dimensions crowd thick, pile into each other like one of those Russian dolls-within-dolls sets. You have to know your way through an increasingly inter-dimensional landscape. It's not just the complex maze of halls and doors—each solid locked door is overlaid with a growing number of Gateway doors, so it's more than knowing the computer codes, you have to be able to scan and adapt to the dimension frequencies or you'll get shredded. Several times, I've followed Major Kalinski into the Seeking Room to find the body of an enemy spy floating in bloody particles. No need for the Legion to set up much of a defence system; the frequencies do it for them.

Once it was one of our own, a Legion General who'd gone seeking past his level of competence. One of his eyes floated, still intact. Major Kalinski made me swallow it so I'd implant the General's vision of death. I felt it too, that moment when all the energy in the General's body exploded into fragments of black, white and colour. The energy of his life was still contained in the dimension he'd attempted to enter, in particles of divided light, scream frequencies.

Today, Major Kalinski has me sit in the Electric Chair and face the screen. The Seeking Room looks a little like the deck of the Starship Enterprise, minus the goodwill. No need to strap me in, I know there's nowhere to go around here. Lights are controlled by thought waves; the Major blips a few of his brain frequencies and the room darkens. As it does, the screen opens to a view of stars, planets, asteroids: space guck. This screen is another Gateway you can't see until the lights are off.

Now the Major tunes his thought waves to mine. Some of mine. If he could find them all, I wouldn't have Seeker Status, I'd be some low level bully Trainer like him. What he finds he moves into, infiltrates like bad breath blown up your nose and mouth, no choice to breathe in anything else. Then he tunes my frequencies for a specific distance and directs them at the screen. A whole new series of space guck comes into focus. Far in the distance, a pale pink light.

"Find it," says Major Kalinski. "Bring it in."

The pain begins. For this type of seeking, there's always applied pain. It's their weapon to force you to go the distance. It's also another frequency tuner, so when you've travelled to the required dimension, you're either at the correct frequency or as close as they can get you. Pain comes in different textures, sounds and colours. Today Major Kalinski tunes The Electric Chair until it's giving me pain close to the frequency of pink I see on the screen. The scream I give off is beyond human hearing range but I can feel it, a live wire in my throat. *Find the pain entering the body, seek it out, face it as it enters the pores—neon pink energy snakes flicking their forked pain tongues, longer than their bodies, tasting flesh, organs, nerves. Move straight into the forked vee, into the pain tongues, the length of each pain snake, deep into the frequency throb. Deep. Deeper. Feel it. Feel it. Become.*

Shot out. Released. The room and the Electric Chair gone. Sudden immense dark. Space guck floating nearby. I'm no longer flesh, I am energy, the neon pink energy of pain, without the nerve tips to feel it. *Freedom.*

Ahead of me glows the pink star. In the Seeking Room, Major Kalinski watches me as a tiny pink blip on a screen. To him, the star I'm hovering around looks like a pale rose light. Up close, this rose terrifies, roars and belches incalculable heat. Without nerve ends I can match it, as long as the body continues to send me pain frequencies that are strong enough. *Focus.* Pick up the frequencies coming out of the rose. Adjust. Move in. Fast. Fast as the energy coming at you. No thought, or only thought. Focused narrow line of thought shot straight into the heat and volume of fear.

Now I'm inside, part of the star, its being. I focus in tight. Then slowly I widen at an even rate, allowing the star to rip a hole into the middle of me, tear my center open. I focus on my edges, keeping the circle firm and strong. That circle gives and it's all over, for me, for the body, for every me in every dimension I carry.

Circle still strong. The star's energy registers as cosmic violence pushing in. Early on I learned the solution to this level of energy: *become hole, become edge of hole.* Let it all into the hole, let the hole become a Channel leading back to the Seeking Room. But not to the body. If this energy was fed directly into flesh, the body would join the now-deceased General's unfortunate fragments, floating in some dimension of Major Kalinski's memory. No, the Channel leads back to a Gateway to the left of the body. This Gateway opens onto a dimension of void, prepared to accept whatever comes to it. The void dimension is encased within several other dimensions; Major Kalinski will see the pink frequency arrive and collect, but he'll be protected from any nasty side effects.

Inside the rose star, I hold the circle firm. Starlight shoves through me and reappears in the Seeking Room. Major Kalinski watches untouched as a pink energy swells behind the Gateway. When he decides enough has been collected, he sends a thought command to the body which is transmitted to me. I suck my circle self together, focus its frequency and leave the star. For a moment, the odd asteroid, absolute silence. Then the Electric Chair shuts down, the pain ceases and the body collapses. There's a *whoosh* and I'm back in the body, sagging into a crying face and demon heartbeat. Piss and shit in my pants, every nerve end withered.

To my left I can see it, a thick pink pulse. Already, Major Kalinski has compacted the star's energy into a small glow. It's only a minute part of that outer space rose, as much as they can handle for now. The Legion will study it, figure out its possibilities, then dilute and hang it over some world region they figure is too peaceful for comfort. Whatever its original pulse, this pink frequency was sought through pain, collected through fear, channelled into the Gateway through terror. Wherever it's sent, its frequency will transmit the message of terror to the local inhabitants. The Legion will rack up more bucks and power selling guns, missiles and planes.

Major Kalinski changes the immediate frequencies in the Seeking Room to scarlet and lets this energy sink deep into me. Deep red is the frequency of life and healing: the restoration process begins. Fibres regain fluid, thicken. Cracks in skin and bone come together. The raw brain grows a new artillery of tentacles, dark and light.

The body fixed, Major Kalinski opens a door onto a luxury bathroom, my choice of bath or shower, thick plush towels. I shower and wash my hair, then pull on a clean uniform. Both the door and the walls to this bathroom are transparent. I know the Major watches what he chooses to watch, The Seeing Eye is part of the Legion routine: *I have no country, I have no family, I have no body, no self. All is owned.*

I return to the Seeking Room, my hair wafting the delicate scents of expensive shampoo. The new uniform moves fresh as morning on my skin, the start of a summer day where far-off sounds call through a bedroom window, hope blooms in a garden, the night has faded, and I've never been anyone except the one I am at this moment—someone of beginnings, no past within seeking range. I sense that something, *some horror*, has taken place, the knowing in me like a coloured transparency held up over a section of my brain. But whatever happened, I've forgotten it, the event is over. I'm clear and clean, the Major smiles at me and tells me to sit down in the Comfort Chair.

The Comfort Chair is the palest blue or the deepest blue, whichever frequency you call in. All its frequencies carry serenity. I close my eyes, relax, and let even the vague sense of what went before fade, ripple out, until there's nothing but an endless stretch of blue surrounding me. The Major talks to me and I answer back, something about the Enemy and their seeking: some of our Gateways have been penetrated. Tomorrow I'll be placed in the Electric Chair and sent out on assignment somewhere over the Pacific to probe several alien dimensions. I hear this conversation as if listening to someone else talk to the Major. My jaw moves and a voice comes out of my mouth but it doesn't seem to have much to do with me, I'm taken up with an effortless heartbeat of endless blue.

The Major keeps track of my frequencies. When I reach equilibrium, he calls me in from the blue, a falcon returned to the glove. We leave the Seeking Room and walk back through the complex series of Gateway frequencies and solid coded doors to the front desk, then on into the general compound area.

When I see the hall leading to the dormitories, something shifts. There's a dizzy swinging motion, memory coming at me from somewhere. All I can think is, *Lennie*. Running down the dormitory hall, I leave Major Kalinski and the day's work behind me. Later, if I focus, I'll remember the Comfort Chair, something about outer space, its vast dark, the neutrality of effortless suspension between times, places, screams. But right now, *Lennie Lennie*, the hall a blur going by.

Lennie twists on our bed, arms wrapped around his groans. Sweat dampens his hair, face, tee shirt. The slow dark dimensions are hell for him to adjust to. At the end of most black triangle days he's moaning until I bring him into equilibrium.

"Lennie?" I pull him in close. His breathing comes in hot jabs on my neck, his face salt acid with tears. I focus on the bluest blue, pull sky in around us, into his mouth and nose so he's breathing it, into his ears so he's hearing it soft sing, into his tongue so he's drinking it down. In through every sweating pore, into fibres, the atoms of bones. Looking for the black hole that spins crazy in each cell.

It's a good place, this dimension of sky. No war planes, no missiles, no radio waves. I keep us here a long time after Lennie's breathing comes human again, long after I know he's slipped into a pale blue dream. Then I bring us back to the dormitory bed and watch him open his eyes. For a moment, there it is in his slow stare, that exact blue.

"All right?" I lick off the dried salt around his mouth and eyes.

"It got so black," he whispers. "So far down. I can't do it, Dorell. I can't do the deep down stuff."

"I'll tell them."

We lie a while longer, just breathing, wait while Lennie rearranges himself, banishes the frequencies he can't handle. Then we head out to the cafeteria and the jumble of the other kids' voices, join Juss and Gwen at a table, caught in the late amber window light.

"What's the shit?" Lennie asks.

"Meatloaf," Juss grins back.

Then I know Lennie's done it, made it through to the dimension of here and now. Pushed the black out of his body into a dimension somewhere around him, another bit of his personal cross. So he's back to his usual fidget-grins and banter. *Normal.*

"Cannibalism's gotta be better than this," Lennie complains. "What's for dessert?"

Dessert is Black Forest Cake. Lennie downs three pieces.

Genesis

"Help me get into her."

Juss lies on his back while he begs, Len kneels over him.

"C'mon, Len, I can't do it myself."

"Juss, let me do you," I say.

"No." Juss doesn't look at me, stares at Len's face like he's got the force to make
   Len move into the shape of his wanting, just through his eyes. Recreate him
   in his own image. And Juss does. He can do that to anyone. Just give him six
   days.

Len looks off, back again, then off, Juss waiting him out. This is almost a last
   wish coming out of Juss's mouth except we all know he's gonna live. *If* he
   doesn't get at that pill bottle again. Grade twelve, Mr. Universe body built
   solid working weights, and Juss is out flat on his back, can barely lift his
   head and hands. Alive because they got to him in time. Alive because his
   mom's a doctor.

I heard them talking in the hall. Still not sure about brain damage.

"I'm gonna marry you and no one's gonna stop me."

Juss has been saying this to me almost daily, it's become the wind and sky, the
   sun coming down to touch us both. Juss repeats it as if saying it more often
   will build it into himself like muscle, he can take this truth in like air, like
   food. Sometimes I think he feels I'm his skin and he lives inside me. I keep
   his face living just inside mine. I know his secret presence, the way I start to
   smile and then his smile slips up through mine. Or I'm watching the wind
   lolligag through the leaves as if it's got all day, nothing to do, and then the
   way Juss watches things—the way he sees life pure in a blade of grass or my
   fingertip, the way he watches as if he can see me down to the molecule—

his way of watching slips into me too, his eyes looking out through mine so I see the basic patterns of things, the beauty of it all, the life will in every-thing, even a pebble on the street.

Juss made this bottle lethal. What they said, talking labels in the hall, was another hour and he would've been beyond their grasp. *Finally.* And their hands are far-reaching, farther than Michelangelo painted Jehovah reaching for Adam. These Doctor Gods reach part way into death.

This time started with an assignment the Kin gave Juss and Len, to see how close Juss and I were getting. Only it wasn't enough that Len bore witness, it had to be the whole Pack. So Len summoned me with the finger snap and two-note whistle. That meant the *reader-dreamer-I-believe-in-Jesus* girl faded out. I surfaced to see Len standing in a school hallway.

"Meet me on Duke Street in ten," he said.

I was by his old green car in five, jacket zipped up, October throwing every-thing into the wind rushing by. Turned into the wind, I let it come at me full force, the whole sky blowing itself through me, cleaning each cell down to a clear settled grey. I didn't hear them come up behind me until Len took my arm. Two of the Pack crowded me into the back seat, a third coming in the opposite door. Couple more got in front with Len and we were driving.

This is what you do when the Pack's on you. You don't fight unless you're look-ing for rage and sometimes you are, sometimes that's all there is. Rage is superhuman, it's love of truth and glory, it's BEAUTY JUSTICE GOD, it's the DARK PULLED FROM THE DEEP FOR ONE MOMENT LIVING IN YOUR BLOOD and you can shake even the Pack while it lasts, but rage in full beauty lasts only as long as you can hold your breath and then you're back to human, Adam coming out of the mud and there's Jehovah's face: you are body getting fucked and beat on.

So you pick and choose times to burn free. That afternoon wasn't one of them. I moved into *Fuck Me* mode, blurred them all into one flesh-toned universe so we became cells fucking, no names, no faces, whatever they did to me, I turned it into whatever I needed to blow the Pack sky-high, let them settle, collect, come back for more.

We ended up at Phil's house, his basement bedroom. Only his mother was home and she lets anything go. Everything went as usual, they rotated on me, a game of poker off to one side. Then the door opened and Juss came in, which was still usual, except he was looking at Len like he was about to cry, like this day had opened wide onto deep pain, he just wanted to stay mud, unnoticed, why did Jehovah have to choose him for the human heart deposit? The guy pumping me finished off; I could tune into the waves going through that room between Juss and Len. Not dark electric, different from the rest of the room's energy. A warm peach colour, smaller curves but more intense. Sorrow. Strong.

"You take her, Juss," said Stan, leader of the Pack. His face has the molten sheen of a Roman general stamped on a coin.

Juss pulled off his rugby shirt, dropped his pants. Going hard as he did—everything in Juss and me goes through a change of state when we're near each other, we breathe a sweeter air. He came down onto me like the sky dropping its gentlest snow across a dark earth aching for touch, for cover. The Pack faded out, even Len, though they stood and watched. They always watch when it's Juss and me, something they can't come close to, they have to watch it happen.

Kissing, just kissing. Juss's mouth wide and full, his lips always the place I find him first.

"Dori."

Said my name once to bring me full to him, I was a flock of scattered birds collecting above the one hand held out with gifts. He took moments into his mouth, making sure this time was all ours, no part of me left floating in what had gone before him, soft pressing his mouth into my neck, along my arm, there on my nipple, stomach, cunt. It all came to him, each part crying for love, together all the parts came together into *me*. Full-blooming, the deepest purple-blue, petals wide open around his cock sliding in deep, deeper, deeper still.

I could tell you with Juss it's all colour moving in slow swirls, it's music I can't describe, as if my body cells release their own singing. He gives me this anywhere and it was ours that afternoon, we moved further and further away from context, deeper into *together we are this*.

Then I remembered it was coming. The Darkness was just ahead. Dark horror had been rising up through our *love beauty fucking joy* the last month or so.

We'd be fucking *wonderlove*, then suddenly Something would be on me, Something with fear force. I never remembered afterward what it had been, it faded fast. Each time so completely gone, I never expected it again until the next lovefuck when it was suddenly there, reaching everywhere, its snarl dark. It happened only with Juss, only Juss had seen it engulf me. At first, when I started to scream he'd pull out, wanting to know how he'd hurt me but I could never say, the Darkness slipped away when his cock left me. They seemed to go together, Juss and the Darkness, so I begged him to keep going, keep moving in me all the way through it, take me through the Dark, he'd be there too, together we'd see what it was. Juss did that for me, stayed in me while I screamed at that Something he couldn't see, Something he couldn't help me with until I broke through it, came out into the pleasure he always gave me. Both of us pulling so close for it, desperate to move together, blow right through each other. After a cum, I'm small sparks of colour floating *in* him, all through him, drifting, settling back down into my body under his, back into me.

He'd ask me every time what the Darkness was, what I'd seen, but the shape and feel of it had vanished, only an aftertaste shifting like black oil. But for the past month we hadn't been able to cum together without moving through it first, sometimes Juss crying all over my face while I screamed and the strange Dark held me fast.

Now it was coming at me again and the Pack would see. Terror is the most private thing, the most tender organ, the innermost face.

"Juss, stop," I whimpered. "Stop. It's coming, I can feel it coming. Stop. Stop."

Juss did what he'd never done to me, turned his face to the wall, leaving mine wide open for the Pack to watch, and he kept moving in me, moving me further into pleasure, beyond it the void opening up.

"Juss, please, please."

Then it was on me, the Darkness leaping, jaws wide. Juss kept moving, moving, moving me straight into fear so huge there was nothing else, no place I could see but this, waves of it coming at me, wave after wave until this place was clogged with fear, thick black fear settled solid around me and there was no moving, nothing. Pinned down and nothing left to breathe.

Far away, at the edge, Juss was still moving, his cock a faint message, pulse almost gone out, the only thing other than Dark filling *mouth nose ears tunnels of the heart*, his moving cock my heartbeat calling, calling me forward, onward to him, to life. In the nothing Dark, a breeze picked up whispering here and there. My heart started to beat, blood move. A little bit of grey now in my mouth, tiny breath in my nose, eyes taking in shapes. Now he was rushing back to me, *colour warmth the sound of Juss* moaning in my ear, "Dori, Dori," and I was back again, splashed full wide into *wonder joy cum.*

Juss blew with me, we drifted and settled. Silence. The room sank back into me—Phil's house, his mom upstairs, the Pack all around. And I remembered the Dark coming, I remembered my begging, oh god I remembered Juss turning his head.

Without looking at me, Juss spoke low into my neck. To the Pack. "There, you've seen it."

Like a slap, I knew he was talking to Stan and Len, Juss had been ordered by the Kin to do this, he'd handed me to the Pack like an olive, splayed and impaled on a toothpick. Straight into its tiny red wish. *Here, take a look at this.*

"Get the fuck off me."

"Dori." He was begging.

"I said get the fuck off."

He got up and I was a wind moving around the room, picking up my clothes, pulling them on. Couple of comments from Stan, his eyes full of what he'd seen, he cums on fear like nothing else. They all wonder about Juss and me, how we do it, travel in such love. The Pack walks all over Juss for the way he lives with his arms around me, and I knew then they were already tasting what they'd throw at him over this. But I was going, he'd let them see it. He was following orders and I knew he had to, but he'd set me up. So I cut out of there. Nobody stopped me, my body turned into the ice of the north wind, nothing you could take into your hands. Or heart. I blew home.

His calls came incessant as the ticks of a clock. I wouldn't answer, it took Dad throwing me around a room before I shoved myself out the side door into the rain, walking toward the pale blur of Juss's car at the end of the driveway. The car door opened onto warmth, *Chicago.*

"I wouldn't be here if I didn't have to."

Inside, I slumped against the door and watched rain overload the windshield. Beside me, Juss's face ran with everything he couldn't hold in. On and on through the evening rain, me keeping my left shoulder solid with a hurt that kept him to his side of the car. When he braked for a Stop sign, I couldn't handle the inertia. Something broke me wide open and I erupted, pushed at the car door and ran down the sidewalk, my body a racing scream.

Juss had me before the end of the block and wrapped his arms around me though I was pulling to be gone, sobs coming through us both, rain knowing nothing coming down. Yellow leaves floated to the gutter, Juss held me tight as my voice ground out its grief. Then the world went quiet, only the rain. He turned me into his wet cold neck.

"I know what it is," I whispered. "The Darkness. I saw it this afternoon. It's a huge black dog and every time I think it's gonna tear out my throat. But it doesn't, Juss, it goes for you. It always tears out yours." A shudder heaved out of the earth, through me. "And then I cum."

Only his breathing for a while, his fingers cold on my neck. All of him cold. Endless rain.

"I'm here, Dori," he said. "I'm always here after."

We went back to the car, touching. He drove, I watched him. The air in his lungs came warm out of my mouth, what I breathed went into his blood. Straight through the fall of leaves spinning the last of their yellow against the twilight, we drove straight to the hotel the Kin owned, rooms at a reduced rate for Family members.

We lay together on a four-poster bed and Juss took me through and out of that Dark over and over. Each time I knew the dog's approach, I knew the sky size of it, the growl coming clear, the teeth, the tongue. Juss's voice talked me all the way through.

"Dori, it's a dog. It's just a dog. No one's gonna die. I'm still here. Dori, I'm alive, you're alive, I'm alive."

Each time, my molecules heard him calling through that Death Dark a little sooner, his voice moving into each cell, picking up the fear that was there, whispering to it, *I'm alive, you're alive, I'm alive.* Each time I could see more of what lived in me. I saw the dog, I saw a fire, I saw the Kin in their white robes. It was years back, I was eleven, twelve. Tied on an altar. Outside. Warm, sometime in summer.

Then finally I saw the boy, naked, stretched out on the ground. I knew his name was Billy Wheeler, that I loved him deep as water travels into the earth, deep as I love Juss. I knew the memory of him came to me through my love for Juss, and I knew Billy was the one the dog leapt for every time, that the dog leapt true.

In each molecule that was me, I saw Billy Wheeler die for the last time. As Juss covered my scream with his hand, I saw how the dog killed, and then the dog was gone.

Leaving me alone with Juss and our love. We could travel straight through it now, swim in it, roll in its October leaves, no dog, no Darkness now that death had been released into the past. For days after, I said his name, "Billy Wheeler, Billy Wheeler," whispered it into time. The only tombstone I could give him was the wind and every time it touched me I thought of him, twelve-year-old boy stretched out dead on the earth.

Juss tried to join him. That night, he and I moved free into each other, there was so much to touch, so many colours in our hands, our mouths. The Kin had to stop it somehow. The hotel door opened and they were there, white robes, white cross, black dog.

They pulled Juss off me, held him to one side. This dog was an ugly one. All I wanted was to get it over with from behind. I knelt and stared at the wall. I could hear Juss plead, twist in their grip; what he wanted was out of his skin into mine. I needed someplace to go, Billy Wheeler kept floating in front of my eyes. Billy Wheeler, Billy Wheeler, his torn-out throat.

Then it came to me, a single yellow oak leaf, its spin in the headlights, wind picking it up before it hit ground. Lifting me with it. Yellow, I was all yellow, circles of wind lifted me high and gentle above that hotel roof.

But not Juss. Fighting those white robes, he saw it all, the dog taking me, its yipping cum.

And he saw Billy Wheeler, dead on the bed with my face, that's what Juss saw.
He still saw it when the Kin pulled the dog off and left. Kept seeing it while
he held and rocked me in the warm slow water of the hotel bathtub. Then
he drove me home and went looking for a skull and crossbones label in his
mom's medicine cabinet.

The Kin wanted Juss in his skin, so he had to stay put. When he woke, my name
was all he'd say, he refused to eat unless they brought me to him. The first
day, he was too weak to pull out the intravenous but he kept trying to get at
it. The second day, they brought me in and left us alone.

I found a pair of scissors on the dresser and cut him out of his tee shirt and gotch.
Then it was everything into my fingertips, touching, touching, Juss watching
me, his eyes glazed blue, his breathing coming so slow out of the mud, back
into his skin. Touching, I gave him what he was to me, stroked it into him,
gave him his arm, his mouth, his nipple, thigh, cock. I loved each part,
wanted his DNA to carry the imprint of my mouth, my fingerprints.

I'm here, Juss. I'm alive, you're alive, I'm alive.

When he could get his mouth around more than my name, what he said was,
"Dori, I'm gonna marry you."

They left me with him three days, just brought in food and drugs, changed his
pee bag. By the end of the first day, Juss could move his head to each side,
then his fingers. By the second, he was lifting his hands, his face could smile
and cry. They took out the intravenous today. I can kiss his cock hard but he
won't let me on him, Juss will never let me on top. He says then he can't
breathe; it scares him. This afternoon Len comes in. He's out of his clothes
halfway across the room.

"Help me into her," Juss says to him. "C'mon, Len, I can't do it myself."

Len looks at him, their eyes holding years of best friends. "That what you want?"
Juss just looks at him.

Len cocks his head at me. "Lie down, Dori."

We roll Juss onto his side, then I lie on my back and cradle Juss's head while Len
lifts his hips. I guide Juss in, his cock so long Len has to hold him a foot from
me, then lower him in slow. Juss can hold up his head though it's working him
hard. I support it with my hands, my cunt beginning to move on him; Juss is

in me, I'm home. I watch his face slip its guarded weariness, ripple now with *wonderjoy*. I rest his head in my neck, just rock him, take him in, further in, curl him where I want to keep him in my deepest pocket, unborn, only mine.

Len is on hands and knees over us, wants to be as close as he can. Breathes with us.

"Juss, Juss, Juss," I'm whispering into his night black hair. "I'm alive, you're alive, I'm alive. I'll take you through this Dark and I'll bring you home. I'll bring you home."

Home is me.

Channels

They strap me on the disc, Counsellor and Almighty, both in their lab coats. We're in the experimental rooms, deep in the base. Tomorrow, my mother will donate the usual excuse note for school records: *Dorene Hall wasn't feeling well yesterday. The Doctor has concerns about her thyroid.* I have concerns about my soul.

Counsellor presses a button, the signal lights flash. There's a hum as the machine warms up. I'm in a *coldcold* sweat. I know where they're sending me and the guy in this dimension is a mean bastard, connects a lot of other clients up on their *meanbastard* frequencies. Something in my throat pumps soft and thick. Pumps as if it's trying to find legs for itself so it can scramble out with my breath, run *awayaway*.

Then I think, *It's my heart, how cliché.*

Behind this thinking, the slow raw throb of black terror. In behind that, the electric sizzle of white.

It starts with circles. No spins yet, I'm lying on my back and I'm gurgle-happy. No words. Colours and shapes, the smell of my fuzzy clean blanket.

The big people come in. The man and woman who take care of me are with them. Some of the people make low moaning sounds and some make high ones. They take their fingers and draw circles on me, starting on the outside of my skin, soft *roundround*. Not hard pressing, soft as their soft sounds. The circles go both ways. Some fast, some slow, all in different places—mouth, head, tummy. Feet. Holes.

Mixing-up. So many feelings, my skin feels like it's moving with their fingertips, I'm turning into tiny river circles of feeling. The river circles go deep under my skin, into my red stuff with its other purple and green globs. I can see inside my body, what happens there. The feeling circles have different colours—there are fast white ones, *slowslow* black, and the red green yellow blue in between. Each colour comes soft as shadow from a big person's fingertips, spins into a river circle of feeling. Deep, deeper, tighter, smaller, until I think I can't breathe, can't see anything outside me, just the spinning circles inside.

Then the circles shoot out of me—the white ones go up, the black ones down, the colour ones straight out. Inside each one goes a little bit of the *feeling me*. Sent out and away. All gone away and I'm cold-shivering, lying in my crib. No more feeling. No more nothing in me but the *deaddeaddead*. I'm cold as the *deaddead* ground.

It takes a while to work up to it, the level of ZAP that will send me far enough out. Counsellor has turned on the Level One force field. The air hums and throbs quicker than usual so I know we're headed into the white, or the upper colours. There's blood on my tongue—I must have bitten it, the salt taste dark. I suck, pull on its slowing frequency, trying to reach a dark counterbalance.

Counsellor pulls the spin lever and the disc begins to rotate to the right. The movie screens on the walls flash their first level trigger signs, cartoon characters from when I was little. The mouse, the dog, the duck. They look angry. Their eyes are mean and they hold knives, guns, whips and chains. Man, do they look mean. Especially the mouse.

Counsellor flicks a switch and we move to force field Level Two. The disc spins faster, the mouse comes and goes quicker, a mean slap at the eyes. I suck on my tongue, chew on it to pull out more of that dark *slowdown* throb.

The spins start in the woman's arms when she's holding me, turning *roundround*. She always sings the same song about rocking a baby. It makes my head dizzy but I get used to it. I pull at the sparkly buttons on her dress. *Sparkle and laugh and all pretty.*

Sometimes they lay me on a disc. They strap my hands and feet in tight belts. The disc turns, longer than the lady. Faster. The lady sings the rocking song.

Always the mouse is there, the big black one. He's as big as a man and walks like one. The mouse leans over me holding a knife and I think he's going to kill me. Other people around the mouse say things over and over.

"Youarebadyouareevilyouarebadyouareevil," they say.

The words get into my head and they live there. Outside, my skin turns into a *whirlingwhirling,* all the outside of me is a black spin going *roundroundround.* In the very middle of me, it's quiet like sleep. I go there to get away from the spin and the mouse and all the scared afraidness. It's dark, nothing, and I sleep.

But the words come in there too.

"Youarebadyouareevil."

The words talk over and over.

"Youarebadyouareevilyouarebadyouareevilyouarebadyouareevil."

Over and over until there's nothing left of me but the words and the *whirling-roundround.*

"Youarebadyouareevil."

Nothing but the words and the dizzy and the bad black mouse.

Almighty has the labyrinth up on the screen. I'm spinning like mad, the screen is a millisecond image repeating itself. I can imprint, no prob. We're up to the Level Four force field, the level that distinguishes the men from the boys. By now, most people shoot out and travel to wherever they're directed, but I can stick around a *longlong* time, know how to weave different colours through the screams in my nerves so everything feels like a fuck. Or love. Ways to convert ugly to beautiful, cum on pain, so I can stick around Here longer. It's an art, an energy art. You take those vivid *wheeling everywhere about* feelings, and with this huge paintbrush called *soul,* brush and stroke those feelings into different shapes. Stroke and stroke over that quivering fear until the *fastfast* waves smooth a little, let you reshape them. Like Michelangelo, I've got a hundred thousand pretty pictures floating around my Sistine Cunt. All of them taken from terror and stroked into a rainbow cum.

Sometimes, when the customer's nice, I don't have to work the feelings into pretty pictures. It just happens. Angels and devils fuck me with gentle cocks. Jehovah reaches down to touch me with His fingertip. Then I call the customer *Dickelangelo.* My highest praise.

Almighty is indicating a move twenty-three dimensions to the left, forty up and sixteen back, so I've got a fix on it now. A long time ago, there was just the six-pointed cross to travel. When I was a kid, it was easy. Now I'm seven-teen, I've got endless fucking labyrinths of frequencies coming out of me every which way. Today we're working on one that travels out and up to my left. A long journey just to get to the dimension where that mean bastard's waiting for me to show. Up there, it's a green-yellow flicker. For that guy waiting, it's probably as far left and up as he can travel. For me, about a third of the way.

He still gets to tell me how everything goes, though. How to moan and spread. Who gets to tune into the Channel with him and suck me dry.

❋

When I'm five, the spins live around me and the messages speak to me inside the spins. Every spin is different—fast or slow, different colours. The messages speak high and fast in the yellow and white, slow and pulled long like gum in the black.

Or there's nothing. Just the quiet.

I'm used to the spins. They live all over me, in my head and arms and tummy and legs. The Kin tells them where to go.

"This spin will live around your nipple," the Doctor says.

I'm on the disc and the spin moves into me and gets small around my little tit. It stays there and keeps going in my tit, even after the disc stops and I get up. I'm used to all the spins, except sometimes I get dizzy headaches. Then the messages that live inside the spins get loud and angry.

"Youarebadyouareevilyouarebadyouareevilyouarebadyouareevil."

I don't want to listen to that even if it's true and God talking to me, so I make the spins go *quickfaster* or *darkslower*. Then my head and tummy hurt real bad but I can't hear the messages anymore.

When I'm five, I'm used to the spins and I can walk with them going all over inside me. Now the Kin tells me I'm old enough to start the Channels.

"What's that?" I ask. We're in the Doctor's office, the Doctor and me.

"Don't ask questions," the Doctor tells me.

So I don't, but I can't help it, I *think* a lot of questions. They go all through my head. The Doctor puts me on the disc and he spins it the dark way. He touches my hole and says he wants the black spin. It comes out of my hole and gets big all around me, going *roundround*, black and slow.

"You are the Devil's child," the Doctor starts to chant.

I don't like this. "No."

He hits me and keeps saying it. "You are the Devil's child. You belong to the Devil. The Devil owns you. The Devil lives in you. The Devil lives in your cunt."

I'm getting very scared. When they talk about the Devil, something bad always happens, but I can't say no or I'll get hit. The air starts to change. The Doctor let some of his own spins out of him into the air. They're black and slow too, and the air gets full of thick dark waves. There's no more light in the lamp. All gone out, but I can still see. When the air gets thick black, shapes turn a red colour in your eyes. Now the Doctor is a red shape.

"I am calling the Devil into you," he keeps saying. "I am calling the Devil to live in your cunt."

I'm very *scaredafraid*, and I can't breathe hardly at all. The air is too heavy and now the whole room is going *roundround*. The Doctor is moving with me, the same way, the whole room is going with him, *roundround*. That's what happens when the Devil comes. He puts everything in a spin so He can come into the room.

But He never came into me before.

The Devil comes up out of the floor. He's darker than the room. I can hardly see him but his eyes are burning red and his mouth is like fire when he opens it. All over he's black but sort of red too. I know he isn't the Doctor playing tricks because I seen their tricks and I can tell when it's the real Devil. The air changes. The Devil is like thick air. You can put your finger through the real Devil and he's still there.

"You are the Devil's child." The Doctor is still saying this. I don't want the Devil to hear it. "You are the Chosen One."

The Devil talks to me. I'm going in my spin, all slow whirling on the outside, all quiet in the middle, so I can hear him good. His voice is very low and black and comes into the quiet nothing place like thunder that makes no noise. Just a feeling sound.

"Are you the daughter of Satan?" he asks me.

I can feel I am. I'm made up of the same black spin waves as the Devil, as if the Devil and I are the same place, there's no beginning and no end.

The Doctor isn't like the Devil and me—his waves can't go this thick and slow. Everything so thick and slow. That's all I am now—thick black waves and the Devil's words.

"Are you the daughter of Satan?" the Devil asks again.

"Yes," I say.

He comes into me. He changes his spin so it's the same as my spin, and he moves into the nothing place with me. Now the spin going around me is my spin *and* the Devil's spin and everything outside is very far out. In the middle of the spin are the Devil and me. I'm nothing and the Devil is ugly black waves, thick and heavy. He sinks down into me. The Devil is so heavy that the nothing place stretches out long and dark and turns into a tunnel. The walls of the tunnel go *roundroundround*. I am the Devil in the long tunnel spin and there's nothing nowhere else.

Then the Devil takes the spinning tunnel and moves it into my hole. The Doctor calls it my *cunt*. I don't like that word. The room stops spinning and the Doctor stops the disc. The lamp comes back on.

I'm out of the nothing place, back to my head and arms and legs. But not my hole. I know what's in there and I won't go there anymore. I feel heavy in my stomach. Sick like I want to throw up. I can't stand up for a while. When I go home, Mommy lets me stay in bed. That day I don't have to go to kindergarten.

✳

The trigger that sends me out of the body is a weird yodel cry at the back of Almighty's throat. They've got the force field at Level Six, and they've lit the light bulb shaped like a white devil head. When I see it, the frequencies in me jump to a panting jiggling *scared kid on high fear*. But it's got to be higher to shoot me out.

Cattle Prod time. The electric dick was inserted before I was strapped in; now Almighty pushes the remote control. My cunt gets the sizzle sear and I'm out like a scream, winging to the left. Behind me, the body keeps spinning at Level Six, the electric dick keeps up its brilliant fuck. Motivation, to ensure I go where I've been called, perform the required service.

I'm a vivid gull winging through dimensions, straight left into the mid-range frequencies—reds, blues, greens. Each dimension is built on a different frequency I sent out in the past—a lot of them little kid stuff, *babygirlfuckmedaddy* dimensions. Sometimes when I'm bored I play hooky from Real and travel to these places on my own, find out what's there, talk to the little kids, tell them how to handle what the Kin throws at them, how to keep themselves sane. What pills to ask for. Who's a friend, who's not.

As I speed twenty-three left, each dimension frequency gets a little slower and darker, the throb changing a little with each one. For instance, everything in a red dimension is tinted red and has a murky taste, but all the colours still pulse there, and a lot of the feelings. You move down to the black, you don't get colour and you don't get mind. You don't get nothing but power, heavy and slow. Everything is a part of it, you're nothing but a part of the power in the deepest places. No mind, no body, no soul.

The same in the upper white—no colours, nothing but sped-up fear. And power. Power so big and huge, nothing holds it in, you sure as hell can't. You're sucked in, you're just part of that God-white fury. No mind, no body, no spirit. Sure as hell no heart.

The further left I go, the further I move into whips and chains, strip and fuck. Saturday night dimensions for the games the Kin plays. These parts of me live as frequencies in dimensions outside the body, except when the Kin pulls the trigger and one of them is called into the body to perform a required service. Descend a couple of dimensions and everything turns into Deadville—vampires, ghouls, open graves. Call one of these selves into the body and it gets pretty ugly. Right now I'm still lateral to body level: number twenty-three is a hotel room of mirrors, four-poster bed, hot tub, torture toys.

I start up.

Daddy explains to me about the Channel. We're driving to another city where I get my training. Daddy takes the day off work so he can drive me. The Kin says I'm supposed to get special training. I'm the Chosen One. I'm extra-special because I try so hard.

Daddy says being the Channel is like being a radio. I'm the radio and lots of stations beam in. He moves the radio knob around so I can hear them all. I'm used to the CBC because Mommy and Daddy always listen to it. Now I hear lots of other ones. I didn't know there were other ones.

"Counsellor will teach you what you need to know," Daddy tells me.

Counsellor is a Lord of the Kin. He dresses like a soldier and I have to salute
him before all my training sessions. First I salute the red flag with the
Swastika, the spinning black cross in the white circle. Then I kneel and kiss
Counsellor's feet and thank him for what I'm about to receive.

"Submit," Counsellor always says.

"Submit," I say back.

"Obey," he says.

"Obey."

"I own you," he says.

"You own me."

"Each station on the radio has a lot of listeners," Daddy says. "Just like we're listening to the CBC right now. There are a lot of people listening to this station at the same time."

I never thought about this before. "How many?"

"Maybe a million," says Daddy.

That's a lot. "Does his throat get sore talking to so many people all at once?"

"No, he just talks. It doesn't matter how many listen," says Daddy. "He just talks
and they all hear it. That's what you'll be doing. You'll be the Channel and
there will be people out there who will come into you."

I don't understand. "How?"

"Counsellor will teach you."

It's a long drive, three hours long. We get to the checkpoint and Daddy shows
his ID. The guard lets us through the gate and we drive in. I turn in the seat
to stare back at the barbed wire. It's an electric shock fence so no one will
climb it. That should work pretty good.

After I kiss Counsellor's feet, he gives me the pills and puts me on the disc.
He takes off his clothes too and he lies on me. He does that almost every
time I come here. It's part of the Service. The disc starts turning to the left,
really slow.

"I am calling the Devil up out of your cunt," Counsellor says.

By now I'm used to this. The tunnel grows in my hole and the whirling comes
out all around and the Devil is here with me and Counsellor. Counsellor
can't last long like this but I'm used to the Devil, I just turn into part of Him.
Everything is slow and ugly. I want to tear things apart, stop hearts from
pumppumppumping, rip little baby kittens to bits, I want to go to my grade

two class and poop on the floor and laugh in all their faces.

I only feel like this when the Devil comes out of me. Or sometimes when he's in my cunt. Makes me want to *fuckfuck* anything, dance the Devil's Jig, push up my shoulders and spin *roundround.*

Counsellor breathes real heavy now and fucks me. When he does, some of the Devil goes into him. A little bit, not much. Counsellor can't hold Him like I can.

In the middle of the fuck, Counsellor starts the Channel in me. "You are looking down a long dark tunnel." He's panting. "Can you see it, Dorell?"

I can always see it. "Yeah, fuck me more daddy." This is Devil Talk. I like talking like this when I'm fucking with the Devil. "More daddy more."

"At the end of the tunnel is a door. Can you see it, Dorell?"

"Yeah, fuck me mister daddy."

"What does it look like?"

"It's round and spinning like the tunnel."

"That's right." Counsellor is happy I've got the right door. "Now you have the key in your hand. Which key is it?"

I look at my hand and see the key. It's the Swastika key with the spinning black cross on the tip. This is the most secret key. "The Key of the Cause," I tell Counsellor.

Counsellor is almost cumming now, I can tell he's holding it. I feel good.

"When you open the door, another Lord of the Service will be waiting there. Open the door."

I put the key in the Swastika keyhole and turn it. The door opens and I see a man's red shape.

"Are you the Chosen One?" this man asks me.

"Yes," I say.

Counsellor keeps fucking me. The man at the door comes down the tunnel to where Counsellor and the Devil and me are all fucking on the disc. The new man lays on top of Counsellor and all of him goes right into Counsellor so they're like one man. They're both fucking me and I can feel the Devil go out of me into both of them.

I don't get scared around the Devil anymore. It's too dark and slow to get scared. It makes me want to fuck a lot more so that's what I do. But later, when the man goes back down the tunnel and Counsellor gets up and the

Devil goes back into my cunt, I lie quiet on the disc. It's not turning now. I'm not dizzy, so I can think. *I don't want to be a Channel. I don't want to fuck two Lords at once.* I'm so scared, I get the shakes all over me, huge big shakes.

Counsellor hits me and tells me to stop. When the shakes go away, I take what happened out of my head. I put my hands around what happened and lift it out of my head. Then I put it into my cunt where the Devil lives. That's where it belongs and now I don't have to think about it *nonomore.*

✳

Forty up. Waves a lot quicker. Lots of crosses around here, the crossbars higher along the vertical beam as you ascend. Not too hot yet, still enough space between waves to think. To know where you are, who you are—if you're travelling on through, that is. Stop and move into a dimension and it will absorb you. Nothing going on for you but that particular place.

Meanwhile, the body is down below at ground level, getting fucked, getting shocked, getting drugged, kissing Counsellor's cock and feet. Where would you rather be?

I've reached forty, a huge old church. Cathedral type, choirs of heaven. Confession and sacrifice for fun. Take it up as a hobby.

I start moving back.

✳

On the plane, Dad won't tell me nothing about where we're going, just that it's for the Service and I'm the Chosen One. He means, *Shut up and live with what you get,* so I peel my eyes for clues. We're in palm tree land, a white limo picks us up. The signal is a white rose on the dash. Driver has a small white triangle pinned to his lapel.

Once we're out of the airport, Dad and the driver gear into backwards talk. That's supposed to get rid of me, trigger one of my chicks from a backwards dimension to come into the body. As she does, there's a heavy pressure at the back of the head and then she's in the eyes, talking backwards out the mouth. But I stick around in a dimension just behind the body, and I listen. I have to keep myself at a frequency close to this backwards chick but not quite the same so she doesn't know I'm here. She'd report me, she's a sucker for the Cause. *Sacrifice* really turns her on. Or rather, *Ecifircas.*

"Krowten." Backwards for the *Network.* Listening backwards is a strain on the brain, a whole different language, but anything on Krowten is worth straining for. The Kin taught Dorene Grace Hall to talk backwards before they taught her forwards. Same with writing. It's second nature to me but first nature for all the backwards chicks that belong to this body.

They're saying there will be a lot of high level officers at the Gathering. Some travelling in on dimension frequencies, but lots in Real. *In the flesh.* Lots of security going up to counteract some new frequency probes that the Enemy's got going.

The Gathering takes place at a country resort hotel. The Kin has rented the whole place, brought in their own personnel. I'm not supposed to know about any of this stuff but I'm hanging around the outside of every one of the chicks they call up. It's hard, I have to keep fighting the chicks who try to put me away, lock me out of what's happening to the body. So I flick in and out of what's going on with Dorene Grace Hall, like a TV flipping between channels. A lot of static.

Dark room. Bonfires. People in black robes, chanting. Swastika flag up front. Everything slow, like dope.

Everything slower, different room. The body on a disc turning counter-clockwise. Six men around the disc, all of them chanting in robes. Air thick and heavy, the room goes into a spin. Suddenly dark tunnels stretch out from me in all directions. Each of the six men now stands at the end of a tunnel but there are more tunnels. Other men appear at the end of the other tunnels and they walk toward me. Thirteen all told, they merge on top of me like shadows coming together, fucking me like one man. All their frequencies together are hard to take. Inside my cunt, doors open onto dimensions of ugly dark power; this energy pours out through the doors into me. The men suck it off me like there's no tomorrow.

Merge work. I'm standing with five other people around a lab, our backs to the wall. I'm the youngest. In the middle is an energy zone, a meeting place. Today we're working on merging in a white energy zone. The room frequencies are sped up to a white scream, each of us sends a white energy self into the meeting place in the middle of the room. There's a hiss and a whine as the white selves merge.

Fear white split wide open hot scream. Something gone wrong. The room goes black as our bodies keel over, hit the floor.

In bed. Hard to open eyes. Doctor talks too loud.

Still in bed. Can sit up. Not allowed to get up though.

Find out one of the six people died. He was pretty old. They're looking for a replacement for further training. Doctor says I can get up tomorrow.

Church. For the religious chicks, so they can get their Jesus-fix. That's why they think they're here, a Jesus retreat.

Orgy.

Training on the shooting range. Targets are naked people. I aim for cocks and cunts. I've got a good shot. Sometimes they send in live animals. You want to kill quick because some of the other shooters are bad shots and there's usually at least five trying for the kill.
Same thing when they send in a person. Just gun it down quick. Best thing you can do for it.

Lord's Supper. I see what's coming and blank out.

Going down to a dimension of ghouls and vampires. Full moon shit. Altars and sacrifice. The feel of black blood and flying, like bass chords in a heavy metal band.
Killing's glee here.

Another Channel session. I recognize some of these guys from newspapers and TV. They rule the world.

Another merge session. They use a lower frequency and we stick it out without collapsing. The replacement is younger. This time I feel the merge take place, the energy of six brains sliding into each other, all thoughts slipped into one pulse. Everything the other five know is suddenly mine, I can see everything they've lived and done, everything they know about the Network in their areas. The other five pull my life from me. What I know and do on this particular frequency.

It's like cramming for exams, one lifetime per millisecond.

A virgin's ball. All the girls in white dresses, the men in white tuxes. The chick who's got the body now doesn't know anything about the Kin or merge work or Channels. She's never seen a Swastika. A gorgeous guy waltzes her close on the dance floor, pulls her out into the garden to lip and tongue. This is what she'll remember about summer vacation, dream it over and over—a hunk with a white car driven far out into the country night, big back seat, white upholstery. Comfy, made-to-order. When she gives it to him, the moon slips whole and sweet into her soft crying-out throat. All she knows is she loves him, she's sure she's doing it for the first time. Pure and true.

And she is.

They found out about me, picked up on my frequency. Spying is treason in the Kin. I'm locked in a stone cellar. Metal collar tight on my throat, chained to the wall. No clothes, no food for two days, though I get some water. There's one window high up. I watch the sky come and go.

Sometimes they send in the dog. It never bites, though it's trained to act like it's always about to. I do what it wants.

They shoot me at dawn. Send me out onto the artillery range. My heartbeat is a semi-automatic. I see rifles, hear shots.

Body going down, bleeding out. Things slow, the ground opens into a raw-cut grave. I sink out of the body, down, down.

Suddenly, I'm shoved up and to the left. The frequencies go jagged, a blade saw whizzing fast. Colours neon. Someone's coming near. Her energy is jagged, crazy-shaped. Her eyes shoot sparks.

"We'll take you in," she says. "You have the skills."

"Am I dead?"

"Yes and no. You'll never return to the body. You're on the Outside now."

"Outside?"

"Outside the body. Outside the Circle. Outside the Network. You're part of the Resistance."

"I didn't die?"

"We faked it for you. They think you're down and out. You would've landed in the grave but we pulled you into this frequency. They can't track us here. We're outside their frequency codes."

This sounds interesting but the frequency is hard to maintain. It's like always being in the middle of a heart attack. Words and thoughts cut like knives and there's pain, an all-over crazy type feeling.

She continues. "The body has forgotten you but you can keep track of it. You can pull information from it to serve the Resistance."

Serve this, serve that.

"Submit?"

Crack of a lightning smile. "Never submit."

Far off, through the hundred dimensions buzzing between me and Real, I can see they're washing blood off Dorene Grace Hall's body. It comes off clean. I can't see any wounds. It must be some sort of paint. So they killed me with emotional stress. Or it's really blood and they regenerated the body. Whatever, the body is still out of it, mouth sagging, eyes rolled up. It disgusts me. The body *always* gives in. It's so full of shit.

"She *submits*," I hiss.

"She wouldn't if she could make it out here," says the Resistance chick. "We can't let you go back to rescue her though. You know this frequency code."

I stare at the far-off body, its limp flesh. Think of the way its bones ache in the morning, the raw cunt, the blood in its shit. Always the mind-sag fatigue, the buzz-saw head. All the cunts in it who know *fucking nothing.*

"Who wants a body?" I ask.

The Resistance chick lights up. "C'mon."

Jagged, I shoot after the spark trail she leaves.

✳

I slide into sixteen back. Green-yellow fibres of energy pulse like strobe lights. The walls of this room are mirrored, catch me in a hundred reflections. Right off, I'm split that many ways. A bit of my energy shoots off like a spark into each mirror. Waiting in each one is a Lord of the Kin, ready for his daily energy fuck. A vitamin pill for the spirit. There's one mean bastard who gets me straight on. He waits by the bed. Circle bed, four-poster with shackles for my hands, feet and throat. All the shock toys. He straps me in, lights my fire.

All the mirror guys have to copy what he does. I'm getting this a hundred times over. Livid shattering cum. Another. Another. Doors in my cunt fall open and the green-yellow dimensions send in their energy. Power: the men suck it off me, again and again.

Down below in Real, Counsellor and Almighty maintain their attack on the flesh. Keeping me connected, body and spirit, Real and *twenty-three left, forty up, sixteen back*. 23L-40U-16B. Combination for this particular Channel.

When all is done, I sink forward, down, right, a sigh coming back into the body. Some of me has been left above in the mirrors. Every one of those reflections is now a new dimension leading off from 23L-40U-16B. Just tack a one onto the end of the code with a mirror direction attached. Now I'm back in Real. Code Zero. No up, no down, no left right back front. Nowhere to go to get away from nerve ends, close-in and personal. Even 23L-40U-16B is better than this.

Almighty pushes a speaker phone. "Send him in."

Lennie's coming now. *My buddy my pal my breath*, coming in to clean me up. He got the day off school, drove me here, delivered me to this shit. They've been feeding him happy drugs to take his mind off. His eyes will be bugged, red raw.

"Take her home," Counsellor tells him. "Make sure she's put to bed and given a sedative. Give her this for the trip back."

Counsellor and Almighty go out.

"Dorell?" Lennie kneels over me, touches my mouth. His face is a blur beyond the slits of my eyes. "Can you talk yet?"

I push out my tongue tip to let him know I hear. He touches it with his finger, then his own tongue.

"You're here," he says.

Network

Hotels circle this downtown university, grey cement in every direction, the occasional green or burgundy awning. As usual, the Ed Psych instructor spent the majority of Dorene's class discussing car makes you can buy on a teacher's salary. It seems he's spent his professional career wet-dreaming about a red Porsche, the back seat possibilities. Wonder if there'll be a question about that on the final exam?

So much for Ed Psych; it's time to take Dorene out, bring in the other side. *Turn the inner knob, turn Dorene out, turn her out.* As the body walks down the front sidewalk, the university—its swinging doors, rushing students, the red Porsche—fades without commercials, without credits. *Leave it all behind, Doll.* Street traffic comes into focus—hotel windows, awnings that glow deep green beneath the streetlights. I surface into skin flickering alert; as I cut across the boulevard, every nerve tip echoes the click of ice in a shot glass. Already I'm breathing the heavy scent of rye, tobacco and aftershave. I enter the hotel by the staff entrance, nod to Room Service.

"Dixie wants you in his office," he says.

Dixie's not the best part of a good day. I knock on the door marked Personnel, step in on command. Wreath of smoke and an inhuman glare; Dixie jabs a cigar.

"Fuck you, bitch."

"What'd I do?"

"You're late."

"You got my schedule. Ed Psych, Thursday night."

"I told you, skip story-time! I got big time guys waiting in the ballroom. Something special tonight and they're waiting for your ass. Now get out there and wiggle. You'll be workin' all night."

"Dix, I got Geography tomorrow at eight thirty."

The desk lurches as Dixie surges up behind it.

"All right all right okay man keep your pants on I'll do it what d'you want me to do just keep your pants on man."

Dixie maintains his menacing lean. "Ballroom, Doll. Special Event. You'll get the details after you're dressed."

"Who are these guys?"

Dixie's stare is atmospheric. "Cock's a cock, cunt. You do your job."

I pause, the slightest infraction of a fraction of time.

"You want I should call your Daddy?" Dixie hisses.

"I'm goin'."

You get the bucks, I get the fucks. Backstage, the usual *boomboom* eats up floors and walls, the dressing room door opens onto odours of grease paint and dead cigarettes. Bare bulbs frame the mirrors, frame the room, frame the inside of my skull. The tiny room is littered with discarded clothing.

"C'mon honey, they're waitin' for ya."

Cherry snuffs her cigarette and comes at me, grabs at zippers and buttons, takes off one skin, hands me another. Today, a minimum of black, sequins and fringes. I check the fastenings, make sure I know where, what, how. *What was it we used to call those question words in language arts?* The thought whirs through my head, a revolving door bringing in the texture of a metal desk seat moulded for a pubescent butt, the singing yellow of poplar and maple at class windows, September scattering itself in handfuls of glad light. So strong, this moment of blue sky, sweet must of earth, grass, leaves. . .I'm lost in a locked stare, yellow dancing across my eyes. Then, the faces of two boys, grinning at me. Two names float through my head. *Lennie. Juss.* The three of us tossing laughter the way trees toss their yellow leaves.

"Doll, wake up!" Cherry slaps my face, not hard. The trees slip their leaves, the boys' faces fade, yellow rots into the ground. My whole gut clenches like hands trying to grab at what's leaving. *Who are those boys?* Their faces flicker in and out of my brain like tiny parts of a kaleidoscope pattern. Every now and then, they surface into me; while they're with me, they're *everything.*

"Sit down, let me do your face."

Cherry works me over, colour and texture taking away this, adding that.

"You're scheduled for a wax Friday morning," she reminds me.

"What time?"

"Nine."

"I can't, I got a lab."

"You talk to Dixie about it."

"Yeah, that'll be serene."

She tips up my chin and darkens the beauty spot on my right cheek. "Now git—the rest of the girls've been going for you long enough. Git out there and give them a break."

Everyone's begging for a break. "Hey Cherry, when was your last vacation?"

"Would ya git?!"

"No, tell me what decade."

"1952."

"I believe it."

I plant a scarlet letter on her crumpled face, avoid her garbage disposal mouth. Smells worse than anything you've ever thrown out. My hand on the door knob, she says, "Doll, you're better than this place."

"We all are."

"But you'll never get out." Her face is dead as an empty mirror. Never no company in it, spirit stolen, sacrificed for who knows whom. You don't argue with wisdom coming at you from beyond the grave.

From the dressing room, it's a short walk to the ballroom. Giff's on tapes, I tell him *Fleetwood Mac.* Surlier than usual, he spins his controls. Everyone's pissed off I'm getting an education. Under the lights, three girls rotate the action on pelvic thrusts, their fatigue is a wound in the air. Half of "The Lady In Red" to go.

Voices to my left, coming down the hall. Dixie and someone. "You think she's ready for this? Her thing's strip and fuck, men and dogs. Most she's done's a donkey. She'll crack."

"She won't crack."

I recognize the other voice—a regular around here. Jake Baldwin, owner of the local hockey team.

"She's tougher than you know, Dix. She's pulling too far off course with that university shit. We're gonna be pulling her in completely. One by one, we'll pull all her pretty chicks over to the other side. That's the program from here on in."

"I dunno. She's pretty stuck on getting educated." Dixie's dubious voice fades as they turn down another hall. I stand a moment, locked into listening, begging for something more, but the clues to the rest of my life disappear with the men's voices. Abruptly, backstage zones back in; I find I'm drooling, wipe my mouth. What's he mean, pull me over to the other side? I thought *this* was the other side.

"Earth to academic, earth to academic," Giff hisses.

"Fuck you." I shove him out of my face, steady my feet. "Giff, what's going on tonight? Special Event?"

Giff splits a grin. "You're the Special, academic."

The dancers come in off stage, give me the glare as they walk by. Then Jake Baldwin's behind me, his hands sudden on my hips, face leaned in around mine. "You listen to me careful now, Doll," he says. "Tonight's a whole new game for you. You're moving up in the world, joining the Inner Circle. It's real tricky in the Inner Circle. One false step and you could be dead. So you do what I tell you and you'll live. Y'hear me?"

My nod breaks my neck, I feel the vertebrae crack all down my spine.

"There's nowhere for you to go," Jake says. "Don't you be thinking about running now." He takes my hand and leads me onto the ballroom floor, packed with tuxes, evening dresses, the sparkle of diamonds under the mirror ball light. Everyone stops dancing and chatting, turns and stares at me. As if I mean something to them, something more than *whore*. There's a sudden ooze in my head, a black door swinging open, something dark with wings flying at me. I slam that door shut, grab tight to Jake's hand like he's my life jacket, but I keep my chin up, my eyes on a separate function from my heart: focus, assess, figure out what's coming here.

Torches—someone's going around lighting torches. Giff shuts off the mirror ball, switches tapes. Just drums now. Hand drums. And then I see it, an altar erected in the middle of the ballroom floor. A whimper out of my mouth and Jake's on me in a flash. I see it in his eyes—he'll kill me if I let out another sound. *So you do what I tell you and you'll live.*

"Lie down," Jake tells me.

I stare at him. Quick as anything, he hits me, his ring cutting my lip. Then he grips my shoulders and pushes me onto the altar. Lying there, I go into a freeze. Time starts to stretch as if there's a millennium between heartbeats; with each one the floor drops out, I'm falling. Falling through shapes dark with wings, falling through screams, fire flickering on all sides. There's dead people, maggots crawling off them, but they're moving, reaching for me. Then I'm pulled back up into the living, onto the altar, everyone standing in a circle around me, Jake cutting off my clothes with a knife.

They're chanting, I can't make out the words. Something in the smoke makes my head swing. Jake's saying something about, "Open your doors for the Dark Lord." He places his palms on my gut and for a second, I light up like a Christmas tree, a million tiny bits of colour glowing in my body, colours of a thousand feelings. Jake touches me thirteen times in different places, still chanting about the Dark Lord. The colours and feelings fade out.

Doors open inside—trap doors falling open. A huge darkness spins up slow from somewhere underneath. Smells bad. Screams and a rushing sound. The spinning gets bigger, closer, it feels full of knives. Then a dark shape lifts up *out of my gut*—black with wings, red eyes. It hovers over me, staring. I can't move, can't think. Stare into red ember eyes staring back at me.

More words from Jake. The demon hisses at him.

It fucks me. Its cock is like a knife, its claws sink into my back, it lifts me up off the altar and fucks me in a spin. I'm one black scream going round and round and while it fucks me, a huge place rips open inside, something dark and ugly pouring out of me into the demon's cock. On and on, it pours. Dark pain. Energy. Power. Then the door closes off and the demon drops me back onto the altar. More words hiss back and forth between the demon and Jake.

The party goes on. I lie bleeding on the altar, guys come and fuck me—blood draws them like flies. I think the demon's still out there, partying with the crowd—I can hear the giant rushing sound on and off, but I can't see much. Cunt of slow black pain, a nothing place, arms, legs, head dissolved into it. No shape, nothing but this hole that gets pushed open, rammed. Each time I feel a dark energy flow out of me into the cock, then there's the cum and I'm left alone.

Jake comes over, pries my eyes open. Ballroom lights are on again, people picking up their clothes. Jake sticks his face close to mine. His words come in huge waves toward me, I'm an ocean shoreline, taking whatever comes. "Doll, you watch this."

He puts his hands on my cunt. Again, I light up but different this time—a blue-white glow lights up in his palms, then sinks into me like goodness, beauty. Everywhere it touches, the pain goes away, the bleeding stops, the torn flesh mends. When he takes his hands off, my body looks as if nothing happened to it—no demon, no bleeding, no orgy.

"See Doll, you're all fixed," Jake grins. "Never no need to worry, Doc Jake'll fix you good every time."

He helps me stand and I need that help. I might look as if nothing happened but my knees give and I ache all over. Jake walks me back to the dressing room, sits me on a chair. At his nod, Cherry goes out, leaving us alone.

"You look at me, Doll."

I don't know why, I'm not seeing much. Everything's a paper dollhouse, something that could shred at a whisper. I slide my eyes onto his paper doll face.

"You're mine, Doll," he says. "Your Daddy's passed you on to me. I own you now. You hear me?"

"Yeah." One word, thick and heavy as a tongue.

"You'll be doing what I tell you. Dix works for me, you work for me. There'll be a lot more of what happened tonight. You'll be getting used to it. It just takes some getting used to. You got the doors to everywhere, Doll. Whatever you call comes to you. And you're mine, all mine."

He straightens in an arc of pleasure, looks at me a moment, slumped in my chair staring at the paper doll floor. *None of this is happening, it's all paper*, is what I'm thinking. *Later I'll tear it up and it'll be gone.*

"Doll, Doll, Doll," he murmurs. "You're the network, the *nerve* network we've been looking for. And now we've found you." He laughs once, a cock's crow. "I'll be sending Cherry back in now. She'll clean you up. You meet me in Room 13 in half an hour."

As he leaves, Cherry walks her thin granny shape through the door. "I've run a bath for you, love," she says. "C'mon."

I hang onto the chair as she pulls me up. Just want to keep everything coming and going in one place for a moment. Just one moment, in one place, in one me.

"Cherry, there was a de—"

"Now Doll, you know I don't discuss nothing that happens around here."

Cherry cuts me off firm, won't look at me but she knows. I can tell she knows what happened in that ballroom.

"Cherry." My corkscrew voice twists on itself.

Cherry hesitates. "I'll tell you this much. It's preordained. It has something to do with who you are."

The words knock me back in my chair and I'm losing it, the paper doll room begins to shred. Two sharp slaps hit my face and Cherry veers back into focus, me blubbering in a little girl voice, clutching at her, dragging her into me like she's some kind of mother and I won't let her go.

Cherry's a pro. "C'mon, Doll, let me get you into your bath. You'll feel better then. You want to feel better, don't you?"

I let her lead me into the adjoining bathroom and settle me into the bubble bath. The water's heat oozes its way into the ache. Cherry wipes my face with a sponge. Breathing, I just think about breathing, that's a small place to be. I can be where it's only breathing, think about Cherry, only Cherry, how nice she is to me, she treats me special, different from the others. Once she even told me she thought of me as her daughter, the one she never had. Cherry lost her one and only chance at a little girl at six months. Exit utero.

"Here, Doll, take these." The pills are her own, for some type of migraine she carries around. "Pain'll go soon. You got ten minutes."

I get ten, Jake and Room 13 get the rest of my life.

"What am I wearing?"

She holds up the long white gown. Some *sacrifice the virgin* wet dream on its way.

"You think I'll never get out?"

"No one does, love. Always a keeper or owner somewhere on your ass." She parts my legs and washes carefully.

"You miss your little girl?"

Cherry dreams of her lost daughter whenever she gets the chance, dreams her in a blue dress, giggles over an ice cream cone, graduation from high school, best in her business class. Dreams she tells only me.

"Not today, Doll. Time to get dressed."

"Cherry, take a look. What's your little girl doing?"

Cherry slides an arm under me, pulls me up.

"Did she go to school, Cherry? Did you read her a story at breakfast today?"

How do you paint the air you breathe? It's our game, Cherry's and mine. Making up her little girl, different ages for different days, never mind about chronology.

"Did she sneak extra brown sugar on her Cornflakes this morning when you weren't looking?"

Cherry's arm slips and everything's the dark slur of my head hitting the side of the tub. "Shit," she hisses.

Darkness rolls, a little girl's face stretches across its surface, *ripples in ripples out.* Screams, fire, dark wings coming. Get a grip, I gotta get a grip. I grab onto that little girl's face and hold on.

"She's sitting in the schoolyard, Cherry. She's opening her sandwiches and she's happy you gave her caramel spread."

My head's still dark but I can hear Cherry crying. I'm searching for sounds, echoes from all the schoolyards I've ever known. I hear a plastic bag slide open, now there's the smell of bread and caramel. Whatever I find I send out into Real, set it up as a pulse shimmering between Cherry and me: caramel heavy in the nose, its taste wrapped around the tongue. Blue sky, yellow trees. The faces of two boys, laughing. The little girl seems to know them, laughs back, pushes her billowing blue skirt tight between her knees.

Cherry stops crying, I feel her smile. Suddenly I see her standing on the playground too, she's watching the little girl eat the caramel sandwich. Cherry's hands smooth her daughter's hair, sculpt it truer.

Somewhere in our dream, a dog barks, the dimension dissolves. Cherry's knees crack as she stands.

"My little girl's lucky I lost her. There are moments in my life I'm thankful for."

I open my eyes. Cherry's a skeleton with a white gown draped over an arm, a watch on a long chain swings like a pendulum and *ticktocks* from her other hand.

"Honey, you got two minutes."

The pills she gave me finally kick in. All the doors, all those nerves, the network shuts down like a little girl heading for sleep, true sleep, where there are no feelings, no dreams, and the darkness takes you in for the nothingness you truly need.

Shock Bitch

Game night at the arena. Sell-out crowd. On the ice, things are heating up.
Sparks fly. "You can feel the electricity in this building!" roars the play-by-
play broadcaster. "They're playing at a higher level tonight!"

Up in a luxury box, Jake and I watch the game. Or rather, Jake watches me work
the team. "Give it more at centre ice, Doll," he orders.

Only second period and it feels like overtime. I've already got the entire arena
flickering with boost frequencies the team is tuned to, dimensions of it con-
centrated on the ice. If you could see the shock pockets I've got stacked in
this arena, it would be like looking at an onion skin under a microscope,
each pocket a jail cell keeping one of my other lives. They pulse everywhere,
inside the player's bodies, throughout the crowd. Long ago, they used to live
inside my body, in my nerves, the electric currents of my brain. Until the
shock machine pulled them out-of-body to live as a current in the air, feed
for the hockey thrill. Each life lives in her energy pocket in the arena, but
she still gets her feed from my body's nerves and currents.

Jake gives me a command. I focus, then throw more breakers in my body, the
shock pockets hiss a more intense frequency. Some of my little kids light up
at centre ice, shooting frenzied energy from their hands, cooking the air.
Near the ceiling, my heavy-duty shock bitches radiate, sending their pulse
down into the team.

If the players tune into the right frequencies, I keep them pulled into speed,
playing high with lightning bolts and shock angels, where they score and
score. But tonight's the third game in four nights. They're tired, their
passes aren't connecting, too many turn-overs in the neutral zone. So I focus
more on merge work, aligning the brain frequencies of each line as it comes
off the bench. Merge them into a network of thought frequencies so they
function as a team. That way they read the ice better, know without looking

where their team mates are, the exact angles of their sticks. I make a holding dimension out of my brain and slide dimensions of their brains into it.
All in one place, their instincts move into the same pulse, they hear each
other think, talk back and forth inside their heads.

I'm going left. Hit me at the circle.

Shooting right.

No! I think at this player. *Goalie's strongest there. Left, upstairs.*

Sudden chorus of *SHOOT IT! SHOOT IT!,* thought by the entire team,
benched or on ice. Coach's groan the loudest.

Puck rebounds off the goalie's pads, gets taken in behind the net. I repeat my
point. *Left, upstairs, like I said. What are you guys, fucking cunts? When I say
left, that's what I mean.*

To these guys, I'm just a voice in their heads, a little god telling them how to
get it right. Believe in me as fact or fiction, just do what I say.

"A miracle pass!" the broadcaster roars. "Look how they communicate with a
glance of the eye. They're playing their A game tonight!"

It's almost the play-offs. Hockey fever has this town in a delirium. Only second
period and the crowd is up and down, throbbing with the play on the ice.
During first intermission, some guy proposed to his girlfriend on the score-
board. *Lorelei Andrews, will you marry me? Jim.* Scoring is what it's all about.
Jim went down on his knees, the crowd oohed and aahed. How could
Lorelei say no? She cried buckets.

"You see everything at a hockey game," the broadcaster chuckled.

Jake's big on the Network these days, gets credit for keeping me down when I get
out of line, cross lines, cross lives. I cross lives as much as possible, use The
Seeing Eye to watch what goes on with my other lives in the other places.
So I know the Network has set up a teaching job for Dorene. Grade four.
She attends a Baptist church big on sacrifice and morality. The "friends" the
Network surrounds her with maintain a constant attack on her self-esteem.
Stand her up, make her phone them. Call her *paranoid* at every opportunity.
Tell her she's got an *overactive imagination.* "It's all in your head, Dorene."
Anything and everything to ensure she never believes she's worth the time
of day. Or believes what she sees inside her head.

Life's rough on both sides of the River Styx.

They're getting nervous about Dorene though. She's starting to wander off
the path, questions the meaning of *sacrifice*. They've got her on the shun
program, trying to drag her back onto the straight and narrow through loneliness. The only place the body gets tenderness is here in hell itself. From Jake.
On a daily basis, gentle once a day. Made that promise to me when he took me
on, and he's kept it. And one of the team players believes in roses, champagne,
foreplay that lasts several hours. Takes my clothes off in a way that makes me
believe in touch. Slow love in pastels and deep blue. He's at centre ice now,
I push another breaker, he lights up, moves in on the goalie, fakes him out.

Left! I hiss.

Lucky for him, he's superstitious, listens to voices.

"He scores!" The broadcaster is approaching heart attack, fans reach a metaphysical cum. Some not so spiritual, closer to the flesh where it belongs, after
all, especially during a game. So everyone can score together.

You feel everything at a hockey game.

As soon as I was officially turned over to him, Jake paraded me in front of the
team. It was just before practice, they were standing in a circle on the ice.
Tall as a ceiling on skates.

"Boys, meet the new Doll."

Jake led me onto the ice, into team snickers. Jake's dolls come and go, life into
death when he tires of them. They're a team perk, a boost available to the
top scorers. I skittered carefully around the inside of that slippery circle,
putting out the turn-on frequencies, pulling them all into Up Fuck dimensions. Jake chooses Network players only for this team, players that are
well-programmed to serve the Dark Lord or the Lord of Light. I could tell
some of them remembered me from Dixie's Network brothel. Some didn't.
Hockey players have a lot of faulty wiring in their brains, need a trigger
right in the face to connect to the obvious.

"I've heard about you," I told the player, touching his chest. The one who
believes in roses. He grinned, remembering me. He'd always asked for me in
the brothel. Always got me, too—he's their top scorer. I kept on, slip-sliding
around the circle, reading their frequencies like a hand of tarot cards. "And

I've heard about you." This one also remembered me but he's a pig, grabbed me, squeezed my ass.

"Enough for now." Jake smiled as he led me off the ice. "You know what you need to do to score, boys."

Behind us, skates knifed ice as the team skated off. Obedient as always to Jake's command, whichever dimension it comes from, whatever he tells them to do. They were all in on the kill. I know, because I used The Seeing Eye to scout out dimensions in Jake's mansion, especially dimensions of the recent past. I came across kill dimensions stacked in Jake's Chamber of Whores, his sub-terranean basement, the secret one under the regular basement with the usual ping pong, TV, pool, kiddy play areas. A secret elevator travels to the Chamber of Whores *going down going down* deep into the dark. No windows underground. A long hall with doors leading off to either side. Each room contains a different type of torture play, guillotine, electric shock, interroga-tion or holding cell. Lot of cameras to give you that Big Brother feeling, as well as dimensions full of Watchers that will report your every move.

First time down, I kept tuning in and out of dimensions that crowded in close and heavy. Some dimensions keep history: step in and watch what happened in this place before you got here. *Know your context.* I kept flipping through them, tracking the kills that had gone down—animals, kids, adults. There's always someone who went before you. *Just* before. Always.

Knew her right off. Shackled to an altar. Gang-banged until she was almost gone but not quite. By the team, so they got the feed off her kill energy. Then Jake did the honours and finished her off. I hear he always finishes his dolls off himself. Makes it more personal.

A little later, Jake showed me the movie he'd made of it. The fun they'd had with the body after. Just so's I'd get the point.

"I hear you're trouble, Doll," he said to me.

"Just enough to keep you interested."

"Submit."

"Submit." Fucking triggers kicked in. Getting wet.

"Obey."

"Obey." Frequencies changing, *fuckmebaby.*

"I own you."

"You own me." Repeat on repeat. He moved in.

The first week, Jake kept me in one of his holding cells. Chained for emphasis. Brought me out for interrogations. Small room, high ceiling, intercom, two-way mirror. They asked, I answered. The rest of the time tapes played rifle fire, gnashing gears, squealing tires, screaming. Non-stop.

Drugs. Shock. Stretching. Needles. Gang-bangs. They pulled dimensions off me the way you'd strip a clump of grapes.

Everyone in the Network moves in their own cluster of dimensions, the cross they carry. Each dimension is an energy place you throw out of yourself, a big ball of feeling. You want to toss love out the quickest, hide it somewhere in the air so they can't get at it in the body. Then you keep that love zone somewhere close, hoping only you know its frequency. That way you can turn it into dreams or daydreams, know what it's like to be loved without investing your skin and bones in it. So it can't be ripped out of you like some nerve end.

If you find someone you want to share more than just nerve ends with, you can take him there. Up in the air to the love dimension. If it's good enough, you sink that love dimension back down into your flesh, your heart. Give him the body and dream together. If you can't stop yourself.

If you're very very stupid.

We were in the player's bed, everything musk flowers and sweat. This fuck was Jake's reward to the player for a hat trick earlier that night.

"Dorene," the player whispered to me suddenly. "Dorene, I found out your real name."

He'd always called me *Doll* like everyone else. Hearing *Dorene*, my stomach tilted, my brain spilled. *Dorene.* Crossing lines, crossing lives. *With him.*

Somewhere in the air around us was the dimension of Dorene, packed safely out of the body for another time and place, far from Jake and all of this.

"Dorene," the player whispered again. "Dorene," into my neck. "Dorene," into the back of my ear. "Dorene," into my mouth.

In the air, Dorene wavered, shifted toward the bed. Called, coming to the name.

"Don't call me that, OK?"

"It's your name."

"Call me Dori, all right?"

"Dori." He slid it around my mouth, tried it out on my nipples. Dori was all right by me, I remembered being called that a lot, in a very distant life. Far as I could place it, Dori knew she had a cunt, knew how to use it.

Dorene retreated, back into further loneliness.

"How'd you find out? You're not supposed to know my real name."

"You know mine."

"Everyone knows yours."

He grinned, likes to be reminded. "I followed you home last week."

"Why?"

"I wanted to know who you were. You're more than this, I know you're more. . . Besides, Doll doesn't fit you right. Doll. . ."

"It's the name for something inflatable?"

Another grin.

"Just pump me up and I'm ready to go," I added.

His grin diminished. Suddenly it hit me, he wanted it more personal, more than the required boost. Something hard in me wavered, broke, I cracked in a whoosh of something warm, tender as the inside of a lip. *Dori.* A goddam fucking dimension of love stacked way far out, *way far out*, slid through thin as rain and filled my heart. *Dori.* All around us, pale silver-pink, streaked with olive, sky blue, glints of green and gold.

"Dori, Dori, Dori." That name whispered from his lips and hands and cock for the rest of that night, it whispered down through every cell as if they were miked. Calling it all in, every part of that lonely love, the blood and bone and gut of it, calling it all to him. *Dori.*

Didn't take Jake long to pick up on the love frequency. Pulled in close to the body, those Dori waves emitted themselves every time I saw the player, a shimmering change in the air. Jake went after those frequencies like a body part he wanted to dismember, but he isn't functional in the pulse of love. Can't come close to it, can't let the throb of love into his skin. Scares him. Jake turns love into terror and rage. That's all he knows.

I toss him other dimensions to keep him off. Raw meat to a dog. Each dimension I throw him has some little bit of me. Say it's a self that learned to like to fuck Daddy when I was four. Jake gets hold of her frequency and trigger codes, pulls her life from me. Stacks the dimension somewhere in his

Chamber of Whores along with all the kill and torture dimensions he's already got stored there. Then he can tune to its specific frequency and send one of his selves into that dimension, fuck and terrorize that four-year-old kid I was. He uses her terror to get at me because I still feel her dimension in the present tense. She may no longer live in Real, in the flesh, but she's an energy part of me going on somewhere in *Around*. Jake can go into my past, my memories, what's happened to almost any part of me, and he can add to the damage, change it, make it worse. I can't stop it. I can't protect any of my kids, not once Jake has hunted them down and pulled off their dimensions.

Sometimes he hires out my dimensions to a business man passing through. Once your dimensions have been stolen and stacked somewhere, you don't have any control over what happens in them. Hell, once your dimensions are stolen, you don't even *remember* a lot of them, it depends on how far from your body they're being kept. When there's activity going on in one of your stolen places, you'll feel a headache, groin ache, back ache, hips sore, can't sleep. Brain like a grinder. Want to die, but you don't know why you're thinking Suicide Heaven. Maybe a few dreams give you clues.

Nowhere is as bad as living in Jake's mansion. My second week here, we were in one of the underground rooms. Some business man and his wife were fucking on the guillotine, the guy playing with the lever, working up a thrill. Lost his focus. Hand slipped.

Talking nearby, Jake and I heard the whiz of the blade. Couple of thuds. Glanced over. Two very clean decapitations.

"Shit," Jake said softly. Cool. A flicker of the eyes, one skipped heartbeat. That was all. Then he called a Network cop and a Network doc and a Network stiff house.

I saw the notice in the paper. Millionaire couple, big donors to the arts. Died in a car crash. Coffins closed, case closed.

Still not enough feed going to the team to win this game. They're starting to lag, doubt dragging at them. Once they start shifting down, they drop into dimensions of the dark under the ice where demons come at them, ready to tear them apart. *Demon feed*. Then the team shatters, it's everyone for himself. I push more breakers and my other lives sizzle, headed for overload.

Jake's still working at setting up new merge dimensions for the team and me. It goes like this. Say he wants the top scorer to move faster on the ice, wants his neurons firing quicker. What I'm giving him isn't enough, they've lost a couple of games. The player gets called to Jake's mansion. So do I, which means *Dorene* calls in sick with the flu, sleeps all day. Wakes up feeling the worse for wear.

I take the body to Check-In where it gets the model make-over, then the limo takes me to Jake's. As we walk into the secret behind-the-bookcase elevator, Jake, the player and I step into an eraser dimension. It seeps through us, taking every thought, every memory of thought, from us and holding it outside in the elevator air, a storage zone. Two floors down, we exit into the Chamber of Whores, cleaned out, removed, nobody. We'll get ourselves back on the way out; now we wait for the next dimension to sink into our brains, tune our frequencies to what is required. Wait for one of our lives trapped in the next dimension to take over.

Jake has stored other lives of the team players here too. That way, when he gets mad at one of them, he comes down here and exacts his revenge. Doesn't have to make a phone call and ream them out. Easier than making a lot of trades, great for contract negotiations.

Jake is impervious to the elevator's eraser dimension but then he set it up, it's coming off his frequencies. I've been beating it more and more, using a concealer frequency. So far, Jake hasn't noticed. Or I haven't noticed he's noticed. I blank my eyes, pretend I'm erasing, send out almost everything I know and remember. Keep enough to hang onto some of me.

The player blanks completely. Jaws and hands go slack. Pupils take over the blue of his eyes. No Man's Land.

As the elevator doors open, Jake snaps his fingers. "Walk."

We step into the dimension set up outside the elevator door. Sometimes it's personal, seduction play. Other times, it's straight into whips and chains and you're running for your life. This time, little kid robots slide into us. Arms swinging, the player and I march down the hall, chanting, "Hup, two, three, four," until Jake barks, "Halt!" He unlocks a door to the right. The player and I pivot and march in.

Another dimension, another switch. Jake has us stand facing the six-pointed star on the wall. We recite the Creed of the Kin, turn to face the Swastika, recite the Code of the Black Cross, turn to face the black circle, recite the Vow of Eternal Life, turn to face the upside-down cross and pledge allegiance to the Network.

Another finger snap and it's back to kid robots. The player and I march out and down the hall. This time, it's a door to the left. This room isn't hot, but the pulse in the air is so fast it feels solid, presses on you. The back of my neck gives off a sharp tingle.

The robots fade out. The player and I glance at each other. What I'd give now for a few roses and a bit of pastel. *Dori.*

We strip. The player stands, his arms stretched out along the white cross in one corner of the room. Jake straps him in. Then he attaches conductor discs all over the player's body, especially the places nerves gather and commune. Since it's speed we're after, I get the other white cross lying flat on the floor. Jake shackles me in, then I get discs in similar places. Extra on my head and cunt, looking for a big energy play.

I decide to use a concealer and watch this out-of-body. I'll do a lot to know, but I'm not into being a hydro plant. So I slip free and move up by the ceiling where I watch the face on my body. Small quivers run through it as it arranges and rearranges everything to prepare for this.

The player has moved into a protector self. He loves Dori, he loves her more than himself, but there's nothing he can do for her here. It's every body for itself. Besides, Jake has him tuned to a frequency ready for the lift. This is how the player gets his jump. Gets his stats. Gets his whole fucking career.

"Sacrifice," says Jake.

"Sacrifice," the player and my body repeat.

Jake throws the breaker. My body gets the shock feed, collects the white scream pattern of nerve ends and sends it out. A sheer dazzle form, vaguely human, floats into a meeting dimension inside a white circle marked on the middle of the floor. She hovers and burns, a new self, *white hot can't think can't talk only burnburnburn*, held within that white circle dimension. Waiting for what, she doesn't know. She's newborn fear.

The player releases an energy self into the circle and the merge takes place. The two energy selves blend into one, the nerve networks overlap, every electric fibre finds its mate. The player is remade, his brain waves change, nerve ends all over his body evolve up the food chain at the speed of light. On the cross, his body hisses and moans. Screams.

The player can handle a unusually high quantity of heat; this is a relatively low level for my body. I watch it teethe on a lightning bolt, endure.

Jake waits it out, then speaks to the joined energy selves. "120 Up, 30 Forward, 72 Right, 67 In," he tells them.

The two selves follow directions, move up, forward, then right. Going *into* dimensions is different—the dimensions grow smaller, their electric blur shrinks and grows more intense. At 66 In, the joined energy selves take their last step into their new home, another dimension of electric burn, fresh off the grill. A new dimension comes into existence, born out of my shock and the player's need to succeed.

"120 Up, 30 Forward, 72 Right, 67 In," Jake repeats. Then he makes a sound in his throat, a new sound. High up; soft but crazed. "This is the sign." He means *trigger*, from now on when Jake makes this noise, it's a breaker to dimension 120U-30F-72R-67I. My body will burn while the player gets the lift of his life.

"Yes, Grandmaster," my body hisses. Still on the current, it'll agree to anything.

The player doesn't have a lot to say about any of this. He may be the one get-
· ting the press and the accolades, but he's just another one of Jake's business toys, a Network poster boy. When he's walking through applause to receive another trophy, he's in another dimension, another self. He doesn't remember this, the shock bitch that gives him the jump, the current that fires his brain. The *sacrifice*. Doesn't remember even though he's merged to me in a hundred different dimensions and carries me with him everywhere.

Sometimes the player's selves who don't know, dream me. Dreams, daydreams, when the mind slips its divisions, moves into different frequencies, and dimensions converge. The player daydreams roses on a dresser. Peach lingerie and a four-poster bed. Pastel love cries coming from a woman's mouth. A woman he daydreams over and over, her musk flesh suddenly there like an unexpected breath, startling, tangible. Feelings light up his palms, lips, thighs. The landscape tilts, he's in a sudden sweat, has to pull the car over to the curb. Or he's walking, turns suddenly, his body in a gesture of reaching. Reaching as if a new direction will take him straight into her, her voice, her skin.

Dizzy, disoriented, tears sting his eyes. *Who are you?*

She fades without reply and he moves out of sensation, freed into common sense, decides she was someone available after a road game. Someone who could really give it.

Dorene is the same. Alone at night, she struggles toward sleep. The barrier is the presence of love, tangible lips that move her mouth. Damp skin everywhere, she's mewing, can almost see him rise above her, hear a voice desperate with her name. "Dori, Dori." No one else calls her this, she requires a full and proper *Dorene*.

She never names him, but why name your fantasy? It's a sin, after all, and you never name that.

It's not enough, this game. I've pushed the breakers to shock dimensions connected to every team member. They're still one goal behind, and we're five minutes from the end of the third period. Jake watches me fry myself to bacon, his almost-smile floating across what he's not saying. A picture of restraint, he pulls out a lighter, flames a cigarette.

The lighter is a trigger for dimensions of fire. Sudden flames flicker around me. I sizzle, try to hold the game in focus. *Sacrifice.*

Fuck it, I think. Pulling on a concealer, I slip out, leave someone else to burn. Up by the ceiling, I scan dimensions. Something is off here; Jake is too complacent. Then I spot a dimension with enough shock cables running into it to feed God, and follow the wires to their source.

It's a control room of sorts, worked by one of my other lives. Her back to me, she's standing at a window overlooking Jake's luxury box. With my concealer up, she doesn't sense any shift in frequencies; she's keeping her eyes on Jake, her ears tuned to his next command.

One scan of the control panel and I've got it. Jake's playing a revenge game against the team or me, punishment, or just general humiliation. Or he's been paid off by the opposing team's owner. All the breakers are on feed, but most of the current that's burning me up has been connected to dimensions that feed the opposing team. Especially their goalie.

The period has a minute and a half to go. I reverse levers, adjust knobs. The current returns to my team. My player, *my love*. He lights up, the team connects.

So do Jake and the control bitch. As she whirls toward the panel, I drop the concealer.

"Who the fuck are you?" she hisses.

"He scores!" the broadcaster squeals. "Under a minute to go."

I don't want to do overtime on this game. Jake will have the body going all night as it is. "I'm your guardian angel," I tell the control bitch. "I have a message for you."

"Get the fuck out of the way!" She lunges for the panel.

In the luxury box, Jake is pulling triggers; all over, my body is calling up its other lives. Kops, Killers, Keepers head for this control room. It's me against my others now.

Someone's crossing lines.

"Maybe they'll try something off the face-off," muses the broadcaster. "Fifty-nine seconds is a lot of time. Remember that game two years ago. . ."

The control bitch comes at me again. I take a cosmic breath, then step straight into her. Her frequency, her dimension. Begin the merge.

I see her life, the interrogations, the beatings. The isolation chamber. No one loves her. Every now and then, she gets offered a smoke. She's sixteen years old.

She sees mine. The roses, the fingertips and tongues, the sweat. Hears the player whisper a name, knows it as her own. "Dori," says the control bitch, losing her virginity to the sweet pulse. She moves deeper into my frequency, accepts this twinning.

"Wait, there's more," I tell her. *Life with Jake. Life as Doll.* But she hasn't waited to get the full picture. Already completely absorbed, she's headed straight for love, leaves me standing in the control room, looking out the window into Jake's face. Behind me, I hear the hiss of Keepers coming close.

But first, there's a game to win. Twenty seconds, nineteen, eighteen. . .I focus on the player's brain, I think of roses, I think of his loving current, that electric dream. Quickly, I bring the full line on the ice into it, merge their brains, doing my guardian angel voice one last time. *Trust each other. Trust the balance. Trust and balance.*

"It's a three on two! Moving in, the pass goes left to—HE SCORES! With seven seconds to go!"

The broadcaster has hit seventh heaven. So has the team. I turn to face the

Keepers coming in the control room door.

"That's it for tonight, folks. Hockey doesn't get better than this. We shocked 'em tonight, we shocked 'em good this time."

I think of the player's cock, the very tip. Where he slows his pulse down to the very last second before it's released, touches and touches me with it, trying to make the moment last, lock it into flesh. Into *knowing*.

I don't know if I'll last this night. Crossing lives is one of the ultimate betrayals; it doesn't take much to be put under the knife and sent down to a dimension of the grave. It'll be just me dying, a bit of the body's knowing lost— the body will come through it alive. There are huge graveyards where decades of selves have been buried. Maybe I'll get a marker with Doll Dori carved into it—a small white cross. Doll Dori Sacrificed.

One thing I do know. Jake might keep me, he might not, but he'll keep my dimensions of love. Someone will be created to replace me and the energy of love will go on. Jake would get rid of these frequencies if he could, but he knows he can't. "Doll's got a heart," he tells his Network superiors. "That's the way to her."

If Jake doesn't decide which one of my selves gets to smell the roses and travel to the player's high-rise suite, then my body will. Jake can pull most of the strings, and he can pretend to pull all of them, but he can't pull love out of this body. Not completely. It would be flesh without nerves. Sleep without dreams.

This body won't sacrifice without them.

The Spin of Spirits

The Club floats in smoke circles the men form carefully in their mouths then
release, to hover, dissipate, fade like a kiss. Another night, the full array of
big city CEO's, several in from Bangkok, Brazil, London. And the local
suits—politicians, business demons, pro athletes. Power cocks of Mother
Earth. Some of them matter; my love sits at one table, Jake at another.
There's a sprinkling of those who'd call me *friend*. On a dark and stormy
night.

Silence settles as the lights go down. I walk onto the dark stage, my soles taking
in the grain of the floor firm beneath me. Holding me up. The air around
me is a membrane of breath, another skin, but more alive. *Alive.* Standing
alone in the drifting smoke, I close my eyes and I feel it, *life* everywhere
around me, pulsing through the wood beneath my feet, the shiver of air on
my neck, tits, upper thighs. *We love you, Doll*, it whispers into every molecule. *We love you, we're proud of you, we're going to take you through this alive.*

One moment before it all starts, alive and alone. Enjoy.

"Mercy Street" begins to fill the Club speakers. The start of a slow rain, notes
splash gently on the walls, floor, here and there on my face. I don't move as
I wait for Gabriel's voice, echoing with empty streets, pale corridors, *words
support like bone.* Wait for his chorus: *dreaming of mercy st.*

I open my eyes as they begin to appear. Up where the walls meet the ceiling,
their soft deep glows, each one separate but in its place in the spectrum, dark
to my left, blue-white to my right. Spirits. Come to this place, to my face,
my cunt, my name. Come to keep me from the absolute shredding of soul.

The men catch sight of them. Chairs creak as they shift to get a better look. No
one is breathing smoke circles now, all breath held in. I raise my arm.

In my body, across its flesh and fibre, its myriad of bone, I feel the Changing
begin, sink into every cell. As always, each cell membrane continues its

constant double spin; the inner circle of dark rotates counter-clockwise, the outer circle of light rotates clockwise. As the spirits approach, the membranes deepen their glow, quickening the two spins. The spirits follow the spectrum, light to dark, one after another descend onto my raised hand, slide along my skin, sink into my flesh. I glow as they continue through to my other arm and foot and release into the air. Blue-white, yellow, pink, green, scarlet, indigo, black, and all that lies between, each a different frequency, force field, presence; each slides into the energy trace left by the others, picks up some of what is left, leaves something of itself behind. For the spirit that follows. For me.

dreaming of mercy st.

wear your inside out

The last spirit glows black, its slow deep throb opens me into a vast chasm. A long time back, I learned fear had nothing to do with the dark, it had to do with the known, not the unknown. The unknown is sanctuary, the tunnels of the heart dark with love, rage, the effort of continuing life. Outside me, the rest of the spirits swoop and dart in the ancient patterns of preparation, my body still a form glowing with dark, dark, the Dark.

tugging at the darkness, word upon word

confessing all the secret things

Now the circle of meeting begins, the spirits of the dark come together around me in a fused counter-clockwise spin. Around them, the spin of light, equal *force presence energy,* spins clockwise. I stand on the stage, surrounded by this whirl of spirits, their whine building to a keen whistle as the light and dark seek one another out. Fast, faster, each pulses toward its opposite through resistance, through all that pushes back, through the invisible *no.* Reaching. Reaching.

'swear they moved that sign

looking for mercy

in your daddy's arms

The void between an impossible place that must be crossed for contact. Reach in, reach across to what waits on the other side. *Presence.* Let it touch you, *the tremble in the hips.*

Touch. Lips. Wet. Warm. Skin. Cock. Opened flesh.

The two spins of spirits merge around me. Dark and light travel through one another, tighter, tighter, until they spin into me, their energy travelling through my flesh, each spirit finding what it needs of the others. They give, they take. I receive, their Receiver, their Joining Place.

Completely opened up, I'm a place of communion, every bit of me an orifice. Spirits come and go through my nostrils, pupils, my cunt, ass, through every fucking pore. Lifted up by their presence, I stream colour, light and dark. Joy, sorrow, pain, the Beyond. I levitate on my back, high above the men. My arms and legs out-stretched, the spirits and I become balance, a dreamy slide-through shimmer. Gradually the spirits float away from me, separate entities once again, and hover, delicate as smoke.

Words are rarely spoken between the spirits and me. They come to me as they've always come, a spectrum of frequencies seeking a Joining Place, a place to spin together, merge and balance. Each time, they spin me into a place where all joins, where the divided circles of dark and light in each cell membrane can temporarily spin into one circle of balance. Sometimes the spirits seem to have the shift of a human face, my face, the pulse of my hands, tits, cunt. These are the oddest moments, when I think these spirits are parts of me, parts lost long ago to what purpose I don't understand. They come back time and time again to spin together into the whole, a moment together, loved.

Whatever, whoever they are, without them, I'd be void.

Below, the men wait. The regulars know this as foreplay. They don't bother with it much in their own lives; here, they have to wait it out. Sometimes, at this point, I get playful, swoop about, pluck off a toupee, levitate a man in his chair, dump a few bowls of soup. Blow out candles with one breath, flame them with the next. Light up into a burning bush, laugh in the gorgeous heat, turn it up, watch the men loosen their shirt collars, sweat amber. Just for a kick, drop into the lap of someone new, leave a burning kiss on his forehead. Singe his eyebrows but not his shirt or pants, leave no other marks. Or rub two fingers together and spark some guy's cigar. So he can tell the story at millionaire poker parties until his quadruple by-pass gives out.

I play, the men ogle, until Behemoth oozes out of the dark corner where he's been waiting. Behemoth, the darkest spirit on the spectrum, my guardian angel, my blood. He was born with me, I came out glowing dark. By the time they washed off my mother's guts, Behemoth had soaked deep into me; at my birth, he formed a protective pocket of dark to keep me safe one moment longer.

Born into the 666, danger eyes of the human race.

Behemoth begins a slow circle around me, counter-clockwise. Flesh of the air, the cosmic pulse, all spirits flow in spins, clockwise at the light end of the spectrum, counter-clockwise at the dark. Both dark and light are necessary as breath, both of them spiral the membrane of every human cell. Listen to the religious talk about the evil dark. Try a day without shadow. No depth perception. All you get is surface. Look at a minister; you see a minister. Look at a doctor; you see Doc. Cop is cop. Lover: lover. Friend: friend.

This crowd of men live split lives, light divided from dark. Light that does not know dark. Dark estranged from light. Life reduced to halves, then set up as antagonistic opposites. Doctor truly believes he's only-doctor when he's in his white lab coat. Here at the Club, he cums on death. Ministers can quote their verses backwards; here, they believe they're god.

My life is also divided, spins both sides of the void. At night I'm the *demon fuck*. On the other side, I'm someone who thinks she's all she is. I might be like the men below, except the spirits have always come to me, giving me a between. Place of balance, being, choice. Power these men don't have because they don't want it, their *own* power. Their *own* being. Choices.

Sometimes the demon fuck is Behemoth. Sometimes it's a dark spirit come from the far east, west, north, south. Sometimes it's a black hole, a shadow growing on a distant planet that drops down to find a Joining Place, communion with light. Just as the light comes, stars seeking their healing opposite.

Behemoth circles, then rises between my legs. His long black cock slides into me, the fingering of twilight, hell into heaven. The gentle dark slips into every cell, cools the bright acid. Together, we begin the slow sex spin, left, always to the left. Arousal like this comes only with the spirits. Behemoth soaks through; everywhere, I'm a black cosmos. Then in each cell, the spectrum lights up, indigo, dandelion, flamingo, suspended nebulae. As the spin gains speed, everything outside is lost, there's only the darklight whirling fast, faster. I lose my arms and legs, tits and cunt.

My skin.

Name.

Now the light is also lost. Only-dark. Behemoth rumbles to a roar, the air sweeps into a vortex, the smoke becomes one tight circle. I'm screaming, losing membranes, each one a jagged tear, everything swung over to the dark. *Losing balance.* In the Club the dark sits so heavy, its energy filters into Behemoth, pulls at him like a magnet. He forgets I'm human. The men's dark energy moves to join Behemoth, increasing the pull, a vacuum pulling me in.

This is what these men seek: the breaking of balance, the banishing of light. The dark trapped deep into itself, the light diminished to a distant surface gleam. Divided knowledge, divided self. But the light comes as it has always come, picks itself up out of shadows like scattered confetti returned to the hand. Specks in every colour, twinkling across the walls, tables, layers of the men's skin. All of it coming together into a circle, beginning the clockwise spin around the outside of the black vortex where I'm trapped, *spun spun, losing human.*

From far off, I feel their push, the massive shoulder of the light pushing against the agony of the dark; *push, keep pushing, the dark needs you, can you hear its sobbing, can you feel the emptiness of your arms without that dark grief to hold and rock, that black rage to take into your hands, a weapon of meaning to point at the lies of only-light, deception of image, what is only surface truth.*

For longer than a human life, the push remains at a standstill, the light hovers as if stilled, the dark screams on and on. Then the huge pinwheel of light begins to move against the slipstream of dark. *Keep going. Keep going.* The two reach equal speed and the void between them begins to shrink. Now, the *touch.* The skins of two who love, mother and baby, the skins of dawn.

Arising from this touch comes the most exquisite sound, a kind of singing, *the longing the wonder* of dark finding light, of light healing its wound. From each molecule, my body releases the same sound. For a moment, the exquisite singing. The vortex dissipates, the two circles spin into one another, then sink through me as before, every part of me again orifice as they come and go through my streets and corridors, no longer empty, no longer pale: *words support like bone.*

dreaming of mercy st.

wear your inside out

dreaming of mercy
in your daddy's arms again

But there are laws in this universe which must be obeyed. I am owned. Jake sits
  below, waiting out my preparation. Now he makes a small gesture with his
  hand. Behemoth moves into me and we float to the stage in slow sex. Spirits
  don't really cum, they spin until they reach their moment of joy. For them,
  it's a matter of movement, kinetics which they reach only through a Joining
  Place. There are many Joining Places scattered across the planet—geo-
  graphic sites, minerals, the movement of water. They can be human, but not
  every human. You don't choose this, it chooses you. Men of the 666 call it
  the power, I'm *the lady with the power*. Born as *the baby the spirits came to*.

Born under attack.

Men of the 666 can't reach the dark straight on, with their skin, their receiving
  orifices. They could if they'd learn to loosen up their pores, let themselves
  be taken, but these guys always gotta be on top.

You don't fuck a spirit; a spirit fucks you.

That's how a spirit's power *becomes* blood, *becomes* flesh, *becomes* bone; it *cums*
  in you. It has to be that deep, you've got to be that taken, opened up, full of
  joy.

Men of the 666 don't *submit.*

So these men reach the power through a human female living with it in her
  flesh. They get their power by sucking it out of her with their cocks. The
  power: it makes men younger, brings the dark circuitry of money to stagnate
  in their hands. Live rich. Live mean. Live forever.

What a life.

Behemoth absorbs into me; again I'm glowing dark, skin of deep night. I float
  in the direction Jake's finger indicates, spread on a table in front of a man
  smelling of another continent, distant water and trees. He stands, unzips and
  enters the shadow of my cunt, its spiral deepening in. Some of these guys
  are divers, some dog paddle; whatever they take, they pay for—deals with
  Jake or straight-up cash.

I watch this guy change. Brown licks through the grey of his hair and there's
  more of it. Lines lift out of his face, the jaw line comes back. Gut recedes
  about ten years. That's all he can last in me—ten years—before the dark

twists him into a cum and I'm lifted up, floating, waiting for Jake's finger, its
tiny codes.

The next guy is familiar—twice a year he makes the trip from Massachusetts.
This is what he gives his wife for her birthday and Christmas—time off his
gut. Meanwhile, she gets to torture herself with aerobics, diets. Panic in the
mirror. Cosmo surgeons and the knife.

Six guys is the limit for one night. Now the show begins.

I float to the stage where I pause, let what's gone before fade. I focus on
Behemoth deepening in my blood. Close my eyes and center through everything shifting exactly into place, waiting for *need*. When I open my eyes, the
pupils and whites are red. Blood red. Not a drug. A mood. *Need*. I put out a
hand and a cigarette floats up from a pack on a nearby table. Snap of my
fingers and I'm lighting it off the flame of my skin. Inhale. Release the circle
of smoke. Club etiquette observed.

"So, how are you tonight, gentlemen? Jet lag? Problems with the ladies? Just
plain bored with the routine?"

I whip my face back one hundred and eighty degrees, snap it front forward
again.

"We'll see if we can liven things up for you. Get you your money's worth. But
a warning to those of you who dream. This will come back to haunt you.
I'm no Pollyanna looking for her Huckleberry Finn."

Start spinning my head three hundred and sixty now, always counter-clockwise,
round and round, move into the motion, push down on it, release. Flames
burst out around me, I sit within them, don't burn. *Smile*. Smoke. Chat.

"So, how d'you like our fine city? Not New York, but it's got its night life. Best
stuff in the churches. After hours, after dark. Jesus goes to sleep and the
Anti-Christ comes out. Resurrects. The Anti-Christ resurrects too, y'know.
Every night she crawls out, more dead than alive. Crucified every morning
against the dawn. That's why the sky lights up red. The silent scream."

There are always a few guys out there jerking their nerves at the idea the Anti-
Christ is a *she*, no cock. Sexist. Better get over it. They're getting the truth
from the burning mouth. Gates of hell. Put your cock in here, boys. Find the
Word.

I exhale, the flames whisper out. The ember on my cigarette is the only glow
on stage. *Behemoth, darken, deepen in*. I press the ember against my leg.

Grimace so they know I feel it. Toss the fag away, show them the leg. No mark.

"Immortal, guys. Don't you just wish you were me? But you have to stay in practice. Keep in shape."

I extend my left hand. The men watch a large-bladed knife float from backstage to settle in my grasp.

"Want to know the secret of eternal life? I know you do. You think you want to live forever. Be a movie star. Replay all your good moments on the golf course. Your best fucks. Your best kills."

I work the blade up and down my left calf. Draw crosses, stars, circles, the one eye radiating blood. This time I don't let it show, the way my flesh hangs on, loving itself, each nerve a pair of lovers' hands being sliced in two. It's not just *my* body, *my* pain I feel here: history leaks some of its wounds. I get flashes of slaves and concubines put to death outside a pyramid; a body floating on a burning pyre on the Ganges; men huddled between their stuck-out ribs in a gas chamber, *going down going down.* Bits of history release into the Club smoke, agony writhes, curls into itself. Now the present tense: somewhere in the world, they're disembowelling someone, a prisoner of war, woman in her forties, long black hair, olive skin, dark eyes going darker. I can take some of that pain from her, let it out here. Another bit of the Anti-Christ scream. For these guys, it's an adrenalin rush. Stiffens their drinks.

One thing they predicted right: when you split skin into light and dark, they both bleed. One thing they didn't: when you split Messiahs, turn Christ into the local currency, stamp his face on every coin you spend to buy more of the status quo, the next Jesus to happen along will be the Anti-Christ. Coming up out of the dark to clean out a few more temples. Clubs. Christ's not doing much these days, someone's got to pick up the slack.

I hold up the knife, blade bleeding.

"Mother forgive them, they *know* what they do."

The blade cleans itself, my leg heals over. No marks. I smile.

Jesus had a fundamental innocence I've had to leave behind. These guys know *exactly* what they're doing. Well, most of them.

"Want to suck on this tit?"

The guy nods. He's a newcomer, his eyelids heavy like he knows what he's get-

ting. Like he's pulling it from me by *his* force of will. I make a clean slice of
it, bottoms up. Instant mastectomy. Hold the lump of flesh, nipple up, in my
hand. The shock of blood surges down my stomach and hand. I smile at the
newcomer, dropped jaw, eyes two balloons bobbing in his face.

"It's all right, honey, you'll get over it. We all do."

I fit the tit back over the wound, hold both palms out clean. No blood, no scars.
No marks. *Smile.*

"Let's see, what shall we do next, gentlemen? I do so like to play."

Time to get bizarre, start sending out the dark call. *Deep, deeper. We're going
underground.* I hold up the knife, stick out one bare foot, cut it off. Live on
the livid pain, move into it, breathe it. *Smile.* Fit the foot back on.

"Seen anything you liked so far, gentlemen?"

Gouge out my left eye, pop it in my mouth, chew it so they can see the juice
spurt. Swallow. Huck it back up whole, return it to the socket. Cut my own
throat. Stab my gut to the hilt. And so it goes. Around the room's edges, it's
going darker. More and more spirits arrive, drawn to the energy of pain. The
men have sunk deep into the darks of their own eyes. The air alters; their
bodies exude a different energy, dimension. *Zone of Shades.*

It's getting hard to breathe. Nostrils of the men flare, their breathing sinks low,
the rhythm synchronizes across the room. Slow. Slower. Over in a corner, a
guy slumps in his chair. Chest pains. No one moves to help him; he may die,
he may not. Coming in here, you take your chances.

I know the Ones approaching tonight. Felt Them shift the ground before dawn,
tease the wind, whine and spin their vast grief. I have to meet Them in their
place of need, the place to which we've exiled Them. To join Them there,
I must push through the membrane of deepest horror. The men's. My own.

Another man groans and slides off his chair. His body jerks on the floor for several moments, then stills. Everything deep in trance. I raise my left arm,
calling the Club's dark spirits into a spin that shuts the light up and out of
this place.

The Dark One coming to me enters city limits. Far off, I feel the One of Light
descend through stars.

Again I point left, calling to me what I need. Onto stage slides the blade saw I
set in the wings. A snap of my fingers and the blade begins its spin. I rise
into the air.

The air is so dense there's no breathing. These men have learned to hold their breath. My cell membranes spin only-black, counter-clockwise, no light anywhere within. The dark spirits swing into a funnel, tip pointed down. Their frequency creates an entry point through which the great Dark One, Nostradamus, rises.

The blade saw is my invitation to Him. I fly straight into the cut, dividing head from cunt, heart from cunt, lungs from cunt, the touching fingers, the *soft speaking your name* tongue from cunt.

Everywhere, blood and scream.

Riding the energy of this death, I fly toward Nostradamus in two parts. Below me the men, sprayed with my blood, lick their faces and hands. Between my legs, the abyss opens. Nostradamus moves into it, deep into the spin of each cell. Carrying the weight of Him, my every molecule becomes a black hole. All across the Club, men drop like flies. Walls wobble, the ceiling sags. Moans rise out of the earth, dark moons.

Extended, stretched out, the dark deepens, until He soaks completely in, all of Nostradamus, all He carries, all we've given Him.

Now the dark funnel slowly lifts itself; within it, I pass through the ceiling into the night. Below, air sinks back into the Club. Men begin to breathe, lift their eyelids, crawl into their chairs. Looking for their heartbeats.

Out here, the stars. Spirits in pinpoints of colour and light. They circle clockwise, spin into a vortex, its tip pointed up. At this pinnacle of light waits the other one. Galactra. Her hair streams comets, the Hounds of Heaven snarl at her heels, her gaze is fierce with light. Overloaded, her heart is burning out.

The dark counter-clockwise funnel begins its journey up through the clockwise spin of light, carrying my halved body to the mid-point. Galactra descends into me, flicker-touches across the surface of every cell. Ripples of light, she sinks into Nostradamus, his suffering, searching, longing. She extends—*fingers tongue cunt*—her suffering, searching, longing.

Found. The two funnels merge and spin through one another. Every part finds its opposite.

Balance. The funnels spin awhile at equal speeds, then dissipate as Galactra and Nostradamus return to themselves.

My parts join. Cunt to head, cunt to heart, cunt to fingertip and tongue. Flesh comes back to me. Now breath. Nerve ends. Muscle defines itself, veins sketch themselves out, blood makes its true way through.

Gently, I'm deposited whole on stage. Nostradamus fades into the rising sun of the east, Galactra into the set of the moon in the west. Across the planet people shift, comforted in their sleep. Rise with tenderness, a moment in their mouths.

In the Club, men stand, straighten ties and toupees, joke their way to the door. Each carries a darker deposit of horror in his nuclei. He'll defend and reinforce it in every aspect of his life, his right to live divided, a living death, his right to live this, ten years longer than anyone else.

Seated in his chair, Jake lights a cigarette. Releases the circle of smoke so that it hovers, whole and still. For one moment, spinning neither one way nor the other. Not even he can pull everything off balance.

"I own you," he says.

"You own me," I reply.

Owned until I find my own way out of this spin, spiralling always one way or the other. Until I find the marks, the scars, and make them last. Find both shores of light and dark, bring the parts together to live the full spectrum of joy, pain, need. Make myself fully mortal, fully human. Able, in time, to truly die, truly live.

dreaming of mercy

To Live Forever

We're scouting the streets, looking for a kill, a last minute order from Jake. Usually these details are managed in advance, but none of the breeders are carrying a life that doesn't already have a claim on it. The rich old geezer who's ordered this life turns sixty-six at midnight; he's in town due to an unforeseen business coup and he wants it done here.

I'm driving, two goons hunch down in the back. Jake's chauffeur, Pete, sits next to me.

"How about her?" One of the goons points at a girl working the corner. Around fourteen under the make-up. A lot of native blood running her veins.

Pete snorts. "White, idiot."

White, underage, looking at least close to virgin.

"Head out to the suburbs?" the goon suggests.

"We'll stick around here," I say. Around here no one misses underage girls, especially if there's money in it. I point at another kid—white, thin, around seventeen. Hyper on the gum. Pete scans what's left of her—not much on those bones, but it's alive.

"She'll do."

He offers her a fifty and she climbs into the front seat, doesn't even glance in the back. As I turn down an alley, Pete clamps a hand over her mouth. One of the goons hands him the chloroform rag and she's out.

"Find the name," I tell Pete.

He goes through her purse. You get a name on a street grab, you hand it to the Network cops so they know who not to look for.

"Melissa Lane," he reads off a library card.

"A library card? She reads?"

Melissa is now in the back seat, tied and gagged for her return to consciousness. Pete flips the card over. "No address listed."

"They don't put addresses on them anymore," I snap. A library card means place of residence means landlord means rent not paid and possible shit.

"Get out and find her pimp. Pay him off, tell him to clean out her place and burn her stuff," I tell a goon. He gets out and grumbles off down the alley.

A lot of girls work independent these days. Fucks up the structure. Breakdowns in the chain of command.

The Chosen gather in the Lodge. These are the city elite, its politicians and millionaires. No back alley strays for them, or so they imagine. Dressed in black robes and a blank stare, they sway and chant in the pews. Melissa is drugged so deep, she's breathing her own flesh. At the funeral home, she was stripped and cleaned, then drugged as deep and slow as life can go. It's mercy, more than she's seen in her time. Now she sprawls loose on the altar, doesn't shift. The sixty-six-year-old grandfather kneels at her feet.

As the high priest finishes the doxology, I step out from where I've been waiting between worlds, waiting to cross from one side to the other. Now I cross over, leaving it all behind, the skin and bones of it, the heartbeat, the brain that hangs onto knowing the specific details of a life and a name. *Dorene Grace Hall: twenty-seven years old, school teacher. Doll: grandmaster's whore, player's love.* Step over to the other side into the other name, the secret name, the name that calls one into being beyond flesh and blood. Here on the other side, no one can follow me, none keep pace—not my grandmaster, not my lover, keeper, trainer, father—none of those who own.

It's a change of state like none other. The face slides off, taking with it the sensation of skin and bone. Flesh turns to dark wounded air, the wound of the other side, the wound that uncared for survives, the wound that pushed beyond redemption goes looking for whatever will keep it alive. Life in its furthest pushed-out-beyond forms. The further out you go, the more power you carry. True power is *outside. Outside* everything that tries to hold you in.

At the altar, I stand at the girl's head, raise the knife and begin the call. My body becomes shadow, a pulsing human shape. Darkness spreads from me, bruises and fills every part of the Lodge. Some core part of me still stands at the altar, knife in hand, but I've moved beyond it so that I am everywhere, I am everything, an uncontained pulse moving into the brain waves of every human in this place, slowing them until they are prepared for the Dark Lord's coming.

As I move into everyone, everyone becomes His approach. There are no limits, none resist. The Dark Lord rises through the stone of the Lodge floor: the floor fades and disappears. He flows through the windows: the windows dissolve. He takes out the ceiling and we're enclosed in His dark circle, we're held within, there is no way out.

He is the stink of death, the horror that creeps slow into the very tips of nerves. He is what waits within flesh, the nucleus of each cell. He is the secret name given to each one of us, the name that is door to the beyond. Beyond flesh, beyond fear, beyond pain. Beyond the known.

I begin the call of secret names, start with Omega, call backwards through to Alpha. At each letter, members of the congregation release what has been summoned. A dark shape swells out around their human form. This shape hovers a moment, larger then life, then floats toward the Dark Lord and is absorbed into His pulse. When I finish the recitation, everyone present has performed the sending, given over their soul. Called by the true names, we become One: one heart, one soul, one mind, One Seeing Eye.

I begin the invocation for a door, a new door just for this sixty-six-year-old coot, a door waiting on the other side for him to open after the last heart attack does him in. He's got nine more years, I can see it in him. He'll be out on the golf course, it'll hit him five minutes before lunch. I begin the call for a lock and a key. As I do, I work the knife along Melissa's tits, cut deep to draw out what is required. Drugged, she doesn't scream, the pain rises off her as energy, you can see it in the air. Slowed by the drug, it takes the shape I command: key, keyhole, door knob.

I begin the description of door, still working the periphery of Melissa's flesh, *pull on pain pull on fear* until enough has been taken from her and the door hangs suspended in the air before the kneeling millionaire.

"Open," I tell the old bastard.

The key floats into his hand, he inserts it into the keyhole, unlocks and opens his door to the afterlife. It looms, empty.

"Kneel." He complies.

I begin the room. This room will feed the old bugger's afterlife with as much energy as I can pull off Melissa's body. Melissa is a little Christ now. Just as Jesus said: *I am the Door to everlasting life. I go to prepare a place for you, a mansion with many rooms...*

Sacrifice: everybody does it. Some of us get more credit than others.

This millionaire wants a resort hotel waiting for him. He's got about half of it built already, each room with its individual key, all built with the kill energy of someone else's sacrifice. There's enough energy left in Melissa to build one bedroom, throw in a hot tub, the usual torture toys. So someone can visit the millionaire in his afterlife, play fuck and scream games with him. Make him feel half alive again. Like the good old days.

The trick is keeping Melissa alive as long as possible, fighting for life. There's still energy left in a body after death, but cold is never as good as warm. These afterlives you build with the energy of sacrifice, they aren't going to last forever. The energy will wait for the customer who's purchased it, but once he dies and starts feeding off it, it dwindles. Like an RSP. So the more pain I can pull off a body before it gives out, the more energy stored for the guy who's paying Jake for my services.

Some of the kill rituals are dedicated to feed Inner Sanctum forefathers already living on the other side: Hitler, Genghis Khan, Cain. Sacrifice energy can be directed into a farmer's crop at seeding, or spilled into finance for business transactions. The possibilities keep the breeding farms busy pumping seed into girls so they churn out the human stuff that provides the kill energy required to maintain the wheels and gears of money, harvest, family, tradition, ancestors, eternal life. All part of the Network machine.

Through the open door, the millionaire watches his room swell in careful detail. Knowing which nerves give off which pulse, I mutilate Melissa's living body with precision. The final article is yet to be designed; commanding the four-poster bed, I cut out the girl's beating heart.

Now the room is complete, but the ritual isn't. The man with the money takes a last look at what's waiting for him, then drooling, locks the door and returns to his pew. I stand holding the dead heart, blood dark on my hands and arms, awaiting the Dark Lord's message. Waiting for my mouth to speak. *The Word.*

Suddenly Melissa's heart lifts from my hands and shoves itself whole into my mouth, down my throat. Tossed into the air, I'm shaken violently, my bones snap, come together, my neck *breaks mends breaks mends*. Finally the divine play ends and I'm levitated mid-air. A voice deep and stinking as the catacombs booms from my mouth.

"FOOLS! You who think you are worthy of death, worthy of My Name. You who kill the innocent for your mangy worthless souls. You are nothing. I spit you out of my mouth. You are not worthy of death. You are not worthy of life. You are not worthy of My Name."

There is a pause. The congregation chants, "Submit. Obey. Sacrifice. Submit. Obey. Sacrifice." Appease the Dark Lord; He's played bowling matches with the bodies of the Chosen before. Tonight He appears to be in a foul mood.

"FOOLS! This is not the purpose for which you were created, for which you came into being. Endless is your search for destruction, your hunger for more death and suffering. YOU are the evil. It comes from your hearts, not Mine."

This is new, not the usual stuff for these occasions, but I can't stop it. Hell, I'm just a door, my body a megaphone for the Dark Lord to yell through from the other side. Below me, the congregation shifts and mutters.

"You think this is the purpose of the Dark? You think this is the purpose for which that tiny pulse of life begins in the babe, beats in her heart and mouth and brain, in every cell? You think this is why nerve ends were created, why they evolved through millennia of careful choices, not this way, not that, moving always toward greater feeling, greater sensation, greater knowledge of what it means to be alive?! FOOLS! You think the purpose of life is doors onto tiny rooms of half-life nothingness? Tiny rooms where you have no skin or bones or heart? No flesh, no feeling, simply scraps of energy that were not even yours to begin with?! You are but shadows, shadows of dead breath, nothingness. You are killing to become more nothing. You are nothing now and you will be nothing forever. FOOLS! You have no names, I take them from you. I name you NOTHING!"

Either the Dark Lord has had an identity crisis or some jerk with a different mind set has grabbed the mike, but I can't stop it. I'm stuck here, mid-air, bellowing blasphemy and rage like I've never felt it. Still biblical as ever, everyone on the other side spouts the King James version. Makes them feel more important.

Down below, the congregation grows uneasy. Jake's giving me The Eye like I'm next for the altar.

Fuck, would ya shut up and go back to your dimension, whoever you are? I'm begging for my own voice but this whiner's got my mouth and He's on a roll.

"FOOLS! I believed as you believe. I took it all in, I wanted to live forever, I wanted power over other men, I killed and slaughtered. I made the children suffer and I built my own fortress out of their screams and tears."

The voice hisses now, knives in my throat. "Well, I live in it. *Forever.* You do not know what this means. Yet. You kill and you torture, you maim, you rape your children, you sell their very souls. You can still choose to walk away from it. You are yet alive, you can yet alter.

"I cannot. I live forever in their agony. I live with a knife in my heart but I live. FOREVER!"

Another pause, then a scream. On and on, it endures, the energy of it coming from every nerve end of every babe, child, teenager and adult I've ever sacrificed. I remember them all, every scream that has been drugged and silenced, all of them now released in one unending plea. For life. For life now.

Tears run down my face, huge, steady. I can't stop them, I can't stop anything.

"I will not allow it," the voice bellows. "It must stop here and now."

Suddenly I'm whirled toward the millionaire's fantasy life. This time the bedroom door opens without a key and I'm shoved into the throb of Melissa's energy. All of it soaks back into me, my being. All the sensation, the pain of each cut slicing deep as feeling goes, and it goes everywhere. There is no way out, no escape. Nothing but the dying, nothing but the fear and pain of it. In the pews, the congregation gets it too, the burn of the knife everywhere a nerve lurks. Until the pain of that room, door, and key have been taken back into me. But the voice has me still. Quieter now, it speaks.

"Fools. You must choose to face your own death. Understand this: *it all ends.* You live and you die. To live beyond death means you live only-death. Forever. But you are already dead. Your hearts beat, but you don't feel what you do. You kill this child and you think this brings you eternal life. Fools, this is the thinking of the already-dead."

The Dark Whiner walks me to the altar, then lays me flat across the dead girl.

"Fools," the voice whispers from my mouth.

The energy begins to leave me. In a steady flow, the stolen life pours back into the girl's body. A giant shudder passes through me and the heart hiccups through my mouth into the chest wound. The cuts close themselves over, the flesh grows warm. Melissa's eyes open. She screams.

I crawl off her and she lunges to her feet. The Dark Whiner collects in around
her and settles into a deep pulse. For a moment Melissa stares at us. She spits.

"Give me that," she hisses at me, pulling on my black robe.

I let her take it, watch wordless as she walks quickly down the aisle and out the
front door, taking the Dark Whiner with her.

Jake comes toward me, stopped momentarily by one last word, bellowed from
my throat. "FOOL!"

Then ceiling, walls, and floor swirl gently together, nothing but black. I dream
of Melissa, I dream her on a downtown street in the long black robe, she
looks left and right, wonders where to go. I dream she hails a cab, the cabby's
a good woman, *sees* what she sees.

"What's your name, honey?" the cabby asks.

"Melissa Lane," says the live girl.

"You come with me, Melissa," says the cabby.

I dream the cabby takes Melissa home, gives her a room to herself, a bed that
is clean and warm, I dream Melissa safe and clean, I dream her alive, wondering, *What will I do now with this skin, this heart, these bones? What do I do
with this Dark that saved me, saved me for life in the here and now?*

I wake to the interrogation. Cement walls, no windows. Tied down, naked as a
cunt, hooked up to machines that whir and hum. Cameras focus on me, tapes
run, record heartbeat, brain waves, voice. Wires run off me everywhere.

Jake is right over me, watching my eyes open, quickly close. He pulls my eyelids open so I can't look away from the blue light he shines straight into
them, can't get away from its pulse.

"Why'd you do it, Doll?"

"Jake, I didn't do it, it was something from the other side, something got in
between—"

Sharp clean slice of shock comes through the wires.

"Why'd you do it, Doll?"

"Jake Jake, it wasn't me, I don't know who it was. Interference, interference—"

Shock, hard-edged as diamond, pain shiny-brilliant.

"You don't allow interference, Doll."

"I didn't want to, Jake, it just came. I didn't know until it got going. I didn't call it."

"You called it."

Bleeding white pain. Pools of it.

"Jake, I didn't. It was just there."

"YOU CALLED IT!"

"No, I just—"

Long white knife of shock.

"You're the Doorkeeper. You control the doors. I control you."

"Yes, Jake."

"Submit."

"Submit."

"Obey."

"Obey."

"I own you."

"You own me."

There's a momentary pause, enough for me to pull into a bit of thought. Arrange my brain. Jake notices, more shock. No mind left, I stare at the blue and release. Release whatever I am now, let it go. Don't make it fight and suffer, don't make it scratch and claw and beg for knowing, for any part of self. Just let it go. *Relief.*

Brain waves change on the monitor. Now my eyes don't waver off the blue light.

"I own you, Doll."

"You own me."

"I'm going to tell you something, Doll, and I expect you to get it right this time. This will be the last time. If it happens again, I'll kill you. You got it?"

"Yes, Jake."

"This has happened before. You remember the last time?"

"No, Jake."

"It was at Christmas."

"I don't remember, Jake."

"I'm telling you it's happened before."

"Yes, Jake."

"I own you. I tell you which doors to open and who can speak from the other side. Last night you disobeyed."

"Yes, Jake."

"You allowed an impostor to speak, a rebel. An infidel."

"Yes, Jake."

"That was your voice, Doll."

Fear lights momentary thought. "No, Jake, not my voice, it wasn't—"

Sometimes shock is delicate, fine membrane patterns of lace.

"That was your voice, Doll. You called it to you."

"Yes, Jake."

"Repeat after me: I will not resist."

"I will not resist."

"I will not resist."

"I will not resist."

I will not resist.

I will not resist.

I will submit.

I will submit.

. . .

Echoes

This airport is an echo of god's footsteps in well-heeled boots. He strides across sky, making sure it's an empty day, well-tiled so every human hears his passing, crawls into a cave, lights a fire and renews vows. Maybe paints a few myths on the walls with the blood from the slit throat of an available child killed to keep god's steel-toed boots from striding into a father's head. The boots will leave after kicking a brain to shit, but the echoes never do.

Faith is believing in echoes.

Sitting in a blue plastic chair, I'm tight head-to-toe black, large silver cross earrings. White pen between my teeth, red purse over the right shoulder. Left ankle crossed over the right knee, waiting. Another plane, another rush of people, eyes staring ahead as they pass. *Take me with you people take me somewhere nice and normal, wherever whatever whoever.*

Running off the last time, I made it through two airports into a city of millions. Asleep in a women's hostel, I woke to hear men's voices at the front desk, the night clerk arguing, refusing them something. "Them's the rules," the old hag kept saying.

Fear haemorrhages, pools inside palms and soles and throat until what you want is a butcher to slice you open, let it all drain away.

"Them's the rules. You can talk to her in the morning. Wake Up is eight A.M."

The men went out, there was the sound of a door, then the scrape of the old hag's chair at the desk. I watched her in my head, watched her giving the evil eye to the front door but it was a guarded glance, she knew they'd be back.

They came with a uniform. Cop walked his badge straight past her and up the stairs, came in the open door headed for my corner. He'd never seen me but he knew exactly which bed I was in. Jake was downstairs using The Seeing Eye, must have told Cop where to find me.

Cop yanked me out of bed. "You're under arrest."

"For what? Don't you have to read me my rights?"

"For possession." A shove. The other women creaked in their beds, some to
watch, some to tunnel back into sleep.

"What'm I possessing?"

Cop dragged me to the dorm door where Jake stood in the dull hall light, something in his hand. Clicked on, the flashlight beam was a startling heavy
white, a force pulling at my eyes, pulling them in.

"Look into the light, Doll." Jake's monotone voice. *Called into the white.*
Everything jiggle-screaming in my body *slowed slowed stopped.* I stared at
that light *so white so pure so white nothing but the pure white path straight into
the light no pain no fear nothing but the pure white pure. . .*

Something with resistance, with wings, shuddered, burst out of me in a long
ahhh, then surrendered and flew into Jake's flashlight beam.

"Walk," said Cop.

I walked. Into the light, into the cold killer whites of Jake's eyes, walked down
those stairs, tee shirt, panties and bare feet, floating in a bubble of pure
white. The stairs white, the railing white, Jake and Cop gone white as angels
with their flaming sword of judgement.

In the lobby, a scraping at the white. The old hag at the desk scratched at the
glare over my eyes, patches of her coming into focus: ratty brown perm,
neon pink shirt, glassy hazel eyes, the reek of a warehouse of smoked cigarettes.

"It's cold out," she said to the men. "Give her your coat."

"What's her stuff?" Cop asked. The old lady handed him my wallet from safe-
keeping behind the desk. Cop passed it to Jake. "Go get the rest of it."

She took a lifetime going up those stairs, collecting my clothes and knapsack,
bringing them back down. Cop tossed me jeans, jacket, shoes. The white
had faded taking with it serenity, my foot jitterbugged around the mouth of
each runner, resisting the shoe.

"You want to walk out in bare feet?" Jake asked softly.

Going out, I looked back. That old lady never took her eyes off me. The beige
brown lobby was a patch of the nondescript and in the middle of it glinted
those old lady eyes, hard, determined. *Holding onto me* as we went out into

the winter street, the whirling specks of snow. *Holding on* as Jake guided me into the limo, Cop driving his official car in the opposite direction. The old lady came to the hostel glass doors, *held onto me* as the limo purred off down the street, Jake's arm along my shoulder gentle as smoke and mirrors.

Still *holds onto me.* Sometimes I feel those hag eyes clamp onto my life. I step into their watching beams, their force field takes me to another place, her apartment where she lives with a TV, Barney the cat, and a closet full of contraband cigarettes. She knits afghans with all the usual ugliness, I wrap myself in one, she rocks in her rocker, Barney warm in her lap. We watch whatever is on the tube.

She keeps me there with all the energy she can muster, wrapped in cigarette smoke and zigzag afghans, moments of canned laughter. *Peace is in between.*

Zigzag off the afghan, I'm back at the airport, tuned into Real. Focus on the job at hand. Passing by, the odd pair of eyes shift in my direction. A man will nod, a woman's nostrils flare. Everyone sniffs out a whore, especially women. Especially feminists. Better at it than any other form of human waste.

High school jobs weren't as complicated as this. The summons a note dropped onto my desk, a drawing of a circle with the time written inside: *3:30.* In the top right corner, the street corner: *Mabel and Orford.* I'd skip French and smoke off the minutes until Len pulled up in his old green car and I climbed into the smell of hot cheap upholstery, *The Doobie Brothers* "Takin' It To The Streets," Len's grin coming in for a kiss. Heading off for another job, we travelled in *The Doobie Brothers* or *Queen* or the *Eagles*: songs could take you anywhere in skin.

"Fucking's not part of the deal." Len stuck up for me whenever he could. Once he stood between me and some men in a cabin, his body working to keep its seventeen years out of an obvious tremble.

"You put the pussy on the table."

"You *got* what you ordered." Whatever it was—drugs, guns, snuff, the latest Network directory—it was there on the table, Len and I were backing for the open door.

"Her daddy said she was available."

"He didn't tell me. I'm her trainer, I say no." Len never argued if he was playing go-boy, delivering me to a john, but if it wasn't in his instructions he didn't pawn me off for extra bucks. Tense in front of me, his arm came back to my shoulder, signalling the dash. He always left the car running in out-of-the-way spots. One shove and we made a bee-line for the car, squealed off down the road, open doors flailing. Then the gunshot and the window shattering into the back seat. It set something off in me, a key turning in a lock, something kicked into gear, rearing through me hot and ugly, twisting hard *can't breathe can't think only one way to shove it back down whatever it is twisting me this way and that on the front seat sweating hot sweating cold so many fingertips jabbing this way that way all over inside skin.*

"Len, stop the car, I gotta, I gotta."

Knives let loose, cutting inside. All the church bells in a fundy town tolling doom in my head.

"Len I gotta I mean it I can't help it I gotta."

The body no longer mine but I had to live in it, the whimpers and groans, hands tearing at my shirt and bra to get them off, get the pants off, the blow *get into the blow it'll take all this shit this place what happened blow it all up into those sky-dancing trees.*

RESISTING THE PROGRAM, MAN ORDERED FUCK, RESISTING THE PROGRAM, MUST FUCK MUST FUCK MUST FUCK, RESISTING THE PROGRAM, PUNISHPUNISHPUNISHPUNISHPUNISHPUNISH.

Len knew the way it kicked in, took over muscles and bones but not my brain, made me watch. "Keep it for ten, I gotta put on some miles." He squealed onto the highway.

For a second, I got out of my body, tuned into the cabin and watched. The men were loading up another shotgun blast, then changed their minds and began to check out the goods.

"Fuck it, man," one asshole said to the other. "We'll get her next time."

The cabin sucked itself away and I was back into body frenzy, PUNISHPUN-ISHPUNISH, the *ticktock* in my head building to alarms and sirens.

"Len, they gave it up, they're not coming. C'mon man, it's killing me—"

He kept driving, his eyes on rear view and side view and me twisting on the front seat like I'd taken bad stuff. *Get with the program get with the program get with the fucking programprogramprogram.* Screwed-up on overload, I was

jacking up and down on my own hand, I couldn't stop, a fuckmachine on frantic function: *fuck or die fuck or die fuck or die.*
"LEN!"
"Five miles, Dori, just five. Then I'll pull off."
My fists pounded the door, the dash, no feeling to them, numb rubber things. Len was running eighty MPH, I yanked at his arm then his head. Giving up, he veered onto the next dirt road, braked around the first bend and was into me before *The Doobie Brothers* hit the chorus.
Key in the lock, behind this door what needed to be let out. *Fuckfuckfuckfuck.* No feeling but *fuckfuck.* Everything building, bells and sirens and whistles. Cities crumbled, earthquakes yawned, wild animals ripped at *flesh cunt a grave openingopeningopening the odour the stench of death bodies rising from graves rotting skin and bones ghosts around me swirled twirled screams moans chain saws fallingrope slice of knife axe on throat gunshot* RELEASED.
Bodies blown, Len and I slumped on the car seat, again two kids, *The Doobie Brothers* off and running into "China Grove."
"You all right now?"
"Sorry."
"All right."
"I'm such a shit."
"Dori." He licked my nose. "Dori, you got another five? Ten? Twenty? We'll do it our way."
I looked at him, his blue eyes held a thousand places, I could see every cell, each a place of blue. Len kept me living in so many of them, constant. I touched his mouth, he whispered, "Dori." The wildest crop of blonde curls stomped up and down his head.
"I feel like a shit."
"I don't," he said. "I feel like this."

Echoes fade, the airport comes back clean and clear. Another plane unloads, feet go by. I see him: a man in his fifties, black tie with goldfish, white hanky in the breast pocket. Carries a briefcase and a large purple teddy bear under his right arm. He walks up to my set of triggers. Hands me the teddy bear, the best money can buy.
"For the grandchild," he says.

I take the pen out of my mouth. "What's the name?"

"Tony Roberto Mandez."

Everything clicks into gear. I stand, nerves glimmering into their programs. "Where's the car?"

"Can I keep the teddy bear?"

He grins slowly. *Earn it*, he says to me, but not with that thin-lipped mouth. In the dimensions around us, "Tony Roberto Mandez" and I have slipped the flesh and begun contact, invisible except to The Seeing Eye.

Oh I will, I reply to the Left, where I'm dressed in red and skin. I offer him an arm, we find the car and chauffeur idling. En route to the hotel, he discusses mundane details about his flight, checks out the inside of my thighs. Using the Seeing Eye, he watches what I release into the places around us, each nerve tip programmed to respond one way in the flesh, another in a dimension of flesh. I let his fingers do the walking, my body a control panel, each nerve tip will take us into the labyrinths beyond. My labyrinths, his choices.

He's into the usual, likes it to the Left and Behind, the type that wants a lot of Daddy's little girl. Dimensions Behind are stacked full of childhood, *just put it all behind you*. Tony sends himself into a dimension that holds my second bedroom, the one with the pink walls, tells the little girl I am there to lie down on the bed and pull up her dress, the yellow one I wore to Sunday School, ruffled and frilled. "You'll like this, little girl," grunts Tony as the bed, the walls, the picture of Jesus knocking at the door of the heart go *up down up down up down*.

So goes the rental car foreplay; I can hardly wait for the hotel room. I focus on pulling him out of Behind to the Left, into red dimensions of whore where I've at least hit puberty. Whatever, keep him out of Ahead, Possible Futures.

The driver says, "Five minutes until we get there." We've fucked once in the flesh, fifteen or twenty times in the dimensions. Tony pays the driver and we go into the hotel, Room 33. Everything has been prepared according to Tony's instructions. Torture toys and the Cattle Prod have been left on the bed. An owner's manual outlines nerve points and programmed responses, which sequence will get Tony the Barking Dog Whore, Daddy's Favourite, Devil's Child. *Cum and get it*, Tony.

From somewhere, Jake is watching; this room has the quality of the inside of his eyeball, rounded, blurred at the edges, colours twisted like a cat's eye marble.

"Come sit in my lap," Tony murmurs, putting down the owner's manual. He picks up a sucker from the bed. "Something sweet for someone sweet."

I sit, take the sucker, play little. Giggle.

"First you get a spanking for wanting it," he decides. "Show me your behind. Let's play a game. You see my finger? It can get bigger. Watch this."

A game, just a game of altered states. Following the owner's manual, Tony presses the suggested sequence of nerve triggers, waves the red garter and says, "Jezebella Samantha Moonshine." The hotel room slips from my eyes, I'm in a long hallway running past a series of doors, the hallway is red, the doors are red, on each one a name: *Jezebella Diana Lynn. Jezebella Mary Sue. Jezebella Luella Ann.* Finally, *Jezebella Samantha Moonshine.*

I knock twice, the door opens.

This Jezebella is three years old. She's been sleeping, yawns and rubs her eyes, but she's ready, dressed in black and red lingerie, a red garter on her left leg.

Tony is getting impatient. On the bed the body is lying quiet, not responding. The summons comes again, the six nerves pressed in sequence, the red garter waved, the name spoken: *Jezebella Samantha Moonshine.*

"Hurry," the little one says.

I dawdle, she pays, so I scoop her up and run back through the red, everywhere red walls and doors, halls splitting off into further halls and walls of red until I reach the entry point, the spinning red gate, step through it and deposit the child in the body. Then I turn away from Real toward my own door and go in. Closing it, I hear Jezebella ask for the sucker.

At the back of my dimension, another door opens onto a high school lunch period when the Pack had gotten me into the guys can and worked me over until Len came looking for me. He knew what had been going on, we always had The Eye on each other, but he'd been trapped in basketball practice. He pushed his way in, yelling and shoving; the guys zipped up and left. Another class skipped, another cruise in Len's car, his foot raging the gas pedal. We stopped at a drugstore, he bought a salve for my mouth. Then we slipped the city, gunned and revved and burned up country roads, sky, fields and grey black asphalt *going by going by.*

Finally he swerved into a stretch of trees and grass, placing poplars between us and the road. Radio on loud, he pulled me out, sat me on the trunk. Then he leaned in against my chest and stared off across that field of sweet breathing grass, his body taut, trembling. Around us, everything stopped moving, sucked in, held its breath. Released something into Len.

"BASTARDS!"

His yell cut out of him, a blade saw slicing his mouth, his face, the landscape in two.

"FUCKING COCK SUCKERS!"

Breathing and heartbeat his gas pedal now, Len raged. Suddenly he twisted in against me, took my face between his hands. Tried to keep his fingertips tender.

"C'mon, Dori, let it loose."

My face was a wobbly acid. I kept my cheeks sucked in, my eyes a burnt stare.

"Dori, let it out. Scream."

I stared at him.

"I do this sometimes," he said. "Just drive out somewhere and scream. C'mon."

"Why?"

"The sky listens," he said. He turned, the scream bending him forward at the waist and dragging him down until it had finished with his body and left him wheezing on his knees. He pulled in another breath, but this time I was ahead of him.

"MY DADDY FUCKS ME."

Then a sound cut out of me, a sound I didn't know I carried; it came out *black blood and raw gut*, blew my face away. No bones left, no brain, no name, just the sound *driving driving driving* its way out.

Grass warm under my cheek, buzz of a nearby fly. Car radio tuning in. "Time in a Bottle." Beside me, Len breathing, just breathing. Something gone now.

The radio switched tunes. Len and I suspended in the scent of grass. *Lighthouse* rejuvenating our minds. Breath a little different now, shuddered deeper in. Len shifted. "Love Hurts." *Nazareth* sang itself out. Len rolled onto his back. I moved an arm, heavy, solid with fatigue. The inner shifting pieces gradually settled into place. *Chicago* drifted past, "Wishin' You Were Here." I grunted as I sat up. My throat shredded on the sound, raw as if raked.

"Not yet." Len reached a slow arm up and pulled me back down against him, the radio played on. Gordon Lightfoot, Joni and "The Circle Game."

Returning to the body bit by bit. Now the hips were back, the sensation of skin.
Fingers at the ends of arms, where were the hands? Grass prickled my neck.
I knew where my ear was, the beginning of thighs, lips in my jeans. Feet still
a long way off. Len slid his hand under my shirt, I found my nipple under
his fingers. Floating on me, not rooted.

"Seasons in the Sun." Flesh sketching itself in deep, nerves coming out of
shock, a network of electrical currents feeling me out. Radio switched the
scene.

"You want to do it to *The Doobie Brothers*, Dori?"

Focus coming clear as Len's cock slid in, colours slipped deep into skin and eye,
grass and sky. Len brought it all home to me, every nerve, every bone, every
bit of lip and brain, breath and air. Voice. The radio accompanying, the sky
listening.

Joni returns me to my dimension behind my door with "Both Sides Now." It
takes a heartbeat to adjust; I focus The Seeing Eye and look out. Tony has
moved into s&m, Jezebella Samantha Moonshine is back behind her
red door, one of the teens getting the Prod, taking the pain waves,
smoothing them, *smoothsmoothsmooth them out rearrange to a different pulse
change the colour change the hills and valleys make it all cumcumcum.* Convert
context, convert meaning, cum on any texture you get given.

Another door slips open, pulls me off again. Len's bed, a Saturday morning, free
time. Len's parents had finished with us for the moment, fucked the kids
then went grocery shopping. Len and I were staring out the window, watching the back yard trees, everything sleepy, when his pulse started to change.
I felt it rise through him, the stuff he was supposed to keep Down and
Behind, seeping into his bones, his brain. His eyes changed colour, the blue
getting lighter, almost white.

The Killer. Len had slipped his programs. Without being triggered, The Killer
had come into his body. His hand began to tighten on my throat.

"No, Len."

He pushed a spot near my mouth and my voice went silent. He pushed a spot
at the base of my spine and paralysis set in. He didn't have to tie me up but
he did anyway, ropes stretched off me, nerve ends tying me to another bed.

Len left the room and returned with his Dad's set of training needles and instruction guide.

"You're gonna die, Dori," was what he said.

The Killer's face was different than Len's—thinner, pulled down, the mouth bigger. I lay staring, mouth locked, the key lost.

Len knew the trigger sequences for most of my ones who loved him. They didn't all have triggers, some just birthed themselves, made their own doors, came and went when they could get past the triggers of the rest of the tribe. But they could all die. Inside my skull, there was a pack of loving eyes staring out at Len's Killer and their love was *fading fading*, the room's colours dying, no breath in the air, no sound, no pulse.

Len pushed the sequence for the one who loved him pure as nerves pulse. She surfaced, a lilting green yellow energy, startled by ropes, then by his eyes. She tried to struggle but the body couldn't move, couldn't scream.

"You're gonna die now." He inserted the needles one by one deep into her trigger sequence, the eight touch points that would bring her alive anywhere any time Len needed her. The Killer had come, he pushed death into each point, she slipped from the body *downdowndown* into the Dark, dimensions of the killed. There was a grave with her name waiting, she went into that coffin and closed the door.

So many times, she has resurrected, spirit returning to flesh, love seeping in pure and true. Nerves splintering alive when they need to go dead, need to pulse at a half-life afterlife pace, something a whore can manage so she doesn't scent off so much musk and pain. When I really need her dead, Len is the dimension I go to; I open the door to his Killer and call that morning in on repeat.

Ready now. Tony has finished with my body, he's called the Devil's Child, communed with a demon or two. Now he's dozing on his side. From my dimension, I watch my body shift carefully to the night table drawer. As it reaches for the small knife behind the false back, the eyes gain an energy clear and focused, full of light. Just like Len's—only-white, no colour, no pain. Nothing but the pure straight path toward the accomplished task, and release.

Tony is amenable, his body slack. The Killer pulls his forehead back and makes the cut low across his throat so a funeral suit collar will cover the damage.

Task complete. The Killer retreats behind her white door, high up and Left. I return to the body, shower and dress in the street clothes that hang waiting in a closet. I pack what I came with, add the knife and the teddy bear. Jezebella earned it.

At the front desk, I hand in the key to Room 33, then tap twice on the desk counter to tune the clerk in.

"Clean up required," I tell her.

Her eyes focus, she nods and watches me stride out of the well-tiled lobby, keeping just ahead of my own echoes.

Here

Ended therapy. Could barely sit near Lois. Voices, *Get out, get out.* Told Lois. "You find it difficult to trust."
Fuck her. Night day asleep awake, trying to trust selves, believe *them.* Go it alone. Voices and D.

Still walking dead. Two years, no smell, taste. Can't bear music, just silence. Too much in head—gears, chain saws, sirens. No depth perception. Careful going down stairs, stepping off curb. Everything grey. Blurry.
Can't think A to B. Can't read, words don't know each other, wander off. Touch something, no texture. Stub toe, no pain. Doc says nervous breakdown—no physical, no emotion. No happiness, no grief, no heart. No me. Summer, winter, same thin place. Quit Prozac. Doc not happy, said try religion again. "It will give you comfort." Gave evil eye, he dropped it. Filled out another form for disability. Panic attacks every renewal date. What if he won't sign?

Deep voices. Felt in gut, lower brain. *We are the Givers. We have something to show you. We are going to drag you down where you cannot swim. We are going to take you where you have not been before. We are going to kill you. Touch us and we will touch you like no one ever has. Listen, D. We have a black song for you to sing. No one will hear it but you and you will never hear sound again. We are your fathers. We are your mothers. We are your sisters and brothers. We surround you and hold you up, pull you down, take you in, let you out. This is not a story you can make up, this is a true tale of horror and skin. This time we will let you in. We will take you in. You will not come out again.*
Now you see you are what we made you. We can unmake you. We have that power. You are the bitch we wear. You are the bitch we wear.
Home.

Blood test. Nurse trouble finding vein, needle deeper and deeper, moving left right inside arm, her face screwed up, waiting scream. Could sense needle moving left right, ripped to shreds, no pain. Hit bone, arm jerked six inches, carrying needle and nurse's hands. Crash landing, no pain. Nurse about fainted, went for other arm.

Something happened tonight. Incredible. *Felt* something. Sitting at table, saw flicker of child in doorway. Not flesh and blood—energy shape. Then all over face, gentlest patting from child's hand. Felt one hundred percent real, little girl's hand touching D's face. *Who is this big dead-alive person?*
Felt her about a minute, then gone.

Do you know the path?
What path?
Beware.

Seeing child and teen selves. Sitting on couch. Toddler put hands on D's knee to balance. She smiled at D. Picked her up, held her before she faded. Could see how wrinkled nose.

Little girls, little girls everywhere, sleeping in D's bed, folded in with D's socks, hanging in closet, stuffed into garbage pail. Plugged into electrical outlets. Sitting on couch, reading books. One spins constant pirouettes.

Memories longer. Can hear Len's words. Len's dad making us fuck. Dad taking pictures.
Grad yearbook. Len and Juss didn't show up for grad photos either. Blank squares beside our write-ups. Pact.

I am going to kill you.
Why warn me?
You must not remember or you will die.
Already dead. Hey, I can see you. You're only ten.
Don't look at me.

Juss liked Chicago. Bought CD. Teens dancing. Decided to join. What a joke—lift rubber feet, swing rubber arms. Damn fucking tombstone. Selves boogieing. Electric light.

Juss came and danced with D. Energy form, teen. Then Lennie. Came through time and touched D *now.*

Waves of *something* going through body. Electric waves, one hundred and eighty. Exhausting. Brain feels scrubbed. Opened.

I am in some cold dark place reaching up toward a small circle of light. Something black and evil approaches. If I reach far enough up, I will be rewarded, lifted up toward the light, out of this place.

Electric shock programming. Little girl body lifted and jerked. Goddam Mommy and Daddy. Goddam egg and sperm. Goddam Ian called. Got religious. *Honour thy father and mother.* Told him never call again.

Same people at black cross and white cross rituals. Thought Satanism and Christianity hated each other.

Feels like writing recipe for meatloaf.

You are, D.

Want to feel fear, want to feel love, want to feel *me.*

Little boy murdered inside white chalk circle. Kin calls inside circle Here. Chanting, "Here, here, here."

Don't ever want to be *here.*

Cat's eye marble grey. Nothing. Nothing-That-Was-Something. Selves are someone—life happened to them. Nothing happens to D. No one.

Billy Wheeler. *Billy.* Billy safe in my body now. Cradle him alive.

Cried three tears. Keep cradling, keep cradling.

I am in a black universe, no stars. Nothing moves, nothing sings. No breath. I hear my
   heartbeat, it is coming from some other place. Taunting me.

Hockey?! *Doll?!*

Player, front page face. Used to stare at it, trance. Never attended games—D
   never did. Who did?

Jake Baldwin, part of the atmosphere.

You are in great danger. You come and go like a breath of air and you do not know it.
   You must learn to breathe deeper, you must learn to breathe all of it, earth, sky, your
   very blood. Even then you may not survive. Others have stood at this doorway and
   fallen into the grave.

What doorway? Who are you?

I am a Giver.

Kneeling, hands tied. Jake swinging live mouse, eyes bugged, shrieking. Legs cut off.
"Slow it down, Doll. Slow it down."

Large slow waves in brain. Blue.

"That's right, slow it down. Down, down. Now open wide. You can do this, Doll. You
   take giant cocks in your throat, this is no different. It's all about control. Absolute
   control of your body. Mind over body, Doll, mind over body."

He plugs nose, mouth opens. Arrow head, frantic pulse, warm, soft stomach, hair.
   Shriek going down throat. Tail forever. Stomach kills it, scrape of bones in bowels.
   Extreme attack of diarrhea.

Outside of this, watching, watching. Something between, clear plastic, thick.
   Push, can't get through. Can't stop it, still happening to her. Doll feels, D
   doesn't.

Dorene got diarrhea. And scraping in bowels. Didn't shit skeleton. Who did?

You do not know who you are.

Ballroom, naked people. Jake presses sequence of triggers in Doll's back.

Push and push but rest is blocked.

Sex and power? Don't buy it.

Wave Maker—gadget emits sound frequencies. Triggers switch. Eyes change colour, yellow-orange, red, green. Voice and body posture different.
You are entering a new layer.
Only feel during memories. Small ripple of feeling in big body. Only someone when them.

Woman called and asked for Dorothy. Third time in two weeks. Keep telling her no Dorothy. Always surprised.
Someone new in head, watching out eyes. Dark energy and knowing in her, not D. When she goes, gone.

Unplugged phone unless calling out. Hang ups, wrong numbers, asking for other names.
Who the fuck is Dorothy?

I am crawling through some sort of control room. Cables, wires everywhere. I disconnect them, one by one.

Something thrown at window. Note sliding under door but no note when look. Knocks on door in middle of night. Smells—rubber burning, perfume in hall outside door. Beeps. Whistles start one note, split into two. Feels like brain dividing. Something shifts and floats off.
Banged funny bone, flicker of pain. Tasting and smelling more. Better focus. Put on Peter Gabriel. Sounds in *SO* never heard before.
You do not know who you are.
It all connects into you.

I crawl into another control room. More wires, thousands. Disconnect, one by one.
Brain feels quieter. Bits of peace.

Eyeballs completely scarlet. Bruises legs, groin. Needle puncture mark left arm. Givers silent.

Someone new next door. Knocks on bedroom wall. Met her in hall. Weird eyes—pupils swelled, voice dropped.

No lost time during day. Nights? Wake feeling beaten up. Can hardly move. Minor bruising, sore throat, bloodshot eyes, headaches. Think vagina's raw, can't feel. Tired, no sleep.

Givers still silent. Nothing solid. Cardboard cut-out streets. Thin sky. People talk, thin minds. Dive into memories. Swim like fish. Breathe memory, get thick.

Lab, bright lights, different colours. Staring into green or blue. Voices—military?— naming stars and galaxies.

Bought security bar. Braced it between door handle and floor. Woke, heard base of bar rubbing. Door forced open. Wanted to get up but huge darkness as if dropped into deep sleep. You don't hear your door being forced open in the middle of the night and go back to sleep. Someone pushed D out.

Screws holding base of chain lock loose. Touched it, touched door, couldn't feel them.

I hold up a hand, it fades away. I look at the feet, they disappear. The rest of the body goes with the next breath. I float, one with the Dark, and I am what I am. In the Black Universe, I am.

Jake *here* last night. First memory of *now*. Sex rituals, beatings. Other guys, younger.

Go to cops?

Do not.

Why?

There will be no help for you there.

They're supposed to——

There will be no help for you.

Declare this: Went to cops, asked to file complaint about sexual assault. Didn't say cults.

"Come back tomorrow." Not who, when or where. Didn't ask name. Five cops within hearing range.

Came to Women's Shelter. Told them harassed by cult. Intake questionnaire,
staff turned question into statement. Looked straight at D. "You will not
want to name your abuser."

"Jake Baldwin. Write that down."

She jerked as if slapped.

Givers silent.

*In the distance, the beginning of red, faint streak of it. It is the colour of a scream.
I cannot hear it but I know this. I am what I am in the Dark and far off I see the
unheard red of my own screaming.*

Groin hurts so bad can hardly stand. At breakfast, night staff came into kitchen,
glared and put finger across throat. Another staff said, "I hear you'll be
returning to your apartment today."

"I want to stay the full three weeks."

She walked away. Went back to room and remembered last night. Two knocks
on door, night staff takes Dorothy out back entrance. Alarm shut off. Jake's
limo waiting. Long long ride.

Declare this: Went to Executive Director. Told her.

"What you said happened DID NOT happen." Crossed one wrist over other,
then pulled apart. "We feel we cannot meet your needs. You'll have to leave."

"I'm not asking you to solve my problems. All I want is a bed. You have empty
beds. I'm not a behaviour problem."

"This has nothing to do with anything you've done. The staff are uneasy. They
say they can't handle any more of this. You have multiple personalities. You
could pull out a butcher knife and STAB someone."

"I have no criminal record. I'm not violent."

"We feel we're out of our depth."

"So this has nothing to do with what I just reported?"

"No. Perhaps you could go to the women's hostel."

"The women's hostel takes women's shelter rejects? That might STAB someone?"

Bitch.

Back here at apartment like staff *heard.* Waiting for Jake. Knees in green waves.

D goes to "sleep," Doll takes it. Want to take it just once for them. Step into *my* life.

Are you nuts?

Lost time in hall today, sure of it. Woman next door coming toward me. She raised her hand. Suddenly she was behind me, going downstairs.

Declare this: Met Special Investigator, "handles cult complaints." First thing he said—"I don't believe multiple personalities exist." Got better. A list of quotables.

"I know I'm not qualified to make that judgement. I just don't think I believe in them."

"Cults aren't sophisticated."

"Jake Baldwin is a man about town. I can see a woman such as yourself having fantasies about him."

Told him could draw floor plan of Jake's home. Jerked like he wanted to clap his hand over D's mouth when said *Chamber of Whores.*

"Don't bother with it. If I could somehow arrange a tour of Jake Baldwin's house for you and we found nothing, what would you do then?"

"Ifs are hard to answer."

Pulled out notebook to take down *important* info. "Who is your therapist?"

"Don't have one." Enjoyed saying that.

Jaw dropped. *Nowhere to go for the crazy label.*

"I don't believe we can help you with your problem."

No wonder no complaints about cults filed in past five years.

Givers silent.

Derellamona tied to bed. Thirteen men, black robes. One man forked tongue and cock. "Satan." Rotated fucking. Brought in two-year-old girl from breeding farm, gutted her on top of Derellamona. Spread her blood, fucked some more.

No skin. Everywhere little girl touched, nothing. Vortex underneath. Spinning. *Move in.*

Younger guys—hockey players from Jake's current team. Trainer and Keeper. Rape and kick the shit out of Dara, only minor bruises but *I know it's hap-*

pening. D aches so bad can hardly move. Dara's thirty-one, players are nine-teen and twenty-one. What's the attraction?

Make love and Dara responds. During memories, feel thin lines of arousal and exhaustion, pain across surface, not down deep. Cellophane wrap, face stretched across it. Heartbeat far away.

You are the Anti-Christ.
Someone's programmed to believe that.
You are the Anti-Christ.

Ticks all over apartment, especially at night. Knocks, thuds. Some on ceiling. Loud ones jerk through D like shock.

You are the Anti-Christ.
What is this, get with the program?

Another streak of colour, far off across the Dark. Green. A low green. Mid-throat.

Jake and Didi in front of fire. Fire demon goes into Didi. Jake fucks Didi. Some of demon's energy leaves her, goes into him.
Cult. Occult.
Fucking slow, D.
Declare this: I am not the goddam Anti-Christ.
You are The Chosen One.

Numerology on birth date: 666.
Cry maybe five tears a month. Each tear a door, opens tiny part of body. Door onto feeling, rooms and hallways and windows of feeling in D's flesh. Then gone.

Every body cell a door. Wandering up and down endless hallways of doors, trying to open. All locked.
D dreams in black and white.

On plane, brain slid into deepest voice ever. *Someone decided differently*——

Plane slammed into something in air. Like solid wall. Another dimension? Thrown back against seat, bounced two inches.

Giver cut off, plane continued. No explanation from pilot, no apology, nothing about air turbulence. Everyone pretty nervous. "What was that?" Not just me.

Guess I'll have to stop thinking on planes.

Like it here. Little ones talking mile a minute, want to colour colour colour. Smiles come and go on D's mouth, each one different. Confetti giggles. Renting bungalow on corner lot. Can turn on music and boogie. Touch more sounds, touch more of me.

Jake here last night. Same shit. Fourteen driving hours. Jet? He'll wear out.

Colours, colours, pulse of purple, blue, yellow. Still far off but now something more than I am the Dark. Each pulse, heartbeat of a different colour.

You do not know who you are. It has all been coded into you.
You are a cosmic blueprint.
You are the Anti-Christ.
Shut up.

Doll steps onto bungalow porch. Row of black cars, headlights off, parked facing bungalow. Cars stretch up street, along avenue, back alley. In front of each car, man dressed in black, arms crossed. Silent. Above tree line rises mass of dark-winged beings.

Two white forms float down and stand between Doll and men. Huge, flickering, white-winged, white-robed. Flaming swords. Two black demons land beside them, just as huge. One roars, throat scarlet with rage. Resisting. With Doll. She looks up to see hers coming to her, hundreds of glowing forms, all colours, black and white, some distant pin points, others landing on bungalow roof, ground. Soft whisper-crackle of spirits flickering air.

Assessment. Unseen signal given. Men get into cars and drive off. Dark alien spirits fade behind tree line but Doll's stay, circling outside bungalow. Some clockwise, some counter-clockwise.

Mine. Feel loved. Not alone.

First time, colours in a memory. Before this, beige, brownish-grey.

Wind touched my face today. There's a shape to me, felt my mouth move.

Trainer inserts gadget into Dorell's vagina. "Fetch me a star."

Feel it pulse. Walls of bone, blood, skin drop away. Suspended in outer space. Travelling toward white glow. Enter. Absorb. Beauty. Singing hope.

Gadget calls Dorell back. Flesh glows white. Trainer fucks, absorbs glow.

"A" game. Higher level. *Star* player.

"A"—white triangle pointed up.

In this Dark, a blue floats through me. As it does, I see myself take shape, a blue winged creature, singing. For that moment I am a blue being, singing a blue note. Then the Dark again, the single I.

Getting double view, superimposed. Constellations pinpoint Real. Colour selves suspended in outer space, superimposed over Here. Some look human, some stars. Black holes.

Back is bad. Tying my shoes, pulled something. Can't straighten, hobbling around.

You are a cosmic blueprint. It all connects in you.

Then disconnect it.

That is not the answer this time.

Footsteps walking across ceiling. Feel submerged.

At the end of a long blurred hall there is a vague pink door. It wafts slightly like a window curtain. I am running toward it. I know if I reach it I will be safe, I will be out of here, I will be out of me.

Declare this: *Nazi flag. Swastika cross. Black robes.* Can't. Yes. *Doorkeeper is mutilating a child on an altar with a knife. STOP. Kill energy rises from body. Doorkeeper shapes it into door. Someone waiting. Transparent, blue-white. Large mustache. Spirit of Hitler.*

Feeding his forever.

Sit and stare. Minute can last long time. Longer than a life.

You have accomplished important things today.

Programs have shapes. Flowers, bells, wheels. Windmills. Knives and forks. Baseball caps, purses, phones. Triangles, stars. Dismantle each one—take apart and dissolve. Electric wave courses through body. Brain opens, small spaces freed. Stars shine through. Dark breathes in. Colours touch tiny places in brain. Feel it, tiny sparks, fingertips.

Programs for movement. Do U-turn backwards, energy balances, program negated. Spin going in head, start up spin opposite way. Spins merge, balance each other out and dissolve.

Mostly programs for crosses, black and white. Get so tired from electric waves. Always another cross.

Swastika—spinning cross.

SIX-pointed cross. SIX ways to leave body. Spatial reference to ticking?

Sports broadcast said Jake's been in L.A. since Sunday. *Here* last night. In Real.

Starting to see huge dimensions of colour around me. Flicker and throb. Want to touch, want to go *there*, walk toward them but just more air. Nothing but D.

You are accomplishing what we need, D.

Am I enough?

You are what we need.

About to fall asleep, sound of chain saw erupted full volume, close to bed. Ran about ten seconds.

Man drove by in Kin headgear, 11 A.M. Church on, streets empty. Wobbled slowly then gunned and took off.

White cloth heavy on my skin. Smell fire. Chanting, low pulse in throat. Brain slows, Time slows.

Opened all doors in bungalow to rooms, closets, dressers, cupboards. Feel opened, more space. Want to sing but no voice comes out. Can hear it though, in my head. Far-off singing, from another place.

Tonight, sound of doors slamming several times. Fuck off.

You got it, man.

What kind of a Giver are you?

Maybe I don't take myself so seriously.

I step into the kitchen of childhood. It is dark, the moon shines through a window, no clocks ticking. Soundless, I cross to a wall cupboard and open it. On each shelf, I see a paper bag. I open one to find a baby made of bread dough, quietly rising. The room fills with the scent of her rising, the sound of her breathing.

Each bag contains a bread dough baby, her tiny breathing. As I take them into my arms, they merge into my flesh.

Doors. Energy doors all around me, different colours. Can't feel them though. Walk through them and I'm still here. Not at the correct frequency?

Thought the Anti-Christ was black energy.

Do you think the Network portrays itself in truth?

I am reaching through and into another dimension. The interface is clear as untroubled water, ripples as my hand passes through. On the other side, Jake's face. I run my fingers over his mouth, his forehead. Wherever I touch, he begins to disappear. When I bring my hand back, there is more of it. Deeper bones.

There are other faces beyond his. Unfamiliar. Military uniforms. I cannot reach them yet. They watch.

Rescuing selves from Interrogation dimensions. Courtroom, doctor's office, radio interviews. Endless reporting.

Lost wanderers too. Winter roads, waiting at bus stops for buses that never come. Lift them out of *there* into *here*, this frequency of me.

Dimensions of shock, demons, sex. Memory. Bring them all home to now. Where do I go when someone else takes the body? Where is D's door?

Colours come and go, pass through me, I flicker through colour shapes, the roar of their songs growing strong in me. Between each colour the Dark, steady, deepening.

Sensation of door handle in my hand so strong. Almost constant. Sometimes, handle begins to turn, then fades out.

Miscarriage yesterday. Nauseous all day. Had bath, felt whoosh. No blood, just something floating. Deep freeze, nothing deeper. Reach for it. Thick, rubbery. White, long as my thumb. Giant blood clot in head. Tiny dangling arms and legs.
In out in out. Real rippled in out, fighting to stay knowing, *here*. Dead, holding dead in my hand. *Deaddeaddead.*
Flushed down toilet. Bury it, they'd dig up and desecrate.

Force-fed abortion pill, curled in ball screaming, "It's dying, it's dying."
Living being dying *inside* me, all night, all day.

Some of the colours sheer pain. The roar, the scrape, I am the shape of sheer screaming colour then the Dark. Peace. Not nothingness. Dark I can reach into, suck in like breath.

Can hear more sounds—*The Doobie Brothers* a whole new group. Orange juice tastes different from water. Today in IGA, bananas glowed vivid yellow. *Felt* the yellow. Fruit and vegetables lit up. Me grinning at the oranges.
Depth perception returning. Space to air, the other side of the room looks like it's over there. Even the inside of a mug stretches down.

My arms stretch out, flicker in unfamiliar colours and a keening comes from them, wild alien voices, the sheer knife-edged wailing of stars.

Yellow door opened and Jake came through. He travels, *in his body*, through doors. He took Doll with him through same yellow door.

Where do I go? What colour is my door?

You have not yet absorbed the correct frequency.

Checking body for bruises, went into moment of staring. Sleepy, dopey.

Came out of it, large fresh bruise on shin. No time passed on clock. Door into bungalow locked. Fresh snowfall, no fresh tracks.

Slip. Slip time, D. Come and go, come and go.

You think you are Real but you are not.

Quit bugging her. She's trying.

Deep trance. Hundreds of needles all over body. Close by, woman hangs from noose, dying. Needles direct nerves to transmit kill energy to some other dimension.

I feel needle pricks all the time.

Screaming screaming yellow give me back my life you fucking bastards.

The stars are screaming, the stars are bleeding. Blood running from them into my flesh. Blood surging through me, tidal wave.

"*I tried to get out, Doll. Once. A long time ago. No one gets out. There is no way out. You just learn to live with it.*"

Jake. Sometimes I feel so close to him. He knows everywhere I've been. He knows me better than I know myself.

He does not understand this Changing. He cannot follow you here.

Felt door handle in my hand. As it turned I saw a door open. Sensation of lifting up, rising. I looked back to see my body below, looking up. Doll, watching D leave.

Door opened onto another bungalow. An energy dimension of this bungalow. Exactly the same as Real. Felt real to D, solid. Energy bungalow is a brain frequency, D is a brain frequency. Ate there, slept, wandered around, even processed some memories about Mom.

Couldn't record in this journal though. This journal exists only in Real.

An amber door appears among the stars, moaning fibres of energy. I speak the words of release. "No more sacrifice." The door shudders and loses its form as the trapped energy, soul or spirit, is released to take on a human shape, the energy of a small boy.

A Resistance member takes this freed one to the Outside, frequencies beyond the Network's range.

repeekrooD.

Well-coifed senior spat on my lawn. Several people in alley yipped like coyotes.

Give me back my door. Voices hiss at me constantly. Some are voices of people I know, people still alive. People that used to be friends.

"My goodness, the cost of this has gone up," said store clerk. A white-light dimension came into focus above us. A white-light version of the clerk was giving one of my selves instructions. I pulled my white-light self back down into my body.

The clerk's body gave me a Real astonished look, then said, "NEXT," very loudly.

I. Eye.

You begin to see.

Green door opens, Len and Juss come through. Make love to Dori and the sky opens, they're fucking suspended in outer space. Stars send rays into their bodies so they glow incredible colours. Doors open in their nerves and the energy travels somewhere else.

Len, Juss, Dori, adults now. Love still passing through, someone else owns it. They faded out the green door in the morning along with their stars.

My feelings still with them. They *keep* Dori's colours. *From* me.

Disability insurance cut me off. Doc told them I refused Prozac. Resisting treatment. Enough in savings for one more year. This year is mine.

I step through a blue door into the Blue Universe. Blue stars, blue planets, blue song. The atmosphere pulses with memories sent into these frequencies.

You are here, says a blue voice. This is yours.

Slowly the blue begins to breathe me. Deeper, deeper, I become the breath of blue, I am
remembering all small things blue. Garden bluebells, blue ceramic egg cup, blue
notes from Ian's cello. Blue bruises, Lennie's eyes, the blue Juss touched in me. The
skies that painted each bedroom window, the doors they became. Now they open
inward and I stand knocking at these doors to my heart, saying, Come unto me, oh
please come unto me and I will give you rest.

I was standing looking at a store window with upside-down paper tulips.
  Lovely spring theme. A man walked up.
"So, are you local?" he asked in low tones.
My voice lowered, face muscles slackened and altered, energy shifted, but
  I *stayed in the body.* "I live around here."
Man stepped in closer and pointed right. "Have you heard of Dod? Have you
  ever been to Dod?"
In out in out. Street in ripples. *Here, here, here. Stay here, D.*
Everything cleared. Standing in same place, looking at same man. He'd stepped
  back in confusion, suddenly turned and walked away.
Something that was supposed to happen didn't.
Dod belongs to the Blue Universe. You are absorbing those frequencies.

Got the rest of that ballroom memory. *Orgy. Jake presses a sequence of nerves on*
  Doll's back. Doors open and dimensions merge. A host of demons appear. Demons
  and humans fucking everywhere. Arousal is incredible.
Sacrifice. Demons always feed, devour me to a fleshy pulp. Doors open and the
  Universes send me life. My corpse glows as I regenerate.
You are the Anti-Christ. Our Anti-Christ.

Lois's office. My body in a trance. She's talking to some of my child selves in a blue
  energy dimension. They speak through my mouth to Lois.
"Did you find the blue door?" Lois asks.
"Yes, we founded it," says a little voice.
"I want you to go in through the door and down the blue stairs. Did you do that?"
"Yes, we didded that. There is a lot of doors down here."
"Open the door to your right and go in. Did you do that?"
"Yes, we are in a blue room."

"There are boxes on the floor. Can you see them?"

"Uh huh. Lots of boxes."

"I want each of you to get into a box."

"I don't want to get into a box," says a little voice.

"I don't like to get into boxes," says a different little voice.

"I want you to get into a box. It will keep you safe when the monsters come. Are you getting in?"

"Yes."

"I don't like it in here."

"Now close the lids," says Lois.

"I don't want to close the lid." The voices are upset. *"It's dark in here."*

As the lids close, an adult figure comes into the blue room. It's Lois, one of her blue energy Keepers. She locks the boxes and goes out.

I unlock the boxes and let my children out into me.

Surrounded by the Red Universe. *Deep red gut pulse of pain. Frequency of black runs through red, forks like lightning.* Crawling around here past four days. Migraines, puking, joints feel pulled apart. Playing music so neighbours won't hear me.

Demons coming home.

Doing Laundry. A man parked outside the laundromat and went into the grocery store. A huge black dog hung out the driver's window, watching me and growling. *It can't come through glass.* Then I realized it *was*, as energy. Sending an energy part of itself at me, attacking.

Something came up in me, a deep black pulse. It turned me to face the dog. Energy left me in an intense flow, went at the dog and pushed down on it. The dog sank back until its head was barely above the bottom of the window, its eyes rolled back, petrified.

I laid off and the dog came at me again. I sent more energy at it and it sank down in the seat. After that, it didn't look at me, just sat staring across the street.

When the dog's owner came out of the store, he stared at me through the window, open-mouthed as if he knew what had just gone on.

The womb a deep dark, then stars come alive in it, stars of many colours and planets
shifting in a slow pattern, moving toward the moment. Two dimensions meet, dark
egg and sperm of light. Every star every planet sends a colour beam into this begin-
ning heartbeat, coding it with their frequencies, their shimmering voices, the possi-
bilities of their call.
My conception. All of it mine.

My neighbour is an inter-dimensional Peeping Tom. She was sitting on her
porch and placed her fingers into a steeple. I couldn't see her eyes—sun-
glasses—but I *felt* her gaze move into my kitchen.
 I stepped back so she couldn't see me—sun on her side of the street. No way
she saw me with normal vision. Gave her the finger. In Real. One quick jab.
Her body jerked as if goosed. Got up and went inside.
There are moments in my life I'm beginning to enjoy.

Daemona steps onto the player's balcony and sends out the dark call. As she keens, the
night shifts and begins to take shape, demons of rage and grief tear the air with their
wings. For a long moment they scream with her, their cry the meeting point of
universes. Claws and fingers interweave, the woman and the demons touch palms,
the pulsing of their nerves interlocks. Daemona absorbs their frequency and the
demons merge into her. She returns to the player's suite, the team and Jake who wait
for her there. Walks past them and steps out of there
into me.

Began to cry today, long long time. Breaking through to air, gulping more and
more of it—the wailing, the grief, pain cracking open a dry sky, rain pouring through.

Transfer Base. Underground. Star charts. Kill energy transmitted to feed other dimen-
sions.

All day long, Callers sending out their sounds, calling colour selves back into
the body. So many of them. My head aches with the ringing of bells.

The Yellow Universe the quick pulse of joy. Laughter skips across it, my pores open into
giggles, all that is child slips in through these doors.

Yellow shock. Twisting yellow snakes. Take them in, become electric snake, pain.

I'm beginning to think Jake will never approach D directly. The Network needs
   her somehow, needs her divided and apart. If D actually saw Jake, there'd
   be a huge merge of frequencies and selves, more than the Network could
   handle. Doll and Dorothy and Dorell would become D.

I look at my arm and I see stars. Pinpoints of colour glow across my body.

Nerve network of stars suspended in outer space. Network members coded to these
   stars, realigned in some sort of metaphysical omniscient nerve network that
   simultaneously triggers all members? Needle pricks?

Jake's team has lost eight games straight. Losing their spark.

I had my eyes closed, focused on a panorama of stars divided into colour
   groups. Slowly, a great shifting began. The stars and planets began to move,
   realign, parts of *my brain* shifting with the stars. It continued until a voice
   said, *Complete.*
Colours had broken their boundaries and scattered their glow across the universe.
   My brain pulsed with a different energy, as if this realignment allowed a natural
   flow of energy to re-establish. As if the *stars* had been shifted out of their
   original positions and now returned to their intended places. The stars and
   my brain, healing together.

Dorell lies on a stretcher, discs on her body, two men in surgical dress leaning over her.
"You mean we haven't got them all?" one man asks.
The other chuckles. "There are large uncharted areas to her brain. We may never get it
   all."
I came back to myself, to Real. A large shuddering sigh began in my body, I shifted
   slowly on the bed. Someone was rising into me, coming from the deep. Our
   eyes opened. My head filled with this voice.
The Anti-Christ is too small.

So is the Christ.

Sinking rising Up Down coming together mix merge dance together Black Universe White Universe Colours moan into one another you are here you are home.

Len, driving his old green car. He looks at me and says, "You got it."

"You're the nerve network we've been looking for."

It's all been coded into you.

Our Anti-Christ.

My frequencies now. Pull out the pins and needles, this flesh, its Stars and Dark are mine.

Just at that moment between dream and waking I heard them, voices of the universes, singing throughout my body. As if every cell became a clear translucent mouth singing the most exquisite colours, my body a shimmering river of sound. Then it faded into Real.

When will I get out? When will I finally be completely out? Maybe the answer isn't *out*, but *in*. Further into my own flesh, my own nerve network, further into the colour universes of me. Nerve by nerve, door by door, self by self, working my way in toward the center, where all doors open and the colours conceive.

I've found love among demons and I've found love among angels. Len, Juss, the player, even Jake. There's love in every frequency, in all the hearts that pulse in the dark, in each dimension of colour and light. Singing their heart song in every frequency, singing their song of the universes, song of another way, of choice, possibility. The only-good heart has always been more than *only* and *good*. It is a heart *human* enough for all the parts, all the colours, voices, frequencies. I name that heart now, I name her *human*, I name her *Dora*, the beginning one who calls us all here. I name her *home*.

Singing. Voice takes me in an exquisite scattering of nerves, an orgasm of notes sung body-wide. The walls of the bungalow drop away and *I* am suspended among the starry dark, *I* am singing, every nerve a colour note. The Stars answer with their shimmering voices, the Dark with its deep cradling throb, and the Universes open their doors, countless rays of Colour stretch toward me, into me, deep into the harp strings quivering within each cell. I vibrate with the song of every Colour come together, their touching place, singing me whole.

Home is me.